C.J. Dennis was b...
tried his hand as a...
before the *Bulletin*...
to the Dandenong... ...... full time, but
success eluded him until publication of *The Sentimental Bloke* in
1915. Overnight, his vernacular verse made him Australia's most
popular poet, and he followed up with eight books in nine years.
Although most of his volumes related to the Bloke, Dennis also
wrote the satirical fantasy *The Glugs of Gosh,* and a children's
collection *A Book for Kids*. He married Olive Herron in 1917, and
built a home in Toolangi in the ranges outside Melbourne. In
1922, Dennis began writing topical verse for the Melbourne
Herald, and moved between the city and the bush. Ill health
forced him to retire to his mountain retreat in 1932, where he
completed *The Singing Garden*, a book of nature poems. He
continued to write for the *Herald* until his death in 1938.

Books by C.J. Dennis

Backblock Ballads and Other Verses (1913)
The Australaise: a Marching Song (1915)
The Songs of a Sentimental Bloke (1915)
The Moods of Ginger Mick (1916)
The Glugs of Gosh (1917)
Doreen (1917)
Digger Smith (1918)
Backblock Ballads and Later Verses (1918)
Jim of the Hills (1919)
A Book for Kids (1921)
Rose of Spadgers (1924)
The Singing Garden (1935)
Selected Verse of C.J. Dennis (1950)

C.J. Dennis

THE COMPLETE SENTIMENTAL BLOKE

EDITED BY
NEIL JAMES

A&R Classics
An imprint of HarperCollins*Publishers*

A&R Classics
An imprint of HarperCollins*Publishers*, Australia

This A&R Classics first edition published in 2001
by HarperCollins*Publishers* Pty Limited
ABN 36 009 913 517
A member of the HarperCollins*Publishers* (Australia) Pty Limited Group
www.harpercollins.com.au

Copyright for introduction and selection © Neil James 2001

This book is copyright.
Apart from any fair dealing for the purposes of private study, research,
criticism or review, as permitted under the Copyright Act, no part may
be reproduced by any process without written permission.
Inquiries should be addressed to the publishers.

HarperCollins*Publishers*
25 Ryde Road, Pymble, Sydney NSW 2073, Australia
31 View Road, Glenfield, Auckland 10, New Zealand
77–85 Fulham Palace Road, London W6 8JB, United Kingdom
Hazelton Lanes, 55 Avenue Road, Suite 2900, Toronto, Ontario, M5R 3L2
and 1995 Markham Road, Scarborough, Ontario, M1B 5M8, Canada
10 East 53rd Street, New York NY 10022, USA

National Library of Australia Cataloguing-in-Publication data:

Dennis, C. J. (Clarence James), 1876–1938.
The complete sentimental bloke.
ISBN 0 207 19735 0.
1. Poetry. I. James, Neil. II. Title.
A821.1

Cover design: Jon Foye, HarperCollins Design Studio
Cover image: Coo-ee Historical Picture Library
Author photo (back cover) courtesy Mitchell Library, State Library of NSW
Printed and bound in Australia by Griffin Press

70gsm Bulky Book Ivory used by HarperCollins*Publishers* is a natural,
recyclable product made from wood grown in sustainable forests. The
manufacturing processes conform to the environmental regulations in the
country of origin, Finland.

7 6 5 4 3 2   08 09 10 11 12

Contents

Introduction   vii

THE SONGS OF A SENTIMENTAL BLOKE   1

Preface to the fifty-first thousand 5 • Foreword 7 • A Spring Song 9 • The Intro 13 • The Stoush o' Day 17 • Doreen 20 • The Play 23 • The Stror 'at Coot 27 • The Siren 32 • Mar 36 • Pilot Cove 40 • Hitched 43 • Beef Tea 47 • Uncle Jim 51 • The Kid 56 • The Mooch o' Life 61

The Australaise: A Marching Song   65

THE MOODS OF GINGER MICK   69

Introduction 73 • Duck an' Fowl 76 • War 80 • The Call of Stoush 84 • The Push 88 • The Battle of the Wazzir 93 • Sari Bair 98 • Ginger's Cobber 102 • The Singing Soldiers 107 • In Spadger's Lane 111 • The Straight Griffin 115 • A Letter to the Front 119 • Rabbits 122 • To the Boys Who Took the Count 128 • The Game 132 • "A Gallant Gentleman" 136

DOREEN   141

Washing Day 145 • Logic and Spotted Dog 148 • Vi'lits 151 • Possum 154

Contents

DIGGER SMITH   159

Before the War 163 • Dummy Bridge 168 • Dad 173 • Digger Smith 177 • West 181 • Over the Fence 185 • A Digger's Tale 188 • Jim's Girl 192 • The Boys Out There 196 • Half A Man 200 • Sawin' Wood 203 • Jim 206 • A Square Deal 210

Armistice   215

ROSE OF SPADGERS   219

Introduction 221 • The Faltering Knight 226 • Termarter Sorce 231 • A Holy War 237 • Nocturne 242 • The Crusaders 248 • "'Ave a 'Eart!" 253 • Rose 259 • The Knight's Return 264 • The Also-ran 269 • A Woman's Way 273 • "Stone the Crows" 277 • Listener's Luck 280 • The Dance 284 • Spike Wegg 288 • Narcissus 293

A Message   297

Glossary   301

A Note on the Text   315

Index of Poems   317

Introduction

When Australian bush ballads were popular during the 1890s, few people realised that many of the "bush" poets were actually city folk. Banjo Paterson was a practising Sydney solicitor. Even Henry Lawson, who made much of his bush childhood, spent most of his adult life in the big smoke. It seems fitting that the first Australian poet to take the city as his subject was a boy from the bush.

Clarence James Dennis was born in the small town of Auburn in South Australia in 1876. His father was an Irish publican, and Clarence a sickly eldest child. Life in frontier pubs was tough, and after losing his mother when he was 13, the sensitive youngster was taken in by four prim and proper maiden aunts. They modelled him on little Lord Fauntleroy, replete with Eton collar, cane and gloves. "Clarrie" Dennis suffered the scorn of the backblock locals, and hated the effeminate sound of his moniker. Too diminutive to fight his childhood tormentors, he embraced the weaponry of words. Dennis began by styling himself "C.J.", or simply "Den".

At 17, Dennis tried his hand as a clerk and a journalist, but soon returned to the family pub. Idle, prone to drink, and wanting to be a poet, he quarrelled with his father and went on the track. By the time he reached Broken Hill, his clothes were scraps and patches. He scraped a bare living from carpentry and mining, photography and fettling, but his slight frame could not take the strain. The drink might have finished him had the aunts not intervened. After recovering in Adelaide, Den completed a writing apprenticeship as editor of *The Gadfly*, a weekly satirical paper. He also began publishing verse in the leading Australian outlets of his day: the *Bulletin* and *The Lone Hand*. It was time to have a crack at the big city.

Dennis lasted a year in Melbourne. There were too many distractions, too much easy fellowship, and too little productive work. At 31, he still hadn't succeeded as a poet, and he yearned for the bush. He moved to Toolangi in the Dandenongs in 1908, living hand to mouth in an abandoned timber-worker's shack. Beset periodically by depression, Den wrote "like blazes to fend off the blues". But the drink was never far away, and whenever money came in, he sought "drug-induced excitement" in the nearest pub. Further decline was prevented by a chance introduction to J.G. Roberts, an official of the Melbourne Tramways Company, whose weekender in Kallista had became a regular home for writers and artists. Dennis moved into one of the decommissioned tram cars on the property. Recognising both his talent and his weakness, Roberts gave Dennis an allowance on the condition that he work at his verse. The result was his first book *Backblock Ballads and Other Verses*; but by 1913, populist bush ballads were no longer a novelty, and the book didn't sell. Its one new note was a sequence of four "songs" about a larrikin of the pushes—the inner city street gangs whose reputation for "stoushin'" was matched by their rough, original argot. Dennis was encouraged to develop the story of his "bloke", and found the *Bulletin* eager to publish each new instalment. After 20 years of rough toil, he was about to become an overnight success.

In 1915 Dennis wrote to the publishers Angus and Robertson suggesting a 300 copy subscription edition of *The Sentimental Bloke*. George Robertson, a fiery Scot with a passion for Australian authors, rejected the scheme but accepted its author. A&R had made its name publishing Paterson and Lawson, and the canny Robertson could see the Bloke's potential. He edited it, added illustrations by Hal Gye, cajoled a Foreword out of Henry Lawson, and released 2,500 copies in October 1915. These sold out in days, and another 5,000 books were printed in November. A further 5,000 copies were needed by Christmas, and yet another 5,000 in January. A&R increased the print run to 7,000 copies in February, but still needed an extra 8,500 in April. The book sold more than 50,000 copies in nine months, a feat never matched by any other Australian poet.

The Bloke's success was a case of the right sentiment at the right time. The recently federated nation was looking for a sense of what it meant to be Australian. The bush ballads of the 1890s had mapped some key Australian values: sardonic humour; pioneering graft; a democratic impulse; spirit of place; and the credo of mateship. Yet Australia was already one of the most urbanised nations on earth, and most readers had little direct experience of the world the ballads depicted. Dennis transplanted the genre to the city, but at the same time recognising that the bush would always loom large in the Australian imagination. When his tough larrikin abandons his life of "gittin' shick", "'eadin' tales", and "stoushin' Johns", he does so for a life on the land. *The Sentimental Bloke* is a form of Australian pastoral that runs deep in the Australian psyche. Like the Bloke, city-dwelling Australians could celebrate:

> ... when the moon comes creepin' o'er the hill,
> An' when the mopoke calls along the creek,
> I takes me cup o' joy an' drinks me fill,
> An' arsts meself wot better could I seek.

The money Dennis made from his book allowed him to ask the same. He married, bought some land in Toolangi, and built a home. After years of struggle, he was keen to capitalise on success. In 1916, the nation was coming to grips with war, where an Australian Imperial Force was fighting for the first time. The casualties were high and debate over conscription was tearing through the community. The country needed a collective conversation to resolve the doubts about its place in the world. Dennis took Bill's best mate Ginger Mick, a minor character in *The Sentimental Bloke*, and sent him off to war. *The Moods of Ginger Mick* sold 42,350 copies in six months. Mick's story helped Dennis put Australia itself under the microscope:

> Becos a crook done in a prince, an' narked an Emperor,
> An' struck a light that set the world aflame;
> Becos the bugles East an' West sooled on the dawgs o' war,
> A bloke called Ginger Mick 'as found 'is game—
> Found 'is game an' found 'is brothers, 'oo wus strangers in 'is sight,
> Till they shed their silly clobber an' put on the duds fer fight.

> Yes, they've shed their silly clobber an' the other stuff they
>   wore
> Fer to 'ide the man beneath it in the past;
> An' each man is the clean, straight man 'is Maker meant 'im for,
> An' each man knows 'is brother man at last.
> Shy stranger, till a bugle blast preached 'oly brother'ood;
> But mateship they 'ave found at last; and they 'ave found it good.

Ginger Mick was the catalyst of the Digger myth. The mateship forged in battle meshed easily with the pioneering qualities mythologised in the 1890s. The redemption of Ginger Mick, the violent larrikin of the pushes who became a decorated hero, was also that of the nation. The book was a rallying point which eased the divisions of class and religion that had split the country. In the central episode, Mick is wounded and unconscious behind enemy lines. He wakes to find upper-class Keith, whose privileges he resented, keeping cover for him. Keith refuses to leave when Mick insists he save himself:

> Keith bites 'is lips; 'e never turns 'is 'ead.
> "Wot in the 'ell;" sez Mick, "'ere wot's yer game?"
> "I'm an Australian," that wus all 'e said,
> An' pride took 'old o' Mick to 'ear that name—
> A noo, glad pride that ain't the pride o' class—
> An' Mick's contempt, it took the count at lars'!

The nation also felt his pride, and a military tradition was born. The Diggers themselves took Mick to heart. Angus and Robertson quickly realised that its standard square book format was too awkward for a soldier's kit, and printed a "Pocket Edition for the Trenches" to fit the Australian uniform. *The Sentimental Bloke* and *Ginger Mick* were issued to Australian troops in September 1916. The books became so popular at the front that the actor "Digger" Ted Scott gave recitals to the troops.

The public was eager for more, so Dennis completed *Doreen*, a gift booklet published for the 1917 Christmas market. It captures some episodes in the early farming life of the Bloke and his wife Doreen. He then extended his focus on the home front with *Digger Smith* in 1918. It looked sympathetically at the returning soldier through a doubting "'arf a man" Smith, struggling to regain his place in society after losing a leg in the War. *Digger Smith* went through three editions and 21,000 copies, but with the War over, sales began to wane. George Robertson steered Dennis towards other material, and he published the satirical fantasy *The Glugs of Gosh*, a children's *Book for Kids*, and the tale of a timber cutter *Jim of the Hills*. It was not until 1924 that he returned to the Bloke, adding *Rose of Spadgers* to the original sequence. Rose was the sweetheart Mick left behind, and the story unites her with the Bloke and Doreen in a post-war Australia.

If it is easy to trace the circumstances that made the Bloke immensely popular when first published, its longevity is a little harder to explain. *The Sentimental Bloke* and *Ginger Mick* in particular remained in print for decades, both in their original forms and in selected editions. Dennis was a steady seller on the Angus and Robertson backlist right through to the 1990s, enjoying periodic surges of interest when a new play, film or musical version was produced. The easy explanation is that Dennis drew from wellsprings that are still running through Australian culture. Anyone struggling to understand why so many young Australians make the pilgrimage to Anzac Cove each April could do no better than to read *Ginger Mick*. But more importantly, Dennis remains readable because his *Sentimental Bloke* is at heart a comedy that transcends its historical setting. The type characters, witty dialogue, comic irony, foiled intrigues and concluding marriages are of the same genre as *A Midsummer Night's Dream*, *The Way of the World*, and *The Importance of Being Ernest*. Unfortunately, comedy has never gained serious recognition from Australian literary historians. H.M. Green, for example, fated the Bloke to fade out as "a phenomenon rather than a landmark in Australian literature." Even Dennis' biographer, Alec Chisholm, wondered whether his vernacular verse would become outmoded. Time has proven them wrong. Today's readers will absorb the dialect verse "through the pores" just as easily as readers of the previous century. What initially seems a barrier—Dennis' phonetic spelling—soon reveals itself as an unerringly accurate rendering of the Australian accent.

Dennis' skill as a poet has always been recognised overseas. An American critic in 1945 was convinced that "the book has more of the eternal values, not to mention humour, than most of the protein-fed or intellectualised literature about which the critics are shouting every day." A review of *The Sentimental Bloke* in the London *Times* argued that "the best thing in his idyll is its extremely skilful versification. Mr Dennis is a fine craftsman. He uses a variety of complicated stanzas and fails in none." By contrast, when Banjo Paterson was paid £100 by George Robertson to write a "bush" version of the Bloke, he soon returned chastened, admitting that he simply couldn't "make the rhymes run". Because Dennis insisted on capturing the slang and the ungrammatical speech patterns of his characters, his skill has long been underrated. His verse forms are among the most sustained achievements in Australian poetry.

There was ample opportunity to test his mettle as a versifier when Den took on the post of staff poet for the Melbourne *Herald* in 1922, an association he maintained over 16 years and with more than 4,000 poems. He would attend morning editorial conferences, then fill up his pipe and his kettle and complete a polished piece of topical verse in time for the evening edition. On one occasion, a cable arrived close to deadline announcing the death of G.K. Chesterton. Dennis wrote four six-line stanzas in just twenty minutes and made the edition! But the grind of the city, his black moods, and the temptations of the bottle once more played havoc with his health. Dennis was forced to retire to his mountain retreat in Toolangi in 1932, but he continued to dictate verse to the *Herald* via the phone. He also completed a book of nature poems, *The Singing Garden*, which captured the songs of the bush birds he loved so well. Hard living, alcohol and asthma finally caught up with him in 1938, when he died aged 62.

2001 is the 125th anniversary of Dennis' birth. The sentiment of the Bloke sequence is as fresh today as when its hopeful author first wrote to Angus and Robertson from his bush shack.

Introduction

Yet incredibly, the five books have never been published together except in limited selections. *The Complete Sentimental Bloke* combines the whole kit and caboodle, including some individual Bloke poems published in the *Herald*. From the original *Sentimental Bloke* to the concluding *Rose of Spadgers*, Dennis' narrative is unified by its characters, its humour and its language. It is arguably the best long poem in Australian literature.

NEIL JAMES
Sydney, 1st September, 2001.

THE SONGS OF A SENTIMENTAL BLOKE

TO

MR. AND MRS. J.G. ROBERTS

La vie est vaine:
Un peu d'amour,
Un peu de haine ...
Et puis—bonjour!

La vie est brève:
U peu d'espoir,
Un peu de rêve ...
Et puis—bonsoir!

Léon montenaeken

Preface to the fifty-first thousand

Nearly a year ago Henry Lawson wrote in his preface to the first edition of these rhymes: "I think a man can best write a preface to his own book, provided he knows it is good."

Now, and at the end of some twelve months of rather bewildering success, I have to confess that I do not know. But I do know that it is popular, and to write a preface to the fifty-first thousand of one's own book is rather a pleasant task; for it is good for a writer to know that his work has found appreciation in his own land, and even beyond.

But far more gratifying than any mere record of sales is the knowledge that has come to me of the universal kindliness of my fellows. The reviews that have appeared in the Australasian and British press, the letters that have reached me from many places—setting aside the compliments and the praise—have proved the existence of a wide-spread sympathy that I had never suspected. It has strengthened a waning faith in the human-kindness of my brothers so that, indeed, I have gained far more than I have given, and my thanks are due twofold to those whose thanks I have received.

I confess that when this book was first published I was quite convinced that it would appeal only to a limited audience, and I shared Mr. Lawson's fear that those minds totally devoted to "boiling the cabbitch storks or somethink" were many in the land, and would miss something of what I endeavoured to say. Happily we were both mistaken.

These letters of which I write have come from men and women of all grades of society, of all shades of political thought and of many religions. But the same impulse has prompted them all, and it is good for one's soul to know that such an impulse moves so universally. I created one "Sentimental Bloke" and he discovered his brothers everywhere he went.

Towards those English men of letters who have written to me or to my publishers saying many complimentary things of my work I feel very grateful. Their numbers, their standing and their unanimity almost convince me that this preface should be written. But even the flattering invitation of so great a man as Mr. H.G. Wells, to come and work in an older land, does not entice me from the task I fondly believe to be mine in common with other writers of Australia. England has many writers: we in Australia have few, and there is big work before us.

But when I stop and read what I have written here the thought occurs to me that, even in this case, the man has not written a preface to his own book, and Mr. Lawson's advice is vain. For I have a picture before me of a somewhat younger man working in a small hut in the Australian bush, and dreaming dreams that he never hopes to realise—dreams of appreciation from his fellow countrymen and from great writers abroad whose works he devours and loves.

And I, the recipient of compliments from high places, of praise from many places, of publisher's reports about the book that bears my name—I, who write this preface, have a kindly feeling for that somewhat younger man writing and dreaming in his little bush hut; and I feel sorry for him because he is out of it. Later perhaps, when strenuous days are over, I shall go back and live with him and tell him about it, and find out what he thinks of it all—if I can find him ever again.

C. J. DENNIS
Melbourne, 1st September, 1916.

Foreword

My young friend Dennis has honoured me with a request to write a preface to his book. I think a man can best write a preface to his own book, provided he knows it is good. Also if he knows it is bad.

The Sentimental Bloke, while runnning through the *Bulletin*, brightened up many dark days for me. He is more perfect than any alleged "larrikin" or Bottle-O character I have ever attempted to sketch, not even excepting my own beloved Benno. Take the first poem for instance, where the Sentimental Bloke gets the hump. How many men, in how many different parts of the world—and of how many different languages—have had the same feeling—the longing for something better—to *be* something better?

The exquisite humour of *The Sentimental Bloke* speaks for itself; but there's a danger that its brilliance may obscure the rest, especially for minds, of all stations, that, apart from sport and racing, are totally devoted to boiling

"The cabbitch storks or somethink"

in this social "pickle found-ery" of ours.
Doreen stands for all good women, whether down in the smothering alleys or up in the frozen heights.

And so, having introduced the little woman (they all seem "little" women), I "dips me lid"—and stand aside.

HENRY LAWSON
Sydney, 1st September, 1915.

A Spring Song

THE world 'as got me snouted jist a treat;
   Crool Forchin's dirty left 'as smote me soul;
An' all them joys o' life I 'eld so sweet
   Is up the pole.
Fer, as the poit sez, me 'eart 'as got
The pip wiv yearnin' fer—I dunno wot.

I'm crook; me name is Mud; I've done me dash;
   Me flamin' spirit's got the flamin' 'ump!
I'm longin' to let loose on somethin' rash....
   Aw, I'm a chump!
I know it; but this blimed ole Springtime craze
Fair outs me, on these dilly, silly days.

The young green leaves is shootin' on the trees,
   The air is like a long, cool swig o' beer,
The bonzer smell o' flow'rs is on the breeze,
   An' 'ere's me, 'ere,
Jist moochin' round like some pore, barmy coot,
Uv 'ope, an' joy, an' forchin destichoot.

I've lorst me former joy in gittin' shick,
   Or 'eadin' browns; I 'aven't got the 'eart
To word a tom; an', square an' all, I'm sick
   Uv that cheap tart
'Oo chucks 'er carkis at a feller's 'ead
An' mauls 'im ... Ar! I wish't that I wus dead! ...

Ther's little breezes stirrin' in the leaves,
    An' sparrers chirpin' 'igh the 'ole day long;
An' on the air a sad, sweet music breaves
    A bonzer song—
A mournful sorter choon thet gits a bloke
Fair in the brisket 'ere, an' makes 'im choke ...

What *is* the matter wiv me? ... I dunno.
    I got a sorter yearnin' 'ere inside,
A dead-crook sorter thing that won't let go
    Or be denied—
A feelin' like I want to do a break,
An' stoush creation for some woman's sake.

The little birds is chirpin' in the nest,
    The parks an' gardings is a bosker sight,
Where smilin' tarts walks up an' down, all dressed
    In clobber white.
An', as their snowy forms goes steppin' by,
It seems I'm seekin' somethin' on the sly.

Somethin' or someone—I don't rightly know;
    But, seems to me, I'm kind er lookin' for
A tart I knoo a 'undred years ago,
    Or, maybe, more.
Wot's this I've 'eard them call that thing? ... Geewhizz!
Me ideel bit o' skirt! That's wot it is!

Me ideel tart! ... An', bli'me, look at me!
    Jist take a squiz at this, an' tell me can
Some square an' honist tom take this to be
    'Er own true man?
Aw, Gawd! I'd be as true to 'er, I would—
As straight an' stiddy as ... Ar, wot's the good?

Me, that 'as done me stretch fer stoushin' Johns,
    An' spen's me leisure gittin' on the shick,
An' 'arf me nights down there, in Little Lons.,
    Wiv Ginger Mick,
Jist 'eadin' 'em, an' doin' in me gilt.
Tough luck! I s'pose it's 'ow a man is built.

It's 'ow Gawd builds a bloke; but don't it 'urt
    When 'e gits yearnin's fer this 'igher life,
On these Spring mornin's, watchin' some sweet skirt—
    Some fucher wife—
Go sailin' by, an' turnin' on 'is phiz
The glarssy eye—fer bein' wot 'e is.

I've watched 'em walkin' in the gardings 'ere—
    Cliners from orfices an' shops an' such;
The sorter skirts I dursn't come too near,
    Or dare to touch.
An', when I see the kind er looks they carst ...
Gorstrooth! Wot is the *use* o' me, I arst?

Wot wus I slung 'ere for? An' wot's the good
    Uv yearnin' after any ideel tart? ...
Ar, if a bloke wus only understood!
    'E's got a 'eart:
'E's got a soul inside 'im, poor or rich.
But wot's the use, when 'Eaven's crool'd 'is pitch?

I tells meself some day I'll take a pull
    An' look eround fer some good, stiddy job,
An' cut the push fer good an' all; I'm full
    Uv that crook mob!
An', in some Spring the fucher 'olds in store,
I'll cop me prize an' long in vain no more.

The Sentimental Bloke

The little winds is stirrin' in the trees,
    Where little birds is chantin' lovers' lays;
The music of the sorft an' barmy breeze....
    Aw, spare me days!
If this 'ere dilly feelin' doesn't stop
I'll lose me block an' stoush some flamin' cop!

The Intro

'ER name's Doreen ... Well, spare me bloomin' days!
     You could er knocked me down wiv 'arf a brick!
Yes, me, that kids meself I know their ways,
     An' 'as a name for smoogin' in our click!
I jist lines up an' tips the saucy wink.
But strike! The way she piled on dawg! Yeh'd think
     A bloke wus givin' back-chat to the Queen. ...
          'Er name's Doreen.

I seen 'er in the markit first uv all,
Inspectin' brums at Steeny Isaacs' stall.
     I backs me barrer in—the same ole way—
     An' sez, "Wot O! It's been a bonzer day.
'Ow is it fer a walk?" ... Oh, 'oly wars!
The sorter *look* she gimme! Jest becors
     I tried to chat 'er, like you'd make a start
          Wiv *any* tart.

An' I kin take me oaf I wus perlite,
An' never said no word that wasn't right,
     An' never tried to maul 'er, or to do
     A thing yeh might call crook. Ter tell yeh true,
I didn't seem to 'ave the nerve—wiv 'er.
I felt as if I couldn't go that fur,
     An' start to sling off chiack like I used ...
          Not intrajuiced!

The Sentimental Bloke

Nex' time I sighted 'er in Little Bourke,
Where she wus in a job. I found 'er lurk
    Wus pastin' labels in a pickle joint,
    A game that—any'ow, that ain't the point.
Once more I tried ter chat 'er in the street,
But, bli'me! Did she turn me down a treat!
    The way she tossed 'er 'ead an' swished 'er skirt!
        Oh, it wus dirt!

A squarer tom, I swear, I never seen,
In all me natchril, than this 'ere Doreen.
    It wer'n't no guyver neither; fer I knoo
    That any other bloke 'ad Buckley's 'oo
Tried fer to pick 'er up. Yes, she was square.
She jist sailed by an' lef' me standin' there
    Like any mug. Thinks I, "I'm out er luck,"
        An' done a duck.

Well, I dunno. It's that way wiv a bloke.
If she'd ha' breasted up ter me an' spoke,
    I'd thort 'er jist a commin bit er fluff,
    An' then fergot about 'er, like enough.
It's jest like this. The tarts that's 'ard ter get
Makes you all 'ot to chase 'em, an' to let
    The cove called Cupid get an 'ammer-lock;
        An' lose yer block.

I know a bloke 'oo knows a bloke 'oo toils
In that same pickle found-ery. ('E boils
    The cabbitch storks or somethink.) Anyway,
    I gives me pal the orfis fer to say
'E 'as a sister in the trade 'oo's been
Out uv a jorb, an' wants ter meet Doreen;
    Then we kin get an intro, if we've luck.
        'E sez, "Ribuck."

The Intro

O' course we worked the oricle; you bet!
But, 'struth, I ain't recovered frum it yet!
    'Twas on a Saturdee, in Colluns Street,
      An'—quite by accident, o' course—we meet.
Me pal 'e trots 'er up an' does the toff—
'E allus wus a bloke fer showin' off.
    "This 'ere's Doreen," 'e sez. "This 'ere's the Kid."
      I dips me lid.

"This 'ere's Doreen," 'e sez. I sez "Good day."
An', bli'me, I 'ad nothin' more ter say!
    I couldn't speak a word, or meet 'er eye.
      Clean done me block! I never been so shy,
Not since I wus a tiny little cub,
An' run the rabbit to the corner pub—
    Wot time the Summer days wus dry an' 'ot—
      Fer me ole pot.

Me! that 'as barracked tarts, an' torked an' larft,
An' chucked orf at 'em like a phonergraft!
    Gorstrooth! I seemed to lose me pow'r o' speech.
      But, 'er! Oh, strike me pink! She is a peach!
The sweetest in the barrer! Spare me days,
I carn't describe that cliner's winnin' ways.
    The way she torks! 'Er lips! 'Er eyes! 'Er hair! ...
      Oh, gimme air!

I dunno 'ow I done it in the end.
I reckerlect I arst ter be 'er friend;
    An' tried ter play at 'andies in the park,
      A thing she wouldn't sight. Aw, it's a nark!
I gotter swear when I think wot a mug
I must 'a' seemed to 'er. But still I 'ug
    That promise that she give me fer the beach.
      The bonzer peach!

Now, as the poit sez, the days drag by
On ledding feet. I wish't they'd do a guy.
   I dunno 'ow I 'ad the nerve ter speak,
   An' make that meet wiv 'er fer Sund'y week!
But strike! It's funny wot a bloke'll do
When 'e's all out.... She's gorn, when I come-to.
   I'm yappin' to me cobber uv me mash....
      I've done me dash!

'Er name's Doreen.... An' me—that thort I knoo
   The ways uv tarts, an' all that smoogin' game!
An' so I ort; fer ain't I known a few?
   Yet some'ow ... I dunno. It ain't the same.
I carn't tell *wot* it is; but, all I know,
I've dropped me bundle—an' I'm glad it's so.
   Fer when I come ter think uv wot I been....
      'Er name's Doreen.

The Stoush o' Day

AR, these is 'appy days! An' 'ow they've flown—
    Flown like the smoke uv some inchanted fag;
Since dear Doreen, the sweetest tart I've known,
    Passed me the jolt that made me sky the rag.
An' ev'ry golding day floats o'er a chap
Like a glad dream of some celeschil scrap.

Refreshed wiv sleep Day to the mornin' mill
    Comes jauntily to out the nigger, Night.
Trained to the minute, confident in skill,
    'E swaggers in the East, chock-full o' skite;
Then spars a bit, an' plugs Night on the point.
Out go the stars; an' Day 'as jumped the joint.

The sun looks up, an' wiv a cautious stare,
    Like some crook keekin' o'er a winder sill
To make dead cert'in everythink is square,
    'E shoves 'is boko o'er an Eastern 'ill,
Then rises, wiv 'is dial all a-grin,
An' sez, " 'Ooray! I knoo that we could win!"

Sure uv 'is title then, the champeen Day
    Begins to put on dawg among 'is push,
An', as 'e mooches on 'is gaudy way,
    Drors tribute from each tree an' flow'r an' bush.
An', w'ile 'e swigs the dew in sylvan bars,
The sun shouts insults at the sneakin' stars.

Then, lo! the push o' Day rise to applaud;
　　An' all 'is creatures clamour at 'is feet
Until 'e thinks 'imself a little gawd,
　　An' swaggers on an' kids 'imself a treat.
The w'ile the lurkin' barrackers o' Night
Sneak in retreat an' plan another fight.

On thro' the hours, triumphant, proud an' fit,
　　The champeen marches on 'is up'ard way,
Till, at the zenith, bli'me! 'E—is—IT!
　　And all the world bows to the Boshter Day.
The jealous Night speeds messidges thro' space
'Otly demandin' terms, an' time, an' place.

A w'ile the champeen scorns to make reply;
　　'E's taken tickets on 'is own 'igh worth;
Puffed up wiv pride, an' livin' mighty 'igh,
　　'E don't admit that Night is on the earth.
But as the hours creep on 'e deigns to state
'E'll fight for all the earth an' 'arf the gate.

Late afternoon ... Day feels 'is flabby arms,
　　An' tells 'imself 'e don't seem quite the thing.
The 'omin' birds shriek clamorous alarms;
　　An' Night creeps stealthily to gain the ring.
But see! The champeen backs an' fills, becos
'E doesn't feel the Boshter Bloke 'e was.

Time does a bunk as us-u-al, nor stays
　　A single instant, e'en at Day's be'est.
Alas, the 'eavy-weight's 'igh-livin' ways
　　'As made 'im soft, an' large around the vest.
'E sez 'e's fat inside; 'e starts to whine;
'E sez 'e wants to dror the colour line.

The Stoush o' Day

Relentless nigger Night crawls thro' the ropes,
    Advancin' grimly on the quakin' Day,
Whose noisy push, shorn of their 'igh-noon 'opes,
    Wait, 'ushed an' anxious, fer the comin' fray.
An' many lusty barrackers uv noon
Desert 'im one by one—traitors so soon!

'E's out er form! 'E 'asn't trained enough!
    They mark their sickly champeen on the stage,
An' narked, the sun, 'is backer, in a huff,
    Sneaks outer sight, red in the face wiv rage.
W'ile gloomy roosters, they 'oo made the morn
Ring wiv 'is praises, creep to bed forlorn.

All faint an' groggy grows the beaten Day;
    'E staggers drunkenly about the ring;
An owl 'oots jeerin'ly across the way,
    An' bats come out to mock the fallin' King.
Now, wiv a jolt, Night spreads 'im on the floor,
An' all the west grows ruddy wiv 'is gore.

A single, vulgar star leers from the sky
    An' in derision, rudely mutters, "Yah!"
The moon, Night's conkerbine, comes glidin' by
    An' laughs a 'eartless, silvery "Ha-ha!"
Scorned, beaten, Day gives up the 'opeless fight,
An' drops 'is bundle in the lap o' Night.

      . . . . . .

So goes each day, like some celeschil mill,
    E'er since I met that shyin' little peach.
'Er bonzer voice! I 'ear its music still,
    As when she guv that promise fer the beach.
An', square an' all, no matter 'ow yeh start,
The commin end of most of us is—Tart.

Doreen

"I WISH'T yeh meant it, Bill." Oh, 'ow me 'eart
    Went out to 'er that ev'nin' on the beach.
I knoo she weren't no ordinary tart,
    My little peach!
I tell yeh, square an' all, me 'eart stood still
To 'ear 'er say, "I wish't yeh meant it, Bill."

To 'ear 'er voice! Its gentle sorter tone,
    Like soft dream-music of some Dago band.
An' me all out; an' 'oldin' in me own
    'Er little 'and.
An' 'ow she blushed! O, strike! it was divine
The way she raised 'er shinin' eyes to mine.

'Er eyes! Soft in the moon; such *boshter* eyes!
    An' when they sight a bloke ... O, spare me days!
'E goes all loose inside; such glamour lies
    In 'er sweet gaze.
It makes 'im all ashamed uv wot 'e's been
To look inter the eyes of my Doreen.

        . . . . . .

The wet sands glistened, an' the gleamin' moon
    Shone yeller on the sea, all streakin' down.
A band was playin' some soft, dreamy choon;
    An' up the town
We 'eard the distant tram-cars whir an' clash.
An' there I told 'er 'ow I'd done me dash.

Doreen

"I wish't yeh meant it." 'Struth! And did I, fair?
    A bloke 'ud be a dawg to kid a skirt
Like 'er. An' me well knowin' she was square.
    It' ud be dirt!
'E'd be no man to point wiv 'er, an' kid.
I meant it honest; an' she knoo I did.

She knoo. I've done me block in on 'er, straight.
    A cove 'as got to think some time in life
An' get some decent tart, ere it's too late,
    To be 'is wife.
But, Gawd! 'Oo would 'a' thort it could 'a' been
My luck to strike the likes of 'er?... Doreen!

Aw, I can stand their chuckin' orf, I can.
    It's 'ard; an' I'd delight to take 'em on.
The dawgs! But it gets that way wiv a man
    When 'e's fair gone.
She'll sight no stoush; an' so I 'ave to take
Their mag, an' do a duck fer 'er sweet sake.

Fer 'er sweet sake I've gone and chucked it clean:
    The pubs an' schools an' all that leery game.
Fer when a bloke 'as come to know Doreen,
    It ain't the same.
There's 'igher things, she sez, for blokes to do.
An' I am 'arf believin' that it's true.

Yes, 'igher things—that wus the way she spoke;
    An' when she looked at me I sorter felt
That bosker feelin' that comes o'er a bloke,
    An' makes 'im melt;
Makes 'im all 'ot to maul 'er, an' to shove
'Is arms about 'er... Bli'me? but it's love!

The Sentimental Bloke

That's wot it is. An' when a man 'as grown
    Like that 'e gets a sorter yearn inside
To be a little 'ero on 'is own;
    An' see the pride
Glow in the eyes of 'er 'e calls 'is queen;
An' 'ear 'er say 'e is a shine champeen.

"I wish't yeh meant it," I can 'ear 'er yet,
    My bit o' fluff! The moon was shinin' bright,
Turnin' the waves all yeller where it set—
    A bonzer night!
The sparklin' sea all sorter gold an' green;
An' on the pier the band—O, 'Ell!... Doreen!

The Play

"WOT'S in a name?" she sez ... An' then she sighs,
   An' clasps 'er little 'ands, an' rolls 'er eyes.
"A rose," she sez, "be any other name
Would smell the same.
Oh, w'erefore art you Romeo, young sir?
Chuck yer ole pot, an' change yer moniker!"

Doreen an' me, we bin to see a show—
The swell two-dollar touch. Bong tong, yeh know.
A chair apiece wiv velvit on the seat;
A slap-up treat.
The drarmer's writ be Shakespeare, years ago,
About a barmy goat called Romeo.

"Lady, be yonder moon I swear!" sez 'e.
An' then 'e climbs up on the balkiney;
An' there they smooge a treat, wiv pretty words
Like two love-birds
I nudge Doreen. She whispers, "Ain't it grand!"
'Er eyes is shinin'; an' I squeeze 'er 'and.

"Wot's in a name?" she sez. 'Struth, I dunno.
Billo is just as good as Romeo.
She may be Juli-er or Juli-et—
'E loves 'er yet.
If she's the tart 'e wants, then she's 'is queen,
Names never count ... But ar, I like "Doreen!"

A sweeter, dearer sound I never 'eard;
Ther's music 'angs around that little word,
Doreen!... But wot was this I starts to say
About the play?
I'm off me beat. But when a bloke's in love
'Is thorts turns 'er way, like a 'omin' dove.

This Romeo 'e's lurkin' wiv a crew—
A dead tough crowd o' crooks—called Montague.
'Is cliner's push—wot's nicknamed Capulet—
They 'as 'em set.
Fair narks they are, jist like them back-street clicks,
Ixcep' they fights wiv skewers 'stid o' bricks.

Wot's in a name? Wot's in a string o' words?
They scraps in ole Verona wiv the'r swords,
An' never give a bloke a stray dog's chance,
An' that's Romance.
But when they deals it out wiv bricks an' boots
In Little Lon., they're low, degraded broots.

Wot's jist plain stoush wiv us, right 'ere to-day,
Is "valler" if yer fur enough away.
Some time, some writer bloke will do the trick
Wiv Ginger Mick,
Uv Spadger's Lane. *'E'll* be a Romeo,
When 'e's bin dead five 'undred years or so.

Fair Juli-et, she gives 'er boy the tip.
Sez she: "Don't sling that crowd o' mine no lip;
An' if you run agin a Capulet,
Jist do a get."
'E swears 'e's done wiv lash; 'e'll chuck it clean.
(Same as I done when I first met Doreen.)

The Play

They smooge some more at that. Ar, strike me blue!
It gimme Joes to sit an' watch them two!
'E'd break away an' start to say good-bye,
An' then she'd sigh
"Ow, Ro-me-o!" an' git a strangle-holt,
An' 'ang around 'im like she feared 'e'd bolt.

Nex' day 'e words a gorspil cove about
A secret weddin'; an' they plan it out.
'E spouts a piece about 'ow 'e's bewitched:
Then they git 'itched ...
Now, 'ere's the place where I fair git the pip!
She's 'is for keeps, en' yet 'e lets 'er slip!

Ar! but 'e makes me sick! A fair gazob!
'E's jist the glarssy on the soulful sob,
'E'll sigh and spruik, an' 'owl a love-sick vow—
(The silly cow!)
But when 'e's got 'er, spliced an' on the straight
'E crools the pitch, an' tries to kid it's Fate.

Aw! Fate me foot! Instid of slopin' soon
As 'e was wed, off on 'is 'oneymoon,
'Im an' 'is cobber, called Mick Curio,
They 'ave to go
An' mix it wiv that push o' Capulets.
They look fer trouble; an' it's wot they gets.

A tug named Tyball (cousin to the skirt)
Sprags 'em an' makes a start to sling off dirt.
Nex' minnit there's a reel ole ding-dong go—
'Arf round or so.
Mick Curio, 'e gets it in the neck,
"Ar rats!" 'e sez, en' passes in 'is check.

The Sentimental Bloke

Quite natchril, Romeo gits wet as 'ell.
"It's me or you!" 'e 'owls, an' wiv a yell,
Plunks Tyball through the gizzard wiv 'is sword,
'Ow I ongcored!
"Put in the boot!" I sez. "Put in the boot!"
" 'Ush!" sez Doreen … "Shame!" sez some silly coot.

Then Romeo, 'e dunno wot to do.
The cops gits busy, like they allwiz do,
An' nose around until 'e gits blue funk
An' does a bunk.
They wants 'is tart to wed some other guy.
"Ah, strike!" she sez. "I wish't that I could die!"

Now, this 'ere gorspil bloke's a fair shrewd 'ead.
Sez 'e "I'll dope yeh, so they'll *think* yer dead."
(I tips 'e was a cunnin' sort, wot knoo
A thing or two.)
She takes 'is knock-out drops, up in 'er room:
They think she's snuffed, an' plant 'er in 'er tomb.

Then things gits mixed a treat an' starts to whirl.
'Ere's Romeo comes back an' finds 'is girl
Tucked in 'er little coffing, cold an' stiff,
An' in a jiff,
'E swallows lysol, throws a fancy fit,
'Ead over turkey, an' 'is soul 'as flit.

Then Juli-et wakes up an' sees 'im there,
Turns on the water-works an' tears 'er 'air,
"Dear love," she sez, "I cannot live alone!"
An' wiv a moan,
She grabs 'is pockit knife, an' ends 'er cares …
"*Peanuts or lollies!*" sez a boy upstairs.

The Stror 'at Coot

AR, wimmin! Wot a blinded fool I've been!
　　I arsts meself, wot else could I ixpeck?
I done me block complete on this Doreen,
　　An' now me 'eart is broke, me life's a wreck!
The dreams I dreamed, the dilly thorts I thunk
Is up the pole, an' joy 'as done a bunk.

Wimmin! O strike! I orter known the game!
　　Their tricks is crook, their arts is all dead snide.
The 'ole world over tarts is all the same;
　　All soft an' smilin' wiv no 'eart inside.
But she fair doped me wiv 'er winnin' ways,
Then crooled me pitch fer all me mortal days.

They're all the same! A man 'as got to be
　　Stric' master if 'e wants to snare 'em sure.
'E 'as to take a stand an' let 'em see
　　That triflin' is a thing 'e won't indure.
'E wants to show 'em that 'e 'olds command,
So they will smooge an' feed out of 'is 'and.

'E needs to make 'em feel 'e is the boss,
　　An' kid 'e's careless uv the joys they give.
'E 'as to make 'em think 'e'll feel no loss
　　To part wiv any tart 'e's trackin' wiv.
That all their pretty ways is crook pretence
Is plain to any bloke wiv common sense.

The Sentimental Bloke

But when the birds is nestin' in the spring,
    An' when the soft green leaves is in the bud,
'E drops 'is bundle to some fluffy thing.
    'E pays 'er 'omage—an' 'is name is Mud.
She plays wiv' im an' kids 'im on a treat,
Until she 'as 'im crawlin' at 'er feet.

An' then, when 'e's fair orf 'is top wiv love,
    When she 'as got 'im good an' 'ad 'er fun,
She slings 'im over like a carst-orf glove,
    To let the other tarts see wot she's done.
All vanity, deceit an' 'eartless kid!
I orter known; an', spare me days, I did!

I knoo. But when I looked into 'er eyes—
    Them shinin' eyes o' blue all soft wiv love—
Wiv *mimic* love—they seemed to 'ipnertize.
    I wus content to place 'er 'igh above.
I wus content to make of 'er a queen;
An' so she seemed them days . . . O, 'struth! . . . Doreen!

I knoo. But when I stroked 'er glossy 'air
    Wiv rev'rint 'ands, 'er cheek pressed close to mine,
Me lonely life seemed robbed of all its care;
    I dreams me dreams, an' 'ope begun to shine.
An' when she 'eld 'er lips fer me to kiss . . .
Ar, wot's the use? I'm done wiv all o' this!

Wimmin! . . . Oh, I ain't jealous! Spare me days!
    Me? Jealous uv a knock-kneed coot like that!
'Im! Wiv 'is cute stror 'at an' pretty ways!
    I'd be a mug to squeal or whip the cat.
I'm glad, I am—glad 'cos I know I'm free!
There ain't no call to tork o' jealousy.

The Stror 'at Coot

I tells meself I'm well out o' the game;
    Fer look, I mighter married 'er—an' then....
Ar strike! 'Er voice wus music when my name
    Wus on 'er lips on them glad ev'nin's when
We useter meet. An' then to think she'd go ...
No, I ain't jealous—but—Ar, I dunno!

I took a derry on this stror 'at coot
    First time I seen 'im dodgin' round Doreen.
'Im, wiv 'is giddy tie an' Yankee soot,
    Ferever yappin' like a tork-machine
About "The Hoffis" where 'e 'ad a grip....
The way 'e smiled at 'er give me the pip!

She sez I stoushed 'im, when I promised fair
    To chuck it, even to a friendly spar.
Stoushed 'im! I never roughed 'is pretty 'air!
    I only spanked 'im gentle, fer 'is mar.
If I'd 'a' jabbed 'im once, there would 'a' been
An inquest; an' I sez so to Doreen.

I mighter took an' cracked 'im in the street,
    When she was wiv 'im there lars' Frid'y night.
But don't I keep me temper when we meet?
    An' don't I raise me lid an' act perlite?
I only jerks me elbow in 'is ribs,
To give the gentle office to 'is nibs.

Stoushed 'im! I owns I met 'im on the quite,
    An' worded 'im about a small affair;
An' when 'e won't put up 'is 'ands to fight—
    ('E sez, "Fer public brawls 'e didn't care")—
I lays 'im 'cross me knee, the mother's joy,
An' smacks 'im 'earty, like a naughty boy.

The Sentimental Bloke

An' now Doreen she sez I've broke me vow,
    An' mags about this coot's pore, "wounded pride."
An' then, o' course, we 'as a ding-dong row,
    Wiv 'ot an' stormy words on either side.
She sez I done it outer jealousy,
An' so, we parts fer ever—'er an' me.

Me jealous? Jealous of that cross-eyed cow!
    I set 'im 'cos I couldn't sight 'is face.
'Is yappin' fair got on me nerves, some'ow.
    I couldn't stand 'im 'angin' round 'er place.
A coot like that!... But it don't matter much,
She's welkim to 'im if she fancies such.

I swear I'll never track wiv 'er no more;
    I'll never look on 'er side o' the street—
Unless she comes an' begs me pardin for
    Them things she said to me in angry 'eat.
She can't ixpeck fer me to smooge an' crawl.
I ain't at *any* woman's beck an' call.

Wimmin! I've took a tumble to their game.
    I've got the 'ole bang tribe uv cliners set!
The 'ole world over they are all the same:
    Crook to the core the bunch of 'em—an' yet
We could 'a' been that 'appy, 'er an' me ...
But, wot's it matter? Ain't I glad I'm free?

A bloke wiv commin-sense 'as got to own
    There's little 'appiness in married life.
The smoogin' game is better left alone,
    Fer tarts is few that makes the ideel wife.
An' them's the sort that loves wivout disguise,
An' thinks the sun shines in their 'usban's' eyes.

But when the birds is matin' in the spring,
    An' when the tender leaves begin to bud,
A feelin' comes—a dilly sorter thing—
    That seems to fairly swamp 'im like a flood.
An' when the fever 'ere inside 'im burns,
Then freedom ain't the thing fer wot 'e yearns.

But I 'ave chucked it all. An' yet—I own
    I dreams me dreams when soft Spring breezes stirs;
An' often, when I'm moonin' 'ere alone,
    A lispin' maid, wiv 'air an' eyes like 'ers,
'Oo calls me "dad," she climbs upon me knee.
An' yaps 'er pretty baby tork to me.

I sorter see a little 'ouse, it seems,
    Wiv someone waitin' for me at the gate ...
Ar, where's the sense in dreamin' barmy dreams,
    I've dreamed before, and nearly woke too late.
Sich 'appiness could never last fer long,
We're strangers—'less she owns that she was wrong.

To call 'er back I'll never lift a 'and;
    She'll never 'ear frum me by word or sign.
Per'aps, some day, she'll come to understand
    The mess she's made o' this 'ere life o' mine.
Oh, I ain't much to look at, I admit.
But 'im! The knock-kneed, swivel-eyed misfit! ...

The Siren

SHE sung a song; an' I sat silent there,
   Wiv bofe 'ands grippin' 'ard on to me chair;
      Me 'eart, that yesterdee I thort wus broke
Wiv 'umpin' sich a 'eavy load o' care,
   Come swellin' in me throat like I would choke.
I felt 'ot blushes climbin' to me 'air.

'Twas like that feelin' when the Spring wind breaves
Sad music in the sof'ly rustlin' leaves.
   An' when a bloke sits down an' starts to chew
Crook thorts, wivout quite knowin' why 'e grieves
   Fer things 'e's done 'e didn't ort to do—
Fair winded wiv the 'eavy sighs 'e 'eaves.

She sung a song; an' orl at once I seen
The kind o' crool an' 'eartless broot I been.
   In ev'ry word I read it like a book—
The slanter game I'd played wiv my Doreen—
   I 'eard it in 'er song; an' in 'er look
I seen wot made me feel fair rotten mean.

Poor, 'urt Doreen! My tender bit o' fluff!
Ar, men don't understand; they're fur too rough;
   Their ways is fur too coarse wiv lovin' tarts;
They never gives 'em symperthy enough.
   They treats 'em 'arsh; they tramples on their 'earts,
Becos their own crool 'earts is leather-tough.

The Siren

She sung a song; an' orl them bitter things
That chewin' over lovers' quarrils brings
    Guv place to thorts uv sorrer an' remorse.
Like when some dilly punter goes an' slings
    'Is larst, lone deener on some stiffened 'orse,
An' learns them vain regrets wot 'urts an' stings.

'Twas at a beano where I lobs along
To drown them memories o' fancied wrong.
    I swears I never knoo that she'd be there.
But when I met 'er eye—O, 'struth, 'twas strong!
    'Twas bitter strong, that jolt o' dull despair!
'Er look o' scorn!... An' then, she sung a song.

The choon was one o' them sad, mournful things
That ketch yeh in the bellers 'ere, and brings
    Tears to yer eyes. The words was uv a tart
'Oo's trackin' wiv a silly coot 'oo slings
    'Er love aside, an' breaks 'er tender 'eart....
But 'twasn't that; it wus the way she sings.

To 'ear 'er voice!... A bloke 'ud be a log
'Oo kep' 'is block. Me mind wus in a fog
    Uv sorrer for to think 'ow I wus wrong;
Ar, I 'ave been a fair ungrateful 'og!
    The feelin' that she put into that song
'Ud melt the 'eart-strings of a chiner dog.

I listens wiv me 'eart up in me throat;
I drunk in ev'ry word an' ev'ry note.
    Tears trembles in 'er voice when she tells 'ow
That tart snuffed out becos 'e never wrote.
    An' then I seen 'ow I wus like that cow.
Wiv sudden shame me guilty soul wus smote.

The Sentimental Bloke

Doreen she never looked my way; but stood
'Arf turned away, an' beefed it out reel good,
    Until she sang that bit about the grave;
"Too late 'e learned 'e 'ad misunderstood!"
    An' then—Gorstrooth! The pleadin' look she gave
Fair in me face 'ud melt a 'eart o' wood.

I dunno 'ow I seen that evenin' thro'.
They muster thort I was 'arf shick, I knoo.
    But I 'ad 'urt Doreen wivout no call;
I seen me dooty, wot I 'ad to do.
    O, strike! I could 'a' blubbed before 'em all!
But I sat tight, an' never cracked a boo.

An' when at larst the tarts they makes a rise,
A lop-eared coot wiv 'air down to 'is eyes
    'E 'ooks on to Doreen, an' starts to roam
Fer 'ome an' muvver. I lines up an' cries,
    "'An's orf! I'm seein' this 'ere cliner 'ome!"
An' there we left 'im, gapin' wiv surprise.

She never spoke; she never said no word;
But walked beside me like she never 'eard.
    I swallers 'ard, an' starts to coax an' plead,
I sez I'm dead ashamed o' wot's occurred.
    She don't reply; she never takes no 'eed;
Jist stares before 'er like a startled bird.

I tells 'er, never can no uvver tart
Be 'arf wot she is, if we 'ave to part.
    I tells 'er that me life will be a wreck.
It ain't no go. But when I makes a start
    To walk away, 'er arms is roun' me neck.
"Ah, Kid!" she sobs. "Yeh nearly broke me 'eart!"

The Siren

I dunno wot I done or wot I said.
But 'struth! I'll not forget it till I'm dead—
    That night when 'ope back in me brisket lobs:
'Ow my Doreen she lays 'er little 'ead
    Down on me shoulder 'ere, an' sobs an' sobs;
An' orl the lights goes sorter blurred an' red.

Say, square an' all—It don't seem right, some'ow,
To say sich things; but wot I'm feelin' now
    'As come at times, I s'pose, to uvver men—
When you 'ave 'ad a reel ole ding-dong row,
    Say, ain't it bonzer makin' up agen?
Straight wire, it's almost worth ... Ar, I'm a cow!

To think I'd ever seek to 'arm a 'air
Of 'er dear 'ead agen! My oath, I swear
    No more I'll roust on 'er in angry 'eat!
But still, she never seemed to me so fair;
    She never wus so tender or so sweet
As when she smooged beneath the lamplight there.

She's never been so lovin' wiv 'er gaze;
So gentle wiv 'er pretty wimmin's ways.
    I tells 'er she's me queen, me angel, too.
"Ah, no, I ain't no angel, Kid," she says.
    "I'm jist a woman, an' I loves yeh true!
An' so I'll love yeh all me mortal days!"

She sung a song.... 'Ere, in me barmy style,
I sets orl tarts; for in me hour o' trile
    Me soul was withered be a woman's frown,
An' broodin' care come roostin' on me dile.
    She sung a song.... Me 'eart, wiv woe carst down,
Wus raised to 'Eaven be a woman's smile.

Mar

"'ER pore dear Par," she sez, " 'e kept a store."
   An' then she weeps an' stares 'ard at the floor.
     " 'Twas thro' 'is death," she sez, "we wus rejuiced
To this," she sez ... An' then she weeps some more.

" 'Er Par," she sez, "me poor late 'usband, kept
An 'ay an' corn store. 'E'd no faults ixcept
     'Im fallin' 'eavy orf a load o' charf
W'ich—killed 'im—on the——" 'Struth! But 'ow she wept.

She blows 'er nose an' sniffs. " 'E would 'a' made"
She sez "a lot uv money in the trade.
     But, 'im took orf so sudden-like, we found
'E'adn't kept 'is life insurince paid.

"To think," she sez, "a child o' mine should be
Rejuiced to workin' in a factory!
     If 'er pore Par 'e 'adn't died," she sobs ...
I sez, "It wus a bit o' luck fer me."

Then I gits red as 'ell, "That is—I mean,"
I sez, "I mighter never met Doreen
     If 'e 'ad not"—an' 'ere I lose me block—
"I 'ope," I sez, " 'e snuffed it quick and clean."

An' that was 'ow I made me first deboo.
I'd dodged it cunnin' fer a month or two.
     Doreen she sez, "You'll 'ave to meet my Mar,
Some day," she sez. An' so I seen it thro'.

Mar

I'd pictered some stern female in a cap
Wot puts the fear o' Gawd into a chap.
    An' 'ere she wus, aweepin' in 'er tea
An' drippin' moistcher like a leaky tap.

Two dilly sorter dawgs made outer delf
Stares 'ard at me frum orf the mantelshelf.
    I seemed to symperthise wiv them there pups;
I felt so stiff an' brittle-like meself.

Clobber? Me trosso, 'ead to foot, wus noo—
Got up regardless, fer this interview.
    Stiff shirt, a Yankee soot split up the back,
A tie wiv yeller spots an' stripes o' blue.

Me cuffs kep' playin' wiv me nervis fears
Me patent leathers nearly brought the tears
    An' there I sits wiv, "Yes, mum. Thanks. Indeed?"
Me stand-up collar sorin' orf me ears.

"Life's 'ard," she sez, an' then she brightens up.
"Still, we 'ave alwus 'ad our bit and sup.
    Doreen's been *sich* a help; she 'as indeed.
Some more tea, Willy? *'Ave* another cup."

Willy! O 'ell! 'Ere wus a flamin' pill!
A moniker that alwus makes me ill.
    "If it's the same to you, mum," I replies
"I answer quicker to the name of Bill."

Up goes 'er 'ands an' eyes, "That vulgar name!
No, Willy, but it isn't all the same,
    My fucher son must be respectable."
"Orright," I sez, "I s'pose it's in the game."

The Sentimental Bloke

"Me fucher son," she sez, "right on frum this
Must not take anythink I say amiss.
  I know me jooty be me son-in-lor;
So, Willy, come an' give yer Mar a kiss."

I done it. Tho' I dunno 'ow I did.
"Dear boy," she sez, "to do as you are bid.
  Be kind to 'er," she sobs, "my little girl!"
An' then I kiss Doreen. Sez she "Ah Kid!"

Doreen! Ar 'ow 'er pretty eyes did shine.
No sight on earth or 'Eaving's 'arf so fine,
  An' as they looked at me she seemed to say
"I'm proud of 'im, I am, an' 'e is mine."

There wus a sorter glimmer in 'er eye,
An 'appy, nervis look, 'arf proud, 'arf shy;
  I seen 'er in me mind be'ind the cups
In our own little kipsie, by an' by.

An' then when Mar-in-lor an' me began
To tork of 'ouse'old things an' scheme an' plan,
  A sudden thort fair jolts me where I live:
"These is my wimmin folk! An' I'm a man!"

It's wot they calls responsibility.
All of a 'eap that feelin' come to me;
  An' somew'ere in me 'ead I seemed to feel
A sneakin' sort o' wish that I was free.

'Ere's me 'oo never took no 'eed o' life,
Investin' in a mar-in-lor an' wife:
  Someone to battle fer besides meself,
Somethink to love an' shield frum care and strife.

It makes yeh solim when yeh come to think
Wot love and marridge means. Ar, strike me pink!
   It ain't all sighs and kisses. It's yer life.
An' 'ere's me tremblin' on the bloomin' brink.

" 'Er pore dead Par," she sez, an' gulps a sob.
An' then I tells 'er 'ow I got a job,
   As storeman down at Jones' printin' joint,
A decent sorter cop at fifty bob.

Then things get 'ome-like; an' we torks till late,
An' tries to tease Doreen to fix the date,
   An' she gits suddin soft and tender-like,
An' cries a bit, when we parts at the gate.

An' as I'm moochin' 'omeward frum the car
A suddin notion stops me wiv a jar—
   Wot if Doreen, I thinks, should grow to be,
A fat ole weepin' willer like 'er Mar!

O, 'struth! It won't bear thinkin' uv! It's crook!
An' I'm a mean, unfeelin' dawg to look
   At things like that. Doreen's Doreen to me,
The sweetest peach on w'ich a man wus shook.

'Er "pore dear Par" ... I s'pose 'e 'ad 'is day,
An' kissed an' smooged an' loved 'er in 'is way.
   An' wed an' took 'is chances like a man—
But, Gawd, this splicin' racket ain't all play.

Love is a gamble, an' there ain't no certs.
Some day, I s'pose, I'll git wise to the skirts,
   An' learn to take the bitter wiv the sweet ...
But, strike me purple! "Willy!" *That's* wot 'urts.

Pilot Cove

"YOUNG friend," 'e sez ... Young friend!
    Well, spare me days!
Yeh'd think I wus 'is own white-'eaded boy—
The queer ole finger, wiv 'is gentle ways.
    "Young friend," 'e sez, "I wish't yeh bofe great joy."
    The langwidge that them parson blokes imploy
Fair tickles me. The way 'e bleats an' brays!
              "Young friend," 'e sez.

"Young friend," 'e sez ... Yes, my Doreen an' me
    We're gettin' hitched, all straight an' on the square.
Fer when I torks about the registry—
    O 'oly wars! yeh should 'a' seen 'er stare;
    "The registry?" she sez, "I wouldn't dare!
I know a clergyman we'll go an' see" ...
              "Young friend," 'e sez.

"Young friend," 'e sez. An' then 'e chats me straight;
    An' spouts uv death, an' 'ell, an' mortal sins.
"You reckernize this step you contemplate
    Is grave?" 'e sez. An' I jist stan's an' grins;
    Fer when I chips, Doreen she kicks me shins.
"Yes, very 'oly is the married state,
              Young friend," 'e sez.

"Young friend," 'e sez. An' then 'e mags a lot
    Of jooty an' the spiritchuil life,
To which I didn't tumble worth a jot.
    "I'm sure," 'e sez, "as you will 'ave a wife
    'Oo'll 'ave a noble infl'ince on yer life.
'Oo is 'er gardjin?" I sez, " 'Er ole pot"—
              "Young friend!" 'e sez.

"Young friend," 'e sez. "Oh fix yer thorts on 'igh!
　　Orl marriages is registered up there!
An' you must cleave unto 'er till yeh die,
　　An' cherish 'er wiv love an' tender care.
　　E'en in the days when she's no longer fair
She's still yer wife," 'e sez. "Ribuck," sez I.
　　　　　　　"Young friend!" 'e sez.

"Young friend," 'e sez—I sez, "Now, listen 'ere:
　　This isn't one o' them impetchus leaps.
There ain't no tart a 'undreth part so dear
　　As 'er. She 'as me 'eart an' soul fer keeps!"
　　An' then Doreen, she turns away an' weeps;
But 'e jist smiles. "Yer deep in love, 'tis clear,
　　　　　　　Young friend," 'e sez.

"Young friend," 'e sez—an' tears wus in 'is eyes—
　　"Strive 'ard. Fer many, many years I've lived.
An' I kin but recall wiv tears an' sighs
　　The lives of some I've seen in marridge gived."
　　"My Gawd!" I sez. "I'll strive as no bloke strivved!
Fer don't I know I've copped a bonzer prize?"
　　　　　　　"Young friend," 'e sez.

"Young friend," 'e sez. An' in 'is gentle way,
　　'E pats the shoulder uv my dear Doreen.
"I've solem'ized grand weddin's in me day,
　　But 'ere's the sweetest little maid I've seen.
　　She's fit fer any man, to be 'is queen;
An' you're more forchinit than you kin say,
　　　　　　　Young friend," 'e sez.

The Sentimental Bloke

"Young friend," 'e sez ... A queer ole pilot bloke,
    Wiv silver 'air. The gentle way 'e dealt
Wiv 'er, the soft an' kindly way 'e spoke
    To my Doreen, 'ud make a statcher melt.
    I tell yeh, square an' all, I sorter felt
A kiddish kind o' feelin' like I'd choke ...
              "Young friend," 'e sez.

"Young friend," 'e sez, "you two on Choosday week,
    Is to be joined in very 'oly bonds.
To break them vows I 'opes yeh'll never seek;
    Fer I could curse them 'usbands 'oo absconds!"
    "I'll love 'er till I snuff it," I responds.
"Ah, that's the way I likes to 'ear yeh speak,
              Young friend," 'e sez.

"Young friend," 'e sez—an' then me 'and 'e grips—
    "I wish's yeh luck, you an' yer lady fair.
Sweet maid." An' sof'ly wiv 'is finger-tips,
    'E takes an' strokes me cliner's shinin' 'air.
    An' when I seen 'er standin' blushin' there,
I turns an' kisses 'er, fair on the lips.
              "Young friend!" 'e sez.

Hitched

"A N'—wilt—yeh—take—this—woman—fer—to—be—
Yer—weddid—wife?"... O, strike me! Will I wot?
Take 'er? Doreen? 'E stan's there *arstin'* me!
    As if 'e thort per'aps I'd rather not!
    Take 'er? 'E seemed to think 'er kind wus got
Like cigarette-cards, fer the arstin'. Still,
    I does me stunt in this 'ere hitchin' rot,
An' speaks me piece: "Righto!" I sez, "I will."

"I will," I sez. An' tho' a joyful shout
    Come from me bustin' 'eart—I know it did—
Me voice got sorter mangled comin' out,
    An' makes me whisper like a frightened kid.
    "I will," I squeaks. An' I'd 'a' give a quid
To 'ad it on the quite, wivout this fuss,
    An' orl the starin' crowd that Mar 'ad bid
To see this solim hitchin' up uv us.

"Fer—rich-er—er—fer—poor-er." So 'e bleats.
    "In—sick-ness—an'—in—'ealth,"... An' there I stands,
An' dunno 'arf the chatter I repeats,
    Nor wot the 'ell to do wiv my two 'ands.
    But 'e don't 'urry puttin'on our brands—
This white-'aired pilot-bloke—but gives it lip,
    Dressed in 'is little shirt, wiv frills an' bands.
"In sick-ness—an'—in—" Ar! I got the pip!

The Sentimental Bloke

An' once I missed me turn; an' Ginger Mick,
   'Oo's my best-man, 'e ups an' beefs it out.
"I will!" 'e 'owls; an' fetches me a kick.
    "Your turn to chin!" 'e tips me wiv a shout.
    An' there I'm standin' like a gawky lout.
(Aw, spare me! But I seemed to be *all* 'ands!)
   An' wonders wot 'e's goin' crook about,
Wiv 'arf a mind to crack 'im where 'e stands.

O, lumme! But ole Ginger was a trick!
   Got up regardless fer the solim rite.
('E 'awks the bunnies when 'e toils, does Mick)
    An' twice I saw 'im feelin' fer a light
    To start a fag; an' trembles lest 'e might,
Thro' force o' habit like. 'E's nervis too;
   That's plain, fer orl 'is air o'bluff an' skite;
An' jist as keen as me to see it thro'.

But, 'struth, the wimmin! 'Ow they love this frill!
   Fer Auntie Liz, an' Mar, o' course, wus there;
An' Mar's two uncles' wives, an' Cousin Lil,
    An' 'arf a dozen more to grin and stare.
    I couldn't make me 'ands fit anywhere!
I felt like I wus up afore the Beak!
   But my Doreen she never turns a 'air,
Nor misses once when it's 'er turn to speak.

Ar, strike! No more swell marriages fer me!
   It seems a blinded year afore 'e's done.
We could 'a' fixed it in the registree
    Twice over 'fore this cove 'ad 'arf begun.
    I s'pose the wimmin git some sorter fun
Wiv all this guyver, an' 'is nibs's shirt.
   But, seems to me, it takes the bloomin' bun,
This stylish splicin' uv a bloke an' skirt.

Hitched

"To—be—yer—weddid—wife—" Aw, take a pull!
    Wot in the 'ell's 'e think I come there for?
An' so 'e drawls an' drones until I'm full,
    An' wants to do a duck clean out the door.
    An' yet, fer orl 'is 'igh-falutin' jor,
Ole Snowy wus a reel good-meanin' bloke.
    If 'twasn't fer the 'oly look 'e wore
Yeh'd think 'e piled it on jist fer a joke.

An', when at last 'e shuts 'is little book,
    I 'eaves a sigh that nearly bust me vest.
But 'Eavens! Now 'ere's muvver goin' crook!
    An' sobbin' awful on me manly chest!
    (I wish she'd give them water-works a rest.)
"My little girl!" she 'owls. "O, treat 'er well!
    She's young—too young to leave 'er muvver's nest!"
"Orright, ole chook," I nearly sez. Oh, 'ell!

An' then we 'as a beano up at Mar's—
    A slap-up feed, wiv wine an' two big geese.
Doreen sits next ter me, 'er eyes like stars.
    O, 'ow I wished their blessed yap would cease!
    The Parson-bloke 'e speaks a little piece,
That makes me blush an' 'ang me silly 'ead.
    'E sez 'e 'opes our lovin' will increase—
I *likes* that pilot fer the things 'e said.

'E sez Doreen an' me is in a boat,
    An' sailin' on the matrimonial sea.
'E sez as 'ow 'e 'opes we'll allus float
    In peace an' joy, frum storm an' danger free.
    Then muvver gits to weepin' in 'er tea;
An' Auntie Liz sobs like a winded colt;
    An' Cousin Lil comes 'round an' kisses me;
Until I feel I'll 'ave to do a bolt.

The Sentimental Bloke

Then Ginger gits end-up an' makes a speech—
    ('E'd 'ad a couple, but 'e wasn't shick.)
"My cobber 'ere," 'e sez, " 'as copped a peach!
    Uv orl the barrer-load she is the pick!
    I 'opes 'e won't fergit 'is pals too quick
As wus 'is frien's in olden days, becors,
    I'm trustin', later on," sez Ginger Mick,
"To celebrate the chris'nin'." ... 'Oly wars!

At last Doreen an' me we gits away,
    An' leaves 'em doin' nothin' to the scran.
(We're honey-moonin' down beside the Bay.)
    I gives a 'arf a dollar to the man
    Wot drives the cab; an' like two kids we ran
To ketch the train—Ah, strike! I could 'a' flown!
    We gets the carridge right agen the van.
She whistles, jolts, an' starts ... An' we're alone!

Doreen an' me! My precious bit o' fluff!
    Me own true weddid wife! ... An' we're alone!
She seems so frail, an' me so big an' rough—
    I dunno wot this feelin' is that's grown
    Inside me 'ere that makes me feel I own
A thing so tender like I fear to squeeze
    Too 'ard fer fear she'll break ... Then, wiv a groan
I starts to 'ear a coot call, "Tickets, please!"

You could 'a' outed me right on the spot!
    I wus so rattled when that porter spoke.
Fer, 'struth! them tickets I 'ad fair fergot!
    But 'e jist laughs, an' takes it fer a joke.
    "We must ixcuse," 'e sez, "new-married folk."
An' I pays up, an' grins, an' blushes red....
    It shows 'ow married life improves a bloke:
If I'd bin single I'd 'a' punched 'is head!

Beef Tea

SHE never magged; she never said no word;
But sat an' looked at me an' never stirred.
   I could 'a' bluffed it out if she 'ad been
Fair narked, an' let me 'ave it wiv 'er tongue;
But silence told me 'ow 'er 'eart wus wrung.
                  Poor 'urt Doreen!
Gorstruth! I'd sooner fight wiv fifty men
Than git one look like that frum 'er agen!

She never moved; she never spoke no word;
That 'urt look in 'er eyes, like some scared bird:
   " 'Ere is the man I loved," it seemed to say.
" 'E's mine, this crawlin' thing, an' I'm 'is wife;
Tied up fer good; an' orl me joy in life
                  Is chucked away!"
If she 'ad bashed me I'd 'a felt no 'urt!
But 'ere she treats me like—like I wus dirt.

'Ow is a man to guard agin that look?
Fer other wimmin, when the'r blokes go crook,
   An' lobs 'ome wiv the wages uv a jag,
They smashes things an' carries on a treat
An' 'owls an' scolds an' wakes the bloomin' street
                  Wiv noisy mag.
But 'er—she never speaks; she never stirs ...
I drops me bundle ... An' the game is 'ers.

The Sentimental Bloke

Jist two months wed! Eight weeks uv married bliss
Wiv my Doreen, an' now it's come to this!
    Wot wus I thinkin' uv? Gawd! I ain't fit
To kiss the place 'er little feet 'as been!
'Er that I called me wife, me own Doreen!
                    Fond dreams 'as flit;
Love's done a bunk, an' joy is up the pole;
An' shame an' sorrer's roostin' in me soul.

'Twus orl becors uv Ginger Mick—the cow!
(I wish't I 'ad 'im 'ere to deal wiv now!
    I'd pass 'im one, I would! 'E ain't no man!)
I meets 'im Choosd'y ev'nin' up the town.
"Wot O," 'e chips me. "Kin yeh keep one down?"
                      I sez I can.
We 'as a couple; then meets three er four
Flash coves I useter know, an' 'as some more.

" 'Ow are yeh on a little gamble, Kid?"
Sez Ginger Mick. "Lars' night I'm on four quid.
    Come 'round an' try yer luck at Steeny's school."
"No," sez me conscience. Then I thinks, "Why not?
An' buy 'er presents if I wins a pot?
                      A blazin' fool
I wus. Fer 'arf a mo' I 'as a fight;
Then conscience skies the wipe ... Sez I "Orright."

Ten minutes later I wus back once more,
Kip in me 'and, on Steeny Isaac's floor,
    Me luck wus in an' I wus 'eadin' good.
Yes, back agen amongst the same old crew!
An' orl the time down in me 'eart I knew
                      I never should ...
Nex' thing I knows it's after two o'clock—
Two in the mornin'! An' I've done me block!

48

Beef Tea

"Wot odds?" I thinks. "I'm in fer it orright."
An' so I stops an' gambles orl the night;
    An' bribes me conscience wiv the gilt I wins.
But when I comes out in the cold, 'ard dawn
I know I've crooled me pitch; me soul's in pawn.
                Me flamin' sins
They 'its me in a 'eap right where I live;
Fer I 'ave broke the solim vow I give.

She never magged; she never said no word.
An' when I speaks, it seems she never 'eard.
    I could 'a' sung a nim, I feels so gay!
If she 'ad only roused I might 'a' smiled.
She jist seems 'urt an' crushed; not even riled.
                I turns away,
An' yanks me carkis out into the yard,
Like some whipped pup; an' kicks meself reel 'ard.

An' then, I sneaks to bed, an' feels dead crook.
Fer golden quids I couldn't face that look—
    That trouble in the eyes uv my Doreen.
Aw, strike! Wot made me go an' do this thing?
I feel jist like a chewed up bit of string,
                An' rotten mean!
Fer 'arf an hour I lies there feelin' cheap;
An' then I s'pose, I muster fell asleep....

" 'Ere, Kid, drink this" ... I wakes, an' lifts me 'ead,
An' sees 'er standin' there beside the bed;
    A basin in 'er 'ands; an' in 'er eyes—
(Eyes that wiv unshed tears is shinin' wet)—
The sorter look I never shall ferget,
                Until I dies.
" 'Ere, Kid, drink this," she sez, an' smiles at me.
I looks—an' spare me days! *It wus beef tea!*

Beef tea! She treats me like a hinvaleed!
Me! that 'as caused 'er lovin' 'eart to bleed.
   It 'urts me worse than maggin' fer a week!
'Er! 'oo 'ad right to turn dead sour on me,
Fergives like that, an' feeds me wiv beef tea ...
                I tries to speak;
An' then—I ain't ashamed o' wot I did—
I 'ides me face ... an' blubbers like a kid.

Uncle Jim

"I GOT no time fer wasters, lad," sez 'e,
    "Give me a man wiv grit," sez Uncle Jim.
'E bores 'is cute ole eyes right into me,
    While I stares 'ard an' gives it back to 'im.
Then orl at once 'e grips me 'and in 'is:
"Some'ow," 'e sez, "I likes yer ugly phiz."

"Yeh got a look," 'e sez, "like you could stay;
    Altho' yeh mauls King's English when yeh yaps,
An' 'angs flash frills on ev'rythink yeh say.
    I ain't no grammarist meself, per'aps,
But langwidge is a 'elp, I owns," sez Unk,
"When things is goin' crook." An' 'ere 'e wunk.

"Yeh'll find it tough," 'e sez, "to knuckle down.
    Good farmin' is a gift—like spoutin' slang.
Yeh'll 'ave to cut the luxuries o' town,
    An' chuck the manners uv this back-street gang;
Fer country life ain't cigarettes and beer."
"I'm game," I sez. Sez Uncle, "Put it 'ere!"

Like that I took the plunge, an' slung the game.
    I've parted wiv them joys I 'eld most dear;
I've sent the leery bloke that bore me name
    Clean to the pack wivout one pearly tear;
An' frum the ashes of a ne'er-do-well
A bloomin' farmer's blossomin' like 'ell.

Farmer! That's me! Wiv this 'ere strong right 'and
    I've gripped the plough; and blistered jist a treat.
Doreen an' me 'as gone upon the land.
    Yours truly fer the burden an' the 'eat!
Yours truly fer upendin' chunks o' soil!
The 'ealthy, 'ardy, 'appy son o' toil!

I owns I've 'ankered fer me former joys;
    I've 'ad me hours o' broodin' on me woes;
I've missed the comp'ny, an' I've missed the noise,
    The football matches an' the picter shows.
I've missed—but, say, it makes me feel fair mean
To whip the cat; an' then see my Doreen.

To see the colour comin' in 'er cheeks,
    To see 'er eyes grow brighter day be day,
The new, glad way she looks an' laughs an' speaks
    Is worf ten times the things I've chucked away.
An' there's a secret, whispered in the dark,
'As made me 'eart sing like a flamin' lark.

Jist let me tell yeh 'ow it come about.
    The things that I've been thro' 'ud fill a book.
Right frum me birf Fate played to knock me out;
    The 'and that I 'ad dealt to me was crook!
Then comes Doreen, an' patches up me parst;
Now Forchin's come to bunk wiv me at larst.

First orf, one night poor Mar gits suddin fits,
    An' floats wivout the time to wave "good-byes."
Doreen is orl broke up the day she flits;
    It tears me 'eart in two the way she cries.
To see 'er grief, it almost made me glad
I never knowed the mar I must 'ave 'ad.

Uncle Jim

We done poor Muvver proud when she went out—
    A slap-up send-orf, trimmed wiv tears an' crape.
An' then fer weeks Doreen she mopes about,
    An' life takes on a gloomy sorter shape.
I watch 'er face git pale, 'er eyes grow dim;
Till—like some 'airy angel—comes ole Jim.

A cherub togged in sunburn an' a beard
    An' duds that shouted " 'Ayseed!" fer a mile:
Care took the count the minute 'e appeared,
    An' sorrer shrivelled up before 'is smile,
'E got the 'ammer-lock on my good-will
The minute that 'e sez, "So, this is Bill."

It's got me beat. Doreen's late Par, some way,
    Was second cousin to 'is bruvver's wife.
Somethin' like that. In less than 'arf a day
    It seemed 'e'd been my uncle orl me life.
'E takes me 'and: "I dunno 'ow it is,"
'E sez, "but, lad, I likes that ugly phiz."

An' when 'e'd stayed wiv us a little while
    The 'ouse begun to look like 'ome once more.
Doreen she brightens up beneath 'is smile,
    An' 'ugs 'im till I kids I'm gettin' sore.
Then, late one night, 'e opens up 'is scheme,
An' passes me wot looks like some fond dream.

'E 'as a little fruit-farm, doin' well;
    'E saved a tidy bit to see 'im thro';
'E's gittin' old fer toil, an' wants a spell;
    An' 'ere's a 'ome jist waitin' fer us two.
"It's 'ers an' yours fer keeps when I am gone,"
Sez Uncle Jim. "Lad, will yeh take it on?"

The Sentimental Bloke

So that's the strength of it. An' 'ere's me now
    A flamin' berry farmer, full o' toil;
Playin' joo-jitsoo wiv an' 'orse an' plough,
    An' coaxin' fancy tucker frum the soil,
An' longin', while I wrestles with the rake,
Fer days when me poor back fergits to ache.

Me days an' nights is full uv schemes an' plans
    To figger profits an' cut out the loss;
An' when the pickin's on, I 'ave me 'an's
    To take me orders while I act the boss;
It's sorter sweet to 'ave the right to rouse....
An' my Doreen's the lady uv the 'ouse.

To see 'er bustlin' 'round about the place,
    Full uv the simple joy o' doin' things,
That thoughtful, 'appy look upon 'er face,
    That 'ope an' peace an' pride o' labour brings,
Is worth the crowd uv joys I knoo one time,
An' makes regrettin' 'em seem like a crime.

An' ev'ry little while ole Uncle Jim
    Comes up to stay a bit an' pass a tip.
It gives us 'eart jist fer to look at 'im,
    An' feel the friendship in 'is warm 'and-grip.
'Im, wiv the sunburn on 'is kind ole dile;
'Im, wiv the sunbeams in 'is sweet ole smile.

"I got no time fer wasters, lad," sez 'e,
    "But that there ugly mug o' yourn I trust."
An' so I reckon that it's up to me
    To make a bloomin' do uv it or bust.
I got to take the back-ache wiv the rest,
An' plug along, an' do me little best.

Uncle Jim

Luck ain't no steady visitor, I know;
    But now an' then it calls—fer look at me!
You wouldn't take me, 'bout a year ago,
    Free gratis wiv a shillin' pound o' tea;
Then, in a blessed 'eap, ole Forchin lands
A missus an' a farm fair in me 'ands.

The Kid

MY son!... Them words, jist like a blessed song,
Is singin' in me 'eart the 'ole day long;
   Over an' over; while I'm scared I'll wake
   Out uv a dream, to find it all a fake.

My son! Two little words, that, yesterdee,
Wus jist two simple, senseless words to me;
   An' now—no man, not since the world begun,
   Made any better pray'r than that.... My son!

My son an' bloomin' 'eir ... Ours! ... 'Ers an' mine!
The finest kid in—Aw, the sun don't shine—
   Ther' ain't no joy fer me beneath the blue
   Unless I'm gazin' lovin' at them two.

A little while ago it was jist "me"—
A lonely, longin' streak o' misery.
   An' then 'twas " 'er an' me"—Doreen, my wife!
   An' now it's " 'im an' us" an'—sich is life.

But 'struth! 'E is king-pin! The 'ead serang!
I mustn't tramp about, or talk no slang;
   I mustn't pinch 'is nose, or make a face,
   I mustn't—Strike! 'E seems to own the place!

Cunnin'? Yeh'd think, to look into 'is eyes,
'E knoo the game clean thro'; 'e seems that wise.
   Wiv 'er 'an nurse 'e is the leadin' man,
   An' poor ole dad's amongst the "also ran."

The Kid

"Goog, goo," 'e sez, and curls 'is cunnin' toes.
Yeh'd be su'prised the 'eaps o' things 'e knows.
    I'll swear 'e tumbles I'm 'is father, too;
    The way 'e squints at me, an' sez "Goog, goo."

Why! 'smornin' 'ere 'is lordship gits a grip
Fair on me finger—give it quite a nip!
    An' when I tugs, 'e won't let go 'is hold!
    'Angs on like that! An' 'im not three weeks old!

"Goog, goo," 'e sez. I'll swear yeh never did
In all yer natcheril, see sich a kid.
    The cunnin' ways 'e's got; the knowin' stare—
    Ther' ain't a youngster like 'im *anywhere!*

An', when 'e gits a little pain inside,
'Is dead straight griffin ain't to be denied.
    I'm sent to talk sweet nuffin's to the fowls;
    While nurse turns 'and-springs ev'ry time 'e 'owls.

But say, I tell yeh straight ... I been thro' 'ell!
The things I thort I wouldn't dare to tell
    Lest, in the tellin' I might feel again
    One little part of all that fear an' pain.

It come so sudden that I lorst me block.
First, it was, 'Ell-fer-leather to the doc.,
    'Oo took it all so calm 'e made me curse—
    An' then I sprints like mad to git the nurse.

By gum; that woman! But she beat me flat!
A man's jist putty in a game like that.
    She owned me 'appy 'ome almost before
    She fairly got 'er nose inside me door.

The Sentimental Bloke

Sweatin' I was! but cold wiv fear inside—
An' then, to think a man could be denied
   'Is wife an' 'ome an' told to fade away
   By jist one fat ole nurse 'oo's in 'is pay!

I wus too weak wiv funk to start an' rouse.
'Struth! Ain't a man the boss in 'is own 'ouse?
   "You go an' chase yerself!" she tips me straight.
   There's nothin' now fer you to do but—wait."

Wait? . . . Gawd! . . . I never knoo wot waitin' meant
In all me life till that day I was sent
   To loaf around, while there inside—Aw, strike!
   I couldn't tell yeh wot that hour was like!

Three times I comes to listen at the door;
Three times I drags meself away once more;
   'Arf dead wiv fear; 'arf filled wiv tremblin' joy . . .
   An' then she beckons me, an' sez—"A boy!"

"A boy!" she sez. "An' bofe is doin' well!"
I drops into a chair, an' jist sez—" 'Ell!"
   It was a pray'r. I feels bofe crook an' glad. . . .
   An' that's the strength of bein' made a dad.

I thinks uv church, when in that room I goes,
'Oldin' me breaf an' walkin' on me toes.
   Fer 'arf a mo' I feared me nerve 'ud fail
   To see 'er lying there so still an' pale.

She looks so frail, at first, I dursn't stir.
An' then, I leans acrost an' kisses 'er;
   An' all the room gits sorter blurred an' dim . . .
   She smiles, an' moves 'er 'ead. "Dear lad! Kiss 'im."

The Kid

Near smothered in a ton uv snowy clothes,
First thing, I sees a bunch o' stubby toes,
   Bald 'ead, termater face, an' two big eyes.
   "Look, Kid," she smiles at me. "Ain't 'e a size?"

'E didn't seem no sorter size to me;
But yet, I speak no lie when I agree;
   " 'E is," I sez, an' smiles back at Doreen,
   "The biggest nipper fer 'is age I've seen."

She turns away; 'er eyes is brimmin' wet.
"Our little son!" she sez. "Our precious pet!"
   An' then, I seen a great big drop roll down
   An' fall—kersplosh!—fair on 'is nibs's crown.

An' still she smiles. "A lucky sign," she said.
"Somewhere, in some ole book, one time I read,
   'The child will sure be blest all thro' the years
   Who's christened wiv 'is mother's 'appy tears.' "

"Kiss 'im," she sez. I was afraid to take
Too big a mouthful of 'im, fear 'e'd break.
   An' when 'e gits a fair look at me phiz
   'E puckers up 'is nose, an' then—Geewhizz!

'Ow *did* 'e 'owl! In 'arf a second more
Nurse 'ad me 'ustled clean outside the door.
   Scarce knowin' 'ow, I gits out in the yard,
   An' leans agen the fence an' thinks reel 'ard.

A long, long time I looks at my two 'ands.
"They're all I got," I thinks, "they're all that stands
   Twixt this 'ard world an' them I calls me own.
   An' fer their sakes I'll work 'em to the bone."

The Sentimental Bloke

Them vows an' things sounds like a lot o' guff.
Maybe, it's foolish thinkin' all this stuff—
    Maybe, it's childish-like to scheme an' plan;
    But—I dunno—it's that way wiv a man.

I only know that kid belongs to me!
We ain't decided yet wot 'e's to be.
    Doreen, she sez 'e's got a poit's eyes;
    But I ain't got much use fer them soft guys.

I think we ort to make 'im something great—
A bookie, or a champeen 'eavy-weight:
    Some callin' that'll give 'im room to spread.
    A fool could see 'e's got a clever 'ead.

I knows 'e's good an' honest; fer 'is eyes
Is jist like 'ers; so big an' lovin'-wise;
    They carries peace an' trust where e'er they goes
    An', say, the nurse she sez 'e's got my nose!

Dead ring fer me ole conk, she sez it is.
More like a blob of putty on 'is phiz,
    I think. But 'e's a fair 'ard case, all right.
    I'll swear I thort 'e wunk at me last night!

My wife an' fam'ly! Don't it sound all right!
That's wot I whispers to meself at night.
    Some day, I s'pose, I'll learn to say it loud
    An' careless; kiddin' that I don't feel proud.

My son!... If there's a Gawd 'Oos leanin' near
To watch our dilly little lives down 'ere,
    'E smiles, I guess, if 'E's a lovin' one—
    Smiles, friendly-like, to 'ear them words—My son.

The Mooch o' Life

THIS ev'nin' I was sittin' wiv Doreen,
   Peaceful an' 'appy wiv the day's work done,
Watchin', be'ind the orchard's bonzer green,
   The flamin' wonder uv the settin' sun.

Another day gone by; another night
Creepin' along to douse Day's golden light;
   Another dawnin', when the night is gone,
   To live an' love—an' so life mooches on.

Times I 'ave thought, when things was goin' crook,
   When 'Ope turned nark an' Love fergot to smile,
Of somethin' I once seen in some ole book
   Where an ole sore-'ead arsts, "Is life worf w'ile?"

But in that stillness, as the day grows dim,
An' I am sittin' there wiv 'er an' 'im—
   My wife, my son! an' strength in me to strive,
   I only know—it's good to be alive!

Yeh live, yeh love, yeh learn; an' when yeh come
   To square the ledger in some thortful hour,
The everlastin' answer to the sum
   Must alwus be, "Where's sense in gittin' sour?"

Fer when yeh've come to weigh the good an' bad—
The gladness wiv the sadness you 'ave 'ad—
   Then 'im 'oo's faith in 'uman goodness fails
   Fergits to put 'is liver in the scales.

The Sentimental Bloke

Livin' an' lovin'; learnin' day be day;
    Pausin' a minute in the barmy strife
To find that 'elpin' others on the way
    Is gold coined fer your profit—sich is life.

I've studied books wiv yearnings to improve,
To 'eave meself out of me lowly groove,
    An' 'ere is orl the change I ever got:
    " 'Ark at yer 'eart, an' you kin learn the lot."

I gives it in—that wisdom o' the mind—
    I wasn't built to play no lofty part.
Orl such is welkim to the joys they find;
    I only know the wisdom o' the 'eart.

An' ever it 'as taught me, day be day,
The one same lesson in the same ole way:
    "Look fer yer profits in the 'earts o' friends,
    Fer 'atin' never paid no dividends."

Life's wot yeh make it; an' the bloke 'oo tries
To grab the shinin' stars frum out the skies
    Goes crook on life, an' calls the world a cheat,
    An' tramples on the daisies at 'is feet.

But when the moon comes creepin' o'er the hill,
    An' when the mopoke calls along the creek,
I takes me cup o' joy an' drinks me fill,
    An' arsts meself wot better could I seek.

An' ev'ry song I 'ear the thrushes sing
That everlastin' message seems to bring;
    An' ev'ry wind that whispers in the trees
    Gives me the tip there ain't no joys like these:

The Mooch o' Life

Livin' an' lovin'; wand'rin' on yer way;
    Reapin' the 'arvest uv a kind deed done;
An' watchin', in the sundown uv yer day,
    Yerself again, grown nobler in yer son.

Knowin' that ev'ry coin o' kindness spent
Bears interest in yer 'eart at cent per cent;
    Measurin' wisdom by the peace it brings
    To simple minds that values simple things.

An' when I take a look along the way
    That I 'ave trod, it seems the man knows best,
Who's met wiv slabs uv sorrer in 'is day,
    When 'e is truly rich an' truly blest.

An' I am rich, becos me eyes 'ave seen
The lovelight in the eyes of my Doreen;
    An' I am blest, becos me feet 'ave trod
    A land 'oo's fields reflect the smile o' God.

Livin' an' lovin'; learnin' to fergive
    The deeds an' words of some un'appy bloke
Who's missed the bus—so 'ave I come to live,
    An' take the 'ole mad world as 'arf a joke.

        . . . . . .

Sittin' at ev'nin' in this sunset-land,
Wiv 'Er in all the World to 'old me 'and,
    A son, to bear me name when I am gone....
    Livin' an' lovin'—so life mooches on.

The Australaise
A MARCHING SONG

**Air: 'Onward Christian Soldiers'
(in march time)**

Dedicated to the Australian Expeditionary Force

FELLERS of Australier,
   Blokes an' coves an' coots,
Shift yer —— carcases,
Move yer —— boots.
Gird yer —— loins up,
Get yer —— gun,
Set the —— enermy
An' watch the blighters run.

Chorus

Get a —— move on,
Have some —— sense.
Learn the —— art of
Self de- —— -fence.

Have some —— brains be-
Neath yer —— lids.
An' swing a —— sabre
Fer the missus an' the kids.
Chuck supportin' —— posts,
An' strikin' —— lights,
Support a —— fam'ly an'
Strike fer yer —— rights.

Chorus

The Sentimental Bloke

Joy is —— fleetin',
    Life is —— short.
Wot's the use er wastin' it
    All on —— sport?
Hitch yer —— tip-dray
    To a ——star.
Let yer —— watchword be
    "Australi- —— -ar!"

Chorus

'Ow's our —— nation
    Goin' to ixpand
Lest us —— blokes an' coves
    Lend a —— 'and ?
'Eave yer —— apathy
    Down a —— chasm;
'Ump yer —— burden with
    Euthusi- —— -asm.

Chorus

W'en old mother Britain
    Calls yer native land
Take a —— rifle
    In yer —— 'and
Keep yer —— upper lip
    Stiff as stiff kin be,
An' speed a —— bullet for
    Pos- —— -terity.

Chorus

The Australaise

W'en the —— bugle
Sounds "Ad- —— -vance"
Don't be like a flock er sheep
In a —— trance.
Biff the —— Kaiser
Where it don't agree.
Spifler- —— -cate him
To Eternity.

Chorus

Fellers of Australier,
Cobbers, chaps an' mates,
Hear the —— German
Kickin' at the gates!
Blow the —— bugle,
Beat the —— drum,
Upper-cut and out the cow
To kingdom- —— -come!

Chorus

Get a —— move on,
Have some —— sense.
Learn the —— art of
Self de- —— -fence.

Note:—Where a dash replaces a missing word, the affective "blessed" may be interpolated. In cases demanding great emphasis, the use of the word "blooming" is permissible. However, any other word may be used that suggests itself as suitable.

THE MOODS OF GINGER MICK

DEDICATED TO

THE BOYS WHO TOOK THE COUNT

Introduction

*Jist to intrajuice me cobber, an' 'is name is Ginger Mick—
A rorty boy, a naughty boy, wiv rude ixpressions thick
In 'is casu'l conversation, an' the wicked sort o' face
That gives the sudden shudders to the lor-abidin' race.*

*'Is name is on the records at the Melbourne City Court,
Fer doin' things an' saying' things no reel nice feller ort;
An' 'is name is on the records uv the Army, over there,
Fer doin' things—same sort o' things that rose the Bench's 'air.*

*They never rung no joy-bells when 'e made 'is first de-boo;
But 'e got free edjication, w'ich they fondly shoved 'im thro';
Then turned 'im loose in Spadger's Lane to 'ang around the street
An' 'elp the cop to re-erlize the 'ardness uv 'is beat.*

*Then 'e quickly dropped 'is haitches, so as not to be mistook
Fer an edjicated person, 'oo 'is cobbers reckoned crook;
But 'e 'ad a trick wiv figgers that ud make a clerk look sick;
So 'e pencilled fer a bookie' an' 'e 'awked a bit, did Mick.*

*A bloke can't be pertick'ler 'oo must battle fer a crust;
An' some, they pinch fer preference, an' some, becos they must,
When times is 'ard, an' some swell coves is richer than they ort;
Well, it's jist a little gamble fer a rise, agin the Court.*

*Now, Mick wus never in it as a reel perfeshnal crook,
But sometimes cops 'as slabs uv luck, so sometimes 'e wus took,
An' 'e got a repitation, thro' 'im bein' twice interned;
But 'e didn't skite about it, 'cos 'e felt it wasn't earned.*

Ginger Mick

I reckerlect one time a Beak slings Mick a slab uv guff,
Wiv "Thirty days or forty bob" (Mick couldn't raise the stuff)—
An' arsts 'im where 'is conshuns is, an' w'y 'e can't be good,
An' Mick jist grins, an' takes it out, an' never understood.

An' that is orl there wus to Mick, wiv orl 'is leery ways.
If I wus up among the 'eads, wiv right to blame or praise,
Whenever some sich bloke as 'im wus tucked away fer good
I'd chalk them words above 'is 'ead: " 'E never understood."

If I was up among the 'eads, wiv right to judge the game,
I'd look around fer chance to praise, an' sling the flamin' blame;
Fer findin' things in blokes to praise pays divvies either way;
An' wot they're blamed fer yesterd'y brings 'earty cheers to-day.

Yes, 'earty cheers frum thortless coots 'oo feel dead sure their
   God
Would never 'ave no time fer crooks 'oo does a stretch in quod;
'Oo reckon 'eaven is a place where orl folk tork correck,
An' Judgment, where the "vulgar" gits it solid in the neck.

An' Ginger Mick wus vulgar. 'Struth! When things wus gettin'
   slow
'E took to 'awkin' rabbits, w'ich is very, very low—
'E wus the sort o' bloke to watch when 'e come in yer gate:
'E 'ad a narsty fightin' face that orl nice people 'ate.

'E 'ad that narsty fightin' face that peaceful folk call grim;
But I 'ave seen it grow reel soft when kiddies spoke to 'im.
'E 'ad them narsty sullen eyes that nice folk can't enjure;
But I 'ave seen a smile in 'em that made our frien'ship sure.

There's men 'oo never knoo ole Mick, an' passed 'im in the street,
An' looks away an' sez, "See 'im? A narsty chap to meet!
'E'd be an ugly customer alone an' after dark!"
An' Mick, 'e'd twitch 'is jor at 'em, 'arf earnest, 'arf a lark.

Introduction

That wus the sort o' character that Mick earned be 'is looks.
The talk uv 'im, the walk uv 'im, put 'im among the crooks.
An' Mick, 'e looks on swank an' style as jist a lot o' flam,
An' snouted them that snouted 'im, an' never give a dam.

But spite uv orl 'is 'ulkin' frame, an' langwidge flowin' free
I seen the thing inside uv Mick that made 'im good to me.
An' spite uv orl the sneerin' ways that leery blokes imploy,
I knoo 'im jist fer wot 'e wus—a big, soft-'earted boy.

Fer when a bloke 'as come to be reel cobbers wiv a bloke,
They sorter swap good fellership wivout words bein' spoke.
I never slung no guff to Mick, 'e never smooged to me,
But we could smoke, an' 'old our jor, an' be reel company.

There 'as bin times that 'e would curse to 'ave recalled by me,
When I 'ave seen 'im doin' things that coves calls charity;
An' there's been times, an' frequent times, in spite uv orl 'is looks,
When I 'ave 'eard 'im saying' things that blokes shoves inter books.

But Ginger Mick wus Ginger Mick—a leery boy, fer keeps,
'Oo 'owled "Wile Rabbee!" in the streets, in tones that give yeh
   creeps.
'E never planned 'is mode uv life, nor chose the Lane fer lair,
No more than 'e designed 'is chiv or colour uv 'is 'air.

So Ginger 'awked, an' Ginger pinched, an' Ginger went to quod,
An' never thort to waste 'is time in blamin' man or God—
An' then there came to Call uv Stoush, or Jooty—wot's a name?
An' Ginger cocked 'is ear to it, an' found 'is flamin' game.

I intrajuice me cobber 'ere; an' don't make no ixcuse
To any culchered click that it's a peb I intrajuice.
I dunno wot 'is ratin' wus in this 'ere soshul plan;
I only know, inside o' me, I intrajuice a man.
MELBOURNE,   THE SENTIMENTAL BLOKE.
   April 25th, 1916

Duck an' Fowl

NOW, when a bloke 'e cracks a bloke fer insults to a skirt,
    An' wrecks a joint to square a lady's name,
They used to call it chivalry, but now they calls it dirt,
    An' the end of it is cops an' quod an' shame.
Fer insults to fair Gwendoline they 'ad to be wiped out;
But Rosie's sort is jist fair game—when Ginger ain't about.

It wus Jimmie Ah Foo's cook-shop, which is close be Spadger's Lane,
    Where a vari'gated comp'ny tears the scran,
An' there's some is "tup'ny coloured," an' some is "penny plain,"
    Frum a lawyer to a common lumper-man.
Or a writer fer the papers, or a slaver on the prowl,
An' noiseless Chows a-glidin' 'round wiv plates uv duck an' fowl.

But if yeh wanted juicy bits that 'ung around Foo's perch
    Yeh fetched 'em down an' wolfed 'em in yer place.
An' Foo sat sad an' solim, like an 'oly man in church,
    Wiv an early-martyr look upon 'is face;
Wot never changed, not even when a toff upon a jag
Tried to pick up Ginger's Rosie, an' collided wiv a snag.

Ginger Mick's bin at the races, an' 'e'd made a little rise,
    'Avin' knowed a bloke wot knowed the trainer's cook.
An' easy money's very sweet, as punters reckernise,
    An' sweetest when yeh've prized it orf a "book."
So Ginger calls fer Rosie, an' to celerbrate 'is win
'E trots 'er down to Ah Foo's joint to splash a bit uv tin.

Duck an' Fowl

There wus lights, an' smells of Asia, an' a strange, Chow-'aunted
 scene;
   Floatin' scraps of forrin lingo 'it the ear;
But Rose sails in an' takes 'er seat like any soshul queen
   Sich as stokes 'erself wiv foy grass orl the year.
"Duck an' Fowl" 's 'er nomination; so ole Ginger jerks 'is frame
'Cross to git some fancy pickin's, an' to give 'is choice a name.

While Ginger paws the tucker, an' 'as words about the price,
   There's a shickered toff slings Rosie goo-goo eyes.
'E's a mug 'oo thinks 'e's 'it a flamin' 'all uv scarlet vice
   An' 'e picks on gentle Rosie fer a prize.
Then 'e tries to play at 'andies, an' arrange about a meet;
But Rosie fetches 'im a welt that shifts 'im in 'is seat.

Ginger's busy makin' bargins, an' 'e never seen the clout;
   'E is 'agglin' wiv Ah Foo fer 'arf a duck;
But the toff's too shick or silly fer to 'eave 'is carkis out,
   An' to fade while goin's good an' 'e's in luck.
Then Ginger clinched 'is bargin, an', as down the room 'e came,
'E seen the toff jump frum 'is seat, an' call the girl a name.

That done it. Less than 'arf a mo, an' 'ell got orf the chain;
   An' the swell stopped 'arf a ducklin' wiv 'is neck,
As Ginger guv the war-cry that is dreaded in the Lane.
   An' the rest wus whirlin' toff an' sudden wreck.
Mick never reely stoushed 'im, but 'e used 'im fer a mop.
Then someone doused the bloomin' glim, an' Foo run fer a cop.

Down the stairs an' in the passidge come the shufflin' feet uv Chows,
   An' a crash, as Ah Foo's chiner found it's mark.
Fer more than Mick 'ad ancient scores left over frum ole rows,
   An' more than one stopped somethin' in the dark.
Then the tabbies took to screamin', an' a Chow remarked
   "Wha' for?"
While the live ducks quacked blue murder frum their corner uv
   the floor.

Ginger Mick

Fer full ten minutes it wus joy, reel willin' an' to spare,
    Wiv noise uv tarts, an' Chows, an' ducks, an' lash;
An' plates uv fowl an' bird's-nest soup went whizzin' thro' the air,
    While 'arf-a-dozen fought to reach Foo's cash.
Then, thro' an open doorway, three Chows' 'eads is framed in light,
An' sudden in Mick's corner orl is gentle peace an' quite.

Up goes the lights; in comes the cops; an' there's a sudden rush;
    But the Johns 'as got 'em safe an' 'emmed 'em in;
An' ev'ryone looks innercent. Then thro' the anxious 'ush
    The toff's voice frum the floor calls fer a gin ...
But Mick an' Rose, O where are they? Arst uv the silent night!
They 'ad a date about a dawg, an' vanished out o' sight.

Then Foo an' orl 'is cousins an' the ducks torks orl at once,
    An' the tabbies pitch the weary Johns a tale,
'Ow they orl is puffick ladies 'oo 'ave not bin pinched fer munce;
    An' the crooks does mental sums concernin' bail.
The cops they takes a name er two, then gathers in the toff,
An' lobs 'im in a cold, 'ard cell to sleep 'is love-quest off.

But down in Rosie's kipsie, at the end uv Spadger's Lane,
    'Er an' Mick is layin' supper out fer two.
"Now, I 'ate the game," sez Ginger, "an' it goes agin the grain;
    But wot's a 'elpless, 'ungry bloke to do?"
An' 'e yanks a cold roast chicken frum the bosom uv 'is shirt,
An' Rosie finds a ducklin' underneath 'er Sund'y skirt.

So, when a bloke fergits 'imself, an' soils a lady's name,
    Altho' Romance is dead an' in the dirt,
In ole Madrid or Little Bourke they treats 'im much the same,
    An' 'e collects wot's comin' fer a cert.
But, spite uv 'igh-falutin' tork, the fact is jist the same:
Ole Ginger Mick wus out fer loot, an' played a risky game.

Duck an' Fowl

To fight an' forage ... Spare me days! It's been man's leadin' soot
    Since 'e learned to word a tart an' make a date.
'E's been at it, good an' solid, since ole Adam bit the froot:
    To fight an' forage, an' pertect 'is mate.
But this story 'as no moral, an' it 'as a vulgar plot;
It is jist a small igzample uv a way ole Ginger's got.

War

'E SEZ to me, "Wot's orl this flamin' war?
   The papers torks uv nothin' else but scraps.
An' wot's ole England got snake-'eaded for?
   An' wot's the strength uv callin' out our chaps ?"
'E sez to me, "Struth! Don't she rule the sea?
Wot does she want wiv us?" 'e sez to me.

Ole Ginger Mick is loadin' up 'is truck
   One mornin' in the markit feelin' sore.
'E sez to me, "Well, mate, I've done me luck;
   An' Rose is arstin', 'Wot about this war?'
I'm gone a tenner at the two-up school;
The game is crook, an' Rose is turnin' cool."

'E, sez to me, " 'Ow is it fer a beer?"
   I tips 'im 'ow I've told me wife, Doreen,
That when I comes down to the markit 'ere
   I dodges pubs, an' chucks the tipple, clean.
Wiv 'er an' kid alone up on the farm
She's full uv fancies that I'll come to 'arm.

" 'Enpecked!" 'e sez. An' then, "Ar, I dunno.
   I wouldn't mind if I wus in yer place.
I've 'arf a mind to give cold tea a go.
   It's no game, pourin' snake-juice in yer face.
But, lad, I 'ave to, wiv the thirst I got.
I'm goin' over now to stop a pot."

War

'E goes acrost to find a pint a 'ome;
    An' meets a pal an' keeps another down.
Ten minutes later, when 'e starts to roam
    Back to the markit, wiv an ugly frown,
'E sprags a soljer bloke 'oo's passin' by,
An' sez 'e'd like to dot 'im in the eye.

"Your sort," sez Mick, "don't know yer silly mind!
    They lead yeh like a sheep; it's time yeh woke—
The 'eads is makin' piles out uv your kind!"
    "Aw, git yer 'ead read!" sez the soljer bloke.
'Struth! 'e wus willin' wus that Kharki chap;
I 'ad me work cut out to stop a scrap.

An' as the soljer fades across the street,
    Mick strikes a light an' sits down on 'is truck,
An' chews 'is fag—a sign 'is nerve is beat—
    An' swears a bit, an' sez 'e's done 'is luck.
'E grouches there ten minutes, maybe more,
Then sez quite sudden, *"Blarst the flamin' war!"*

Jist then a motor car goes glidin' by
    Wiv two fat toffs be'ind two fat cigars.
Mick twigs 'em frum the corner uv 'is eye.
    "I 'ope," 'e sez, "the 'Uns don't git *my* cars.
Me di'mon's, too, don't let me sleep a wink ...
Ar, 'Struth! I'd fight fer that sort—I *don't* think."

'E sits there while I 'arness up me prad,
    Chewin' 'is fag an' starin' at the ground.
I tumbles that 'e's got the joes reel bad,
    An' don't say nothin' till 'e comes around.
'E sez 'is luck's a nark, an' swears some more,
An' then: "Wot is the strength uv this 'ere war?"

Ginger Mick

I tells 'im wot I read about the 'Uns,
    An' wot they done in Beljum an' in France,
Wiv drivin' Janes an' kids before their guns,
    An' never givin' blokes a stray dawg's chance;
An' 'ow they think they've got the whole world beat.
Sez 'e, "I'll crack the first Dutch cow I meet!"

Mick listens, while I tells 'im 'ow they starts
    Be burnin' pore coves 'omes an' killin' kids,
An' comin' it reel crook wiv decent tarts,
    An' fightin' foul, as orl the rules forbids,
Leavin' a string uv stiff-uns in their track.
Sez Mick, "The dirty cows! They *wants* a crack!"

'E chews it over solid fer a bit,
    Workin' 'is copper-top a double shift.
I don't need specs to see that 'e wus 'it
    Be somethin' more than Rosie's little rift.
"If they'd done that," 'e sez, "out 'ere—Ar, rats!
Why don't ole England belt 'em in the slats?"

Then Mick gits up an' starts another fag.
    "Ar, well," 'e sez, "it's no affair uv mine,
If I don't work they'd pinch me on the vag;
    But I'm not keen to fight so toffs kin dine
On pickled olives ... *Blarst* the flamin' war!
I ain't got nothin' worth the fightin' for.

"So long," 'e sez. "I got ter trade me stock;
    An' when yeh 'ear I've took a soljer's job
I give yeh leave to say I've done me block
    An' got a flock uv weevils in me knob."
An' then, orf-'anded-like, 'e arsts me: "Say,
Wot are they slingin' soljers fer their pay?"

War

I tells 'im; an' 'e sez to me, "So long.
    Some day this rabbit trade will git me beat."
An' Ginger Mick shoves thro' the markit throng,
    An' gits 'is barrer out into the street.
An', as 'e goes, I 'ears 'is gentle roar:
"*Rabbee! Wile Rabbee!* ... Blarst the flamin' war!"

The Call of Stoush

WOT price ole Ginger Mick? 'E's done a break—
    Gone to the flamin' war to stoush the foe
Wus it fer glory, or a woman's sake?
    Ar, arst me somethin' easy! I dunno.
'Is Kharki clobber set 'im off a treat,
That's all I know; 'is motive's got me beat.

Ole Mick e's trainin' up in Cairo now;
    An' all the cops in Spadger's Lane is sad.
They miss 'is music in the midnight row
    Wot time the pushes mix it good an' glad.
Fer 'e wus one o' them, you understand,
Wot "soils the soshul life uv this fair land."

A peb wus Mick; a leery bloke wus 'e,
    Low down, an' given to the brimmin' cup;
The sort o' chap that coves like you an' me
    Don't mix wiv, 'cos of our strick bringin's-up.
An' 'e wus sich becos unseein' Fate
Lobbed 'im in life a 'undred years too late.

'E wus a man uv vierlence, wus Mick,
    Coarse wiv 'is speech an' in 'is manner low
Slick wiv 'is 'ands, an' 'andy wiv a brick
    When bricks wus needful to defeat a foe.
An' now 'e's gone an' mizzled to the war,
An' some blokes 'as the nerve to arst "Wot for?"

The Call of Stoush

Wot for? Gawstruth! 'E wus no patriot
    That sits an' brays advice in days uv strife;
'E never flapped no flags nor sich like rot
    'E never sung "Gawsave" in all 'is life.
'E wus dispised be them that make sich noise;
But now—O strike!—'e's "one uv our brave boys".

'E's one uv our brave boys, all right, all right.
    'Is early trainin' down in Spadger's Lane
Done 'im no 'arm fer this 'ere orl-in fight;
    'Is loss o' culcher is 'is country's gain.
'Im wiv 'is carst-ir'n chiv an' leery ways—
An' swell tarts 'eavin' 'im sweet words o' praise.

Why did 'e go? 'E 'ad a decent job,
    'Is tart an' 'im they could 'a' made it right.
Why does a wild bull fight to guard the mob?
    Why does a bloomin' bull-ant look fer fight?
Why does a rooster scrap an' flap an' crow?
'E went becos 'e dam well *'ad* to go.

'E never spouted no 'igh-soundin' stuff
    About stern jooty an' 'is country's call;
But, in 'is way, 'e 'eard it right enough
    A-callin' like the shout uv "On the Ball!"
Wot time the footer brings the clicks great joy,
An' Saints er Carlton roughs it up wiv 'Roy.

The call wot came to cave-men in the days
    When rocks wus stylish in the scrappin' line;
The call wot knights 'eard in the minstrel's lays,
    That sent 'em in tin soots to Palerstine;
The call wot draws all fighters to the fray
It come to Mick, an' Mick 'e must obey.

The Call uv Stoush!... It's older than the 'ills.
    Lovin' an' fightin'—there's no more to tell
Concernin' men. An' when that feelin' thrills
    The blood uv them 'oo's fathers mixed it well,
They 'ave to 'eed it—bein' 'ow they're built—
As traders 'ave to 'eed the clink uv gilt.

An' them whose gilt 'as stuffed 'em stiff wiv pride
    An' 'aughty scorn uv blokes like Ginger Mick—
I sez to them, put sich crook thorts aside,
    An' don't lay on the patronage too thick.
Orl men is brothers when it comes to lash
An' 'aughty scorn an' Culcher does their dash.

War ain't no giddy garden feete—it's war:
    A game that calls up love an' 'atred both.
An' them that shudders at the sight o' gore,
    An' shrinks to 'ear a drunken soljer's oath,
Must 'ide be'ind the man wot 'eaves the bricks,
An' thank their Gawd for all their Ginger Micks.

Becos 'e never 'ad the chance to find
    The glory o' the world by land an' sea,
Becos the beauty 'idin' in 'is mind
    Wus not writ plain fer blokes like you an' me,
They calls 'im crook; but in 'im I 'ave found
Wot makes a man a man the world around.

Be'ind that dile uv 'is, as 'ard as sin,
    Wus strange, soft thorts that never yet showed out;
An' down in Spadger's Lane, in dirt an' din,
    'E dreamed sich dreams as poits sing about.
'E's 'ad 'is visions uv the Bonzer Tart;
An' stoushed some coot to ease 'is swellin' 'eart.

The Call of Stoush

Lovin' an' fightin' ... when the tale is told,
    That's all there is to it; an' in their way
Them brave an' noble 'ero blokes uv old
    Wus Ginger Micks—the crook 'uns uv their day.
Jist let the Call uv Stoush give 'im 'is chance
An' Ginger Mick's the 'ero of Romance.

So Ginger Mick 'e's mizzled to the war;
    Joy in 'is 'eart, an' wild dreams in 'is brain;
Gawd 'elp the foe that 'e goes gunnin' for
    If tales is true they tell in Spadger's Lane—
Tales that ud fairly freeze the gentle 'earts
Uv them 'oo knits 'is socks—the Culchered Tarts.

The Push

BECOS a crook done in a prince, an' narked an Emperor,
    An' struck a light that set the world aflame;
Becos the bugles East an' West sooled on the dawgs o' war,
    A bloke called Ginger Mick 'as found 'is game—
Found 'is game an' found 'is brothers, 'oo wus strangers in 'is sight,
Till they shed their silly clobber an' put on the duds fer fight.

Yes, they've shed their silly clobber an' the other stuff they wore
    Fer to 'ide the man beneath it in the past;
An' each man is the clean, straight man 'is Maker meant 'im for,
    An' each man knows 'is brother man at last.
Shy strangers, till a bugle blast preached 'oly brother'ood;
But mateship they 'ave found at last; an' they 'ave found it good.

So the lumper, an' the lawyer, an' the chap 'oo shifted sand,
    They are cobbers wiv the cove 'oo drove a quill;
The knut 'oo swung a cane upon the Block, 'e takes the 'and
    Uv the coot 'oo swung a pick on Broken 'Ill;
An' Privit Clord Augustus drills wiv Privit Snarky Jim—
They are both Australian soljers, w'ich is good enough fer 'im.

It's good enough fer orl uv 'em, as orl uv 'em 'ave seen
    Since they got the same glad clobber next their skins;
An' the bloke 'oo 'olds the boodle an' the coot wivout a bean,
    Why, they knock around like little Kharki twins.
An' they got a common lingo, w'ich is growin' mighty thick
Wiv ixpressive contributions frum the stock uv Ginger Mick.

The Push

'E 'as struck it fer a moral. Ginger's found 'is game at last,
    An' 'e's took to it like ducklin's take to drink;
An' 'is slouchin' an' 'is grouchin' an' 'is loafin' uv the past—
    'E's done wiv 'em, an' dumped 'em down the sink.
'E's a bright an' shinin' sample uv a the'ry that I 'old:
That ev'ry 'eart that ever pumped is good fer chunks o' gold.

Ev'ry feller is a gold mine if yeh take an' work 'im right:
    It is shinin' on the surface now an' then;
An' there's some is easy sinkin', but there's some wants
        dynermite,
    Fer they looks a 'opeless prospect—yet they're men.
An' Ginger—'ard-shell Ginger's showin' signs that 'e will pay;
But it took a flamin' world-war fer to blarst 'is crust away.

But they took 'im an' they drilled 'im an' they shipped 'im
        overseas
    Wiv a crowd uv blokes 'e never met before.
'E rowed wiv 'em, an' scrapped wiv 'em, an' done some tall C.B.'s,
    An' 'e lobbed wiv 'em on Egypt's sandy shore.
Then Pride o' Race lay 'olt on 'im, an' Mick shoves out 'is chest
To find 'imself Australian an' blood brothers wiv the rest.

So I gits some reel good readin' in the letter wot 'e sent—
    Tho' the spellin's pretty rotten now an' then.
"I 'ad the joes at first," 'e sez; "but now I'm glad I went,
    Fer it's shine to be among reel, livin' men.
An' it's grand to be Australian, an' to say it good an' loud
When yeh bump a forrin country wiv sich fellers as our crowd.

" 'Struth! I've 'ung around me native land fer close on thirty year,
    An' I never knoo wot men me cobbers were:
Never knoo that toffs wus white men till I met 'em over 'ere—
    Blokes an' coves I sort o' snouted over there.
Yes, I loafed aroun' me country; an' I never knoo 'er then;
But the reel, ribuck Australia's 'ere, among the fightin' men.

"We've slung the swank fer good an' all; it don't fit in our plan;
    To skite uv birth an' boodle is a crime.
A man wiv us, why, 'e's a man becos 'e *is* a man,
    An' a reel red-'ot Australian ev'ry time.
Fer dawg an' side an' snobbery is down an' out fer keeps.
It's grit an' reel good fellership that gits yeh friends in 'eaps.

"There's a bloke 'oo shipped when I did; 'e wus lately frum 'is ma,
    'Oo 'ad filled 'im full uv notions uv 'is birth;
An' 'e overworked 'is aitches till 'e got the loud 'Ha-ha'
    Frum the fellers, but 'e wouldn't come to earth.
I bumped 'is lordship, name o' Keith, an' 'ad a little row,
An' 'e lost some chunks uv beauty; but 'e's good Australian now.

"There is Privit Snifty Thompson, 'oo wus once a Sydney rat,
    An' 'e 'ung around the Rocks when 'e wus young.
There's little Smith uv Collin'wood, wiv fags stuck in 'is 'at,
    An' a string uv dirty insults on 'is tongue.
A corperil took them in 'and—a lad frum Lameroo.
Now both is nearly gentlemen, an' good Australians too.

"There's one, 'e doesn't tork a lot, 'e sez 'is name is Trent,
    Jist a privit, but 'e knows 'is drill a treat;
A stand-orf bloke, but reel good pals wiv fellers in 'is tent;
    But 'is 'ome an' 'istoree 'as got 'em beat.
They reckon when 'e starts to bleed 'e'll stain 'is Kharki blue;
An' 'is lingo smells uv Oxford—but 'e's good Australian too.

"Then there's Lofty Craig uv Queensland, 'oo's a special pal uv
  mine;
    Slow an' shy, an' kind o' nervous uv 'is height;
An' Jupp, 'oo owns a copper show, an' arsts us out to dine
    When we're doo fer leave in Cairo uv a night.
An' there's Bills an' Jims an' Bennos, an' there's Roys an'
  'Arolds too,
An' they're cobbers, an' they're brothers, an' Australians thro' an'
  thro'.

"There is farmers frum the Mallee, there is bushmen down frum
  Bourke,
    There's college men wiv letters to their name;
There is grafters, an' there's blokes 'oo never done a 'ard day's
  work
    Till they tumbled, wiv the rest, into the game—
An' they're drillin' 'ere together, men uv ev'ry creed an' kind.
It's Australia! Solid! Dinkum! that 'as left the land be'ind.

"An' if yeh want a slushy, or a station overseer,
    Or a tinker, or a tailor, or a snob,
Or a 'andy bloke wiv 'orses, or a minin' ingineer,
    Why, we've got the very man to do yer job.
Butcher, baker, undertaker, or a Caf' de Pary chef,
'E is waitin', keen an' ready, in the little A.I.F.

"An' they've drilled us. Strike me lucky! but they've drilled us fer
  a cert!
    We 'ave trod around ole Egypt's burnin' sand
Till I tells meself at evenin', when I'm wringin' out me shirt,
    That we're built uv wire an' green-'ide in our land.
Strike! I thort I knoo 'ard yakker, w'ich I've tackled many ways,
But uv late I've took a tumble I bin dozin' orl me days.

Ginger Mick

"It's a game, lad," writes ole Ginger, "It's a game I'm likin' grand.
    An' I'm tryin' fer a stripe to fill in time.
I 'ave took a pull on shicker fer the honour uv me land,
    An' I'm umpty round the chest an' feelin' prime.
Yeh kin tell Rose, if yeh see 'er, I serloots 'er o'er the foam,
An' we'll 'ave a cray fer supper when I comes a-marchin' 'ome."

So ole Ginger sends a letter, an' 'is letter's good to read,
    Fer the things 'e sez, an' some things 'e leaves out;
An' when a bloke like 'im wakes up an' starts to take a heed
    Well, it's sort o' worth the writin' 'ome about.
'E's one uv many little things Australia chanced to find
She never knoo she 'ad around till bugles cleared 'er mind.

Becos ole Europe lost 'er block an' started 'eavin' bricks,
    Becos the bugles wailed a song uv war,
We found reel gold down in the 'earts uv orl our Ginger Micks
    We never thort worth minin' fer before.
An' so, I'm tippin' we will pray, before our win is scored:
"Thank God fer Mick, an' Bill an' Jim, an' little brother Clord."

The Battle of the Wazzir

IF ole Pharoah, King of Egyp', 'ad been gazin' on the scene
   'E'd 'ave give the A.I.F. a narsty name
When they done their little best to scrub 'is dirty Kingdom clean,
   An' to shift 'is ancient 'eap uv sin an' shame.
An' I'm tippin' they'd 'ave phenyled *'im*, an' rubbed it in 'is 'ead.
But old Pharoah, King uv Egyp', 'e is dead.

So yeh don't 'ear much about it; an' it isn't meant yeh should,
   Since 'is Kingship wusn't there to go orf pop;
An' this mishunery effert fer to make the 'eathen good
   Wus a contract that the fellers 'ad to drop.
There wus other pressin' matters, so they 'ad to chuck the fun,
But the Battle uv the Wazzir took the bun.

Now, Ginger Mick 'e writes to me a long, ixcited note,
   An' 'e writes it in a whisper, so to speak;
Fer I guess the Censor's shadder wus across 'im as 'e wrote,
   An' 'e 'ad to bottle things that musn't leak.
So I ain't got orl the strength uv it; but sich as Ginger sends
I rejooce to decent English fer me friends.

It wus part their native carelessness, an' part their native skite;
   Fer they kids themselves they know the Devil well,
'Avin' met 'im, kind uv casu'l, on some wild Australian night—
   Wine an' women at a secon'-rate 'otel.
But the Devil uv Australia 'e's a little woolly sheep
To the devils wot the desert children keep.

Ginger Mick

So they mooches round the drink-shops, an' the Wazzir took their
    eye,
    An' they found old Pharoah's daughters pleasin' Janes;
An' they wouldn't be Australian 'less they give the game a fly ...
    An' Egyp' smiled an' totted up 'is gains.
'E doped their drinks, an' breathed on them 'is aged evil breath ...
An' more than one woke up to long fer death.

When they wandered frum the newest an' the cleanest land on
    earth,
    An' the filth uv ages met 'em, it wus 'ard.
Fer there may be sin an' sorrer in the country uv their birth;
    But the dirt uv cenchuries ain't in the yard.
They wus children, playin' wiv an asp, an' never fearin' it,
An' they took it very sore when they wus bit.

First, they took the tales fer furphies when they got around the
    camp,
    Uv a cove done in fer life wiv one night's jag,
But when the yarns grew 'ot an' strong an' bore the 'all-mark
    stamp
    Uv dinkum oil, they waved the danger flag.
An' the shudder that a clean man feels when 'e's su'prized wiv
    dirt
Gripped orl the camp reel solid; an' it 'urt.

There wus Bill from up the Billabong, 'oo's dearest love wus
    cow,
    An' 'oo lived an' thought an' fought an' acted clean.
'E wus lately frum 'is mother wiv 'er kiss wet on 'is brow;
    But they snared 'im in, an' did 'im up reel mean.
Fer young Bill wus gone a million, an' 'e never guessed the
    game ...
For 'e's down in livin' 'ell, an' marked fer shame.

The Battle of the Wazzir

An' Bill wus only one uv 'em to fall to Eastern sin:
    Ev'ry comp'ny 'ad a rotten tale to tell,
An' there must be somethin' doin' when the strength uv it sunk in
    To a crowd that ain't afraid to clean up 'ell.
They wus game to take a gamble; but this dirt dealt to a mate,
Well, it riled 'em; an' they didn't 'estitate.

'Ave yeh seen a crowd uv fellers takin' chances on a game,
    Crackin' 'ardy while they thought it on the square?
'Ave yeh 'eard their 'owl uv anguish when they tumbled to the
    same,
    'Avin' found they wus the victums uv a snare?
It wus jist that sort uv anger when they fell to Egyp's stunt;
An', remember, they wus trainin' fer the front.

I 'ave notions uv the Wazzir. It's as old as Pharoah's tomb;
    It's as cunnin' as the oldest imp in 'ell;
An' the game it plays uv lurin' blokes, wiv love-songs, to their
    doom
    Wus begun when first a tart 'ad smiles to sell.
An' it stood there thro' the ages; an' it might be standin' still
If it 'and't bumped a clean cove, name o' Bill.

An' they done it like they done it when a word went to the push
    That a nark 'oo'd crooled a pal wus run to ground.
They done it like they done it when the blokes out in the bush
    Passed a telegraft that cops wus nosin' round.
There wus no one rung a fire-bell, but the tip wus passed about;
An' they fixed anight to clean the Wazzir out.

Yes, I've notions uv the Wazzir. It's been pilin' up its dirt
    Since it mated wiv the Devil in year One,
An' spawned a brood uv evil things to do a man a 'urt
    Since the lurk uv snarin' innercents begun.
But it's sweeter an' it's cleaner since one wild an' woolly night
When some Aussie scavengers put up a fight.

Ginger Mick

Now, it started wiv some 'orseplay. If the 'eads 'ad seen the look,
   Dead in earnest, that wus underneath the fun,
They'd 'ave tumbled there wus somethin' that wus more than
     commin crook,
   An' 'ave stopped the game before it 'arf begun.
But the fellers larfed like school-boys, tho' they orl wus more
     than narked,
An' they 'ad the 'ouses well an' truly marked.

Frum a little crazy balkiney that clawed agin a wall
   A chair come crashin' down into the street;
Then a woman's frightened screamin' give the sign to bounce the
     ball,
   An' there come a sudden rush uv soljers' feet.
There's a glimpse uv frightened faces as a door caved in an' fell;
An' the Wazzir wus a 'owlin' screamin' 'ell.

Frum a winder 'igh above 'em there's a bloke near seen feet,
   Waves a bit uv naked Egyp' in the air.
An' there's squealin' an' there's shriekin' as they chased 'em
     down the street,
   When they dug 'em out like rabbits frum their lair.
Then down into the roadway gaudy 'ouse'old gods comes fast,
An' the Wazzir's Great Spring Cleanin' starts at last.

Frum the winders came pianners an' some giddy duchess pairs;
   An' they piled 'em on the roadway in the mire,
An' 'eaped 'em 'igh wiv fal-de-rals an' pretty parlor chairs,
   Which they started in to purify wiv fire.
Then the Redcaps come to argue, but they jist amused the mob;
Fer the scavengers wus warmin' to their job.

The Battle of the Wazzir

When the fire-reels come to quell 'em—'struth! They 'ad no
    bloomin' 'ope;
  Fer they cut the 'ose to ribbons in a jiff;
An' they called upon the drink-shops an' poured out their rotten
    dope,
  While the nigs 'oo didn't run was frightened stiff.
An' when orl wus done an' over, an' they wearied uv the strife,
The old Wizzir'd 'ad the scourin' uv its life.

Now, old Ginger ain't quite candid; 'e don't say where *'e* came in;
  But 'e mentions that 'e don't get no C.B.,
An' 'e's 'ad some pretty practice dodgin' punishment fer sin
  Down in Spadger's since 'is early infancy.
So I guess, if they went after 'im, they found 'im snug in bed;
Fer old Ginger 'as a reel tactician's 'ead.

An' 'e sez that when 'e wandered down the Wazzir later on
  It wus like a 'ome where 'oliness reposed;
Fer its sinfulness wus 'idden, an' its brazenness wus gone,
  An' its doors, wiv proper modesty, wus closed.
If a 'ead looked out a winder, as they passed, it quick drew in;
Fer the Wazzir wus a wowser, scared from sin.

If old Pharoah, King uv Egyp', 'e 'ad lived to see the day
  When they tidied up 'is 'eap uv shame an' sin,
Well, 'e mighter took it narsty, fer out fellers 'ave a way
  Uv completin' any job that they begin.
An' they might 'ave left 'is Kingship nursn' gravel-rash in bed ...
But old Pharoah, King uv Egyp', 'e is dead.

Sari Bair

SO, they've struck their streak o' trouble, an' they
   got it in the neck,
An' there's more than one ole pal o' mine 'as
   'anded in 'is check;
But Ginger still takes nourishment; 'e's well,
   but breathin' 'ard.
An' so 'e sends the strength uv it scrawled on
   a chunk uv card.

"On the day we 'it the transport there wus cheerin' on the pier,
An' the girls was wavin' hankies as they dropped a partin' tear,
An' we felt like little 'eroes as we watched the crowd recede,
Fer we sailed to prove Australia, an' our boastin' uv the breed.

"There was Trent, ex-toff, uv England; there wus Green, ex-pug,
   uv 'Loo;
There wus me, an' Craig uv Queensland, wiv 'is 'ulkin' six-foot-
   two;
An' little Smith uv Collin'wood, 'oo 'owled a rag-time air,
On the day we left the Leeuwin, bound nor'-west for Gawd-
   knows-where.

"On the day we come to Cairo wiv its niggers an' its din,
To fill our eyes wiv desert sand, our souls wiv Eastern sin,
There wus cursin' an' complainin'; we wus 'ungerin' fer fight—
Little imertation soljers full uv vanity an' skite.

"Then they worked us—Gawd! they worked us, till we knoo wot drillin' meant;
Till men begun to feel like men, an' wasters to repent,
Till we grew to 'ate all Egyp', an' its desert, an' its stinks:
On the days we drilled at Mena in the shadder uv the Sphinx.

"Then Green uv Sydney swore an oath they meant to 'old us tight,
A crowd uv flamin' ornaments wivout a chance to fight;
But little Smith uv Collin'wood, he whistled 'im a toon,
An' sez, 'Aw, take a pull, lad; there'll be whips o' stoushin' soon.'

"Then the waitin', weary waitin', while we itched to meet the foe!
But we'd done wiv fancy skitin' an' the comic op'ra show.
We wus soljers—finished soljers, an' we felt it in our veins
On the day we trod the desert on ole Egyp's sandy plains.

"An' Trent 'e said it wus a bore, an' all uv us wus blue,
An' Craig, the giant, never joked the way 'e used to do.
But little Smith uv Collin'wood 'e 'ummed a little song,
An' said, 'You leave it to the 'eads. O now we sha'n't be long!'

"Then Sari Bair, O Sari Bair, 'twas you wot seen it done,
The day the transports rode yer bay beneath a smilin' sun.
We boasted much, an' toasted much; but where yer tide line creeps,
'Twus you, me dainty Sari Bair, that seen us play fer keeps.

"We wus full uv savage skitin' while they kep' us on the shelf—
(Now I tell yeh, square an' 'onest, I was doubtin' us meself);
But we proved it, good an' plenty, that our lads can do an' dare,
On the day we walloped Abdul o'er the sands o' Sari Bair.

"Luck wus out wiv Green uv Sydney, where 'e stood at my right
    'and,
Fer they plunked 'im on the transport 'fore 'e got a chance to
    land.
Then I saw 'em kill a feller wot I knoo in Camberwell,
Somethin' sort o' went inside me—an' the rest wus bloody 'ell.

"Thro' the smoke I seen 'im strivin', Craig uv Queensland, tall
    an' strong,
Like an 'arvester at 'ay-time singin', swingin' to the song.
An' little Smith uv Collin'wood, 'e 'owled a fightin' tune,
On the day we chased Mahomet over Sari's sandy dune.

"An' Sari Bair, O Sari Bair, you seen 'ow it wus done,
The transports dancin' in yer bay beneath the bonzer sun;
An' speckled o'er yer gleamin' shore the little 'uddled 'eaps
That showed at last the Southern breed could play the game fer
    keeps.

"We found 'im, Craig uv Queensland, stark, 'is 'and still on 'is
    gun.
We found too many more besides, when that fierce scrap wus
    done.
An' little Smith uv Collin'wood, he crooned a mournful air,
The night we planted 'em beneath the sands uv Sari Bair.

"On the day we took the transport there wus cheerin' on the pier,
An' we wus little chiner gawds; an' now we're sittin' 'ere,
Wiv the taste uv blood an' battle on the lips uv ev'ry man
An' ev'ry man jist 'opin fer to end as we began.

"Fer Green is gone, an' Craig is gone, an' Gawd! 'ow many more!
Who sleep the sleep at Sari Bair beside that sunny shore!
An' little Smith uv Collin'wood, a bandage' round 'is 'ead,
He 'ums a savage song an' vows quick vengeance fer the dead.

"But Sari Bair, me Sari Bair, the secrets that you 'old
Will shake the 'earts uv Southern men when all the tale is told;
An' when they git the strength uv it, there'll never be the need
To call too loud fer fightin' men among the Southern breed."

Ginger's Cobber

"'*E WEARS perjarmer soots an' cleans 'is teeth,*"
    That's wot I reads. It fairly knocked me flat,
"*Me soljer cobber, be the name o' Keith.*"
    Well, if that ain't the limit, strike me fat!
The sort that Ginger Mick would think beneath
'Is notice once. Perjarmers! Cleans 'is teeth!

Ole Ginger Mick 'as sent a billy-doo
    Frum somew'ere on the earth where fightin's thick.
The Censor wus a sport to let it thro',
    Considerin' the choice remarks o' Mick.
It wus that 'ot, I'm wond'rin' since it came
It didn't set the bloomin' mail aflame.

I'd love to let yeh 'ave it word fer word;
    But, strickly, it's a bit above the odds;
An' there's remarks that's 'ardly ever 'eard
    Amongst the company to w'ich we nods.
It seems they use the style in Ginger's trench
Wot's written out an' 'anded to the Bench.

I tones the langwidge down to soot the ears
    Of sich as me an' you resorts wiv now.
If I should give it jist as it appears
    Partic'lar folk might want ter make a row.
But say, yeh'd think ole Ginger wus a pote
If yeh could read some juicy bits 'e's wrote.

Ginger's Cobber

It's this noo pal uv 'is that tickles me;
    'E's got a mumma, an' 'is name is Keith.
A knut upon the Block 'e used to be,
    'Ome 'ere; the sort that flashes golden teeth,
An' wears 'ot socks, an' torks a lot o' guff;
But Ginger sez they're cobbers till they snuff.

It come about like this: Mick spragged 'im first
    Fer swankin' it too much aboard the ship.
'E 'ad nice manners an' 'e never cursed;
    Which set Mick's teeth on edge, as you may tip.
Likewise, 'e 'ad two silver brushes, w'ich
'Is mumma give 'im, 'cos 'e fancied sich.

Mick pinched 'em. Not, as you will understand,
    Becos uv any base desire fer loot,
But jist becos, in that rough soljer band,
    Them silver-backed arrangements didn't soot:
An' etiket must be observed always.
(They fetched ten drinks in Cairo, Ginger says.)

That satisfied Mick's honour fer a bit,
    But still 'e picks at Keith fer exercise,
An' all the other blokes near 'as a fit
    To see Mick squirm at Keith's perlite replies,
Till one day Keith 'owls back "You flamin' cow!"
Then Mick permotes 'im, an' they 'as a row.

I sez "permotes 'im," fer, yeh'll understand
    Ole Ginger 'as 'is pride o' class orl right;
'E's not the bloke to go an' soil 'is 'and
    Be stoushin' any coot that wants to fight.
'Im, that 'as 'ad 'is chances more'n once
Up at the Stajum, ain't no bloomin' dunce.

Ginger Mick

Yeh'll 'ave to guess wot sort o' fight took place.
    Keith learnt 'is boxin' at a "culcher" school.
The first three rounds, to save 'im frum disgrace,
    Mick kids 'im on an' plays the gentle fool.
An' then 'e outs 'im wiv a little tap,
An' tells 'im, 'e's a reg'lar plucky chap.

They likes each other better after that,
    Fer Ginger alwiz 'ad a reel soft spot
Fer blokes 'oo 'ad some man beneath their 'at,
    An' never whined about the jolts they got.
Still, pride o' class kept 'em frum gettin' thick.
It's 'ard to git right next to Ginger Mick.

Then comes Gallipoli an' wot Mick calls
    "An orl-in push fight multerplied be ten;"
An' one be one the orfficers they falls,
    Until there's no one left to lead the men.
Fer 'arf a mo' they 'esitates stock still;
Fer 'oo's to lead 'em up the flamin' 'ill?

'Oo is to lead 'em if it ain't the bloke
    'Oo's 'eaded pushes down in Spadger's Lane,
Since 'e first learnt to walk an' swear an' smoke,
    An' mixed it willin' both fer fun an' gain—
That narsty, ugly, vi'lent man, 'oo's got
Grip on the minds uv men when blood runs 'ot?

Mick led 'em; an' be'ind 'im up the rise,
    'Owlin' an' cursin', comes that mumma's boy,
'Is cobber, Keith, with that look in 'is eyes
    To give the 'eart uv any leader joy.
An' langwidge! If 'is mar at 'ome 'ad 'eard
She would 'a' threw a fit at ev'ry word.

Ginger's Cobber

Mick dunno much about wot 'appened then,
    Excep' 'e felt 'is Dream uv Stoush come true;
Fer 'im an' Keith they fought like fifty men,
    An' felt like gawds wiv ev'ry breath they drew.
Then Ginger gits it solid in the neck,
An' flops; an' counts on passin' in 'is check.

When 'e come to, the light wus gettin' dim,
    The ground wus cold an' sodden underneath,
Someone is lyin' right 'longside uv 'im.
    Groanin' wiv pain, 'e turns, an' sees it's Keith—
Keith, wiv 'is rifle cocked, an' starin' 'ard
Ahead. An' now 'e sez " 'Ow is it, pard?"

Mick gently lifts 'is 'ead an' looks around.
    There ain't another flamin' soul in sight,
They're covered be a bit o' risin' ground,
    An' rifle-fire is cracklin' to the right.
"Down!" sez the mumma's joy. "Don't show yer 'ead!
Unless yeh want it loaded full o' lead."

Then, bit be bit, Mick gits the strength uv it.
    They wus so occupied wiv privit scraps,
They never noticed 'ow they come to git
    Right out ahead uv orl the other chaps.
They've bin cut orf, wiv jist one little chance
Uv gittin' back. Mick seen it at a glance.

" 'Ere, Kid," 'e sez, "you sneak around that 'ill.
    I'm down an' out; an' you kin tell the boys;"
Keith don't reply to 'im but jist lies still,
    An' signs to Ginger not to make a noise.
" 'Ere, you!" sez Mick, "I ain't the man to funk—
I won't feel 'ome-sick. Imshee! Do a bunk!"

Keith bites 'is lips; 'e never turns 'is 'ead.
  "Wot in the 'ell;" sez Mick, " 'ere, wot's yer game?"
"I'm an Australian," that wus all 'e said,
  An' pride took 'old o' Mick to 'ear that name—
A noo, glad pride that ain't the pride o' class—
An' Mick's contempt, it took the count at lars'!

All night they stayed there, Mick near mad wiv pain,
  An' Keith jist lettin' up 'is watchful eye
To ease Mick's wounds an' bind 'em up again,
  An' give 'im water, w'ile 'imself went dry.
Brothers they wus, 'oo found their brother'ood
That night on Sari Bair, an' found it good.

Brothers they wus. I'm wond'rin', as I read
  This scrawl uv Mick's, an' git its meanin' plain,
If you, 'oo never give these things no 'eed,
  Ain't got some brothers down in Spadger's Lane—
Brothers you never 'ad the chance to meet
Becos they got no time fer Collins Street.

"I'm an Australian." Well, it takes the bun!
  It's got that soft spot in the 'eart o' Mick.
But don't make no mistake; 'e don't gush none,
  Or come them "brother'ood" remarks too thick.
'E only writes, *This Keith's a decent coot,
Cobber o' mine, an' white from cap to boot."*

" *'E wears perjarmers an' 'e cleans 'is teeth,"*
  The sort o' bloke that Ginger once dispised!
But once a man shows metal underneath,
  Cobbers is found, an' brothers reckernised.
Fer, when a bloke's soul-clobber's shed in war,
'E looks the sort o' man Gawd meant 'im for.

The Singing Soldiers

"WHEN I'm sittin' in me dug-out wiv me rifle on
    me knees,
An' a yowlin', 'owlin' chorus comes a-floatin' up the breeze—
    Jist a bit o' 'Bonnie Mary' or 'Long Way to Tipperary'—
Then I know I'm in Australia, took an' planted overseas.
    They've bin up agin it solid since we crossed the flamin'
        foam;
    But they're singin'—alwiz singin'—since we left the wharf
        at 'ome.

"O, it's 'On the Mississippi' or 'Me Grey 'Ome in the West.'
If it's death an' 'ell nex' minute they must git it orf their chest.
    'Ere's a snatch o' 'When yer Roamin'—When yer Roamin'
        in the Gloamin'.'
'Struth! The first time that I 'eard it, wiv me 'ead on Rosie's
    breast,
    We was comin' frum a picnic in a Ferntree Gully train ...
    But the shrapnel made the music when I 'eard it sung again."

So I gits it straight frum Ginger in 'is letter 'ome to me,
On a dirty scrap o' paper wiv the writin' 'ard to see.
    "Strike!" sez 'e. "It sounds like skitin'; but they're singin'
        while they're fightin'";
An' they socks it into Abdul to the toon o' 'Nancy Lee.'
    An' I seen a bloke this mornin' wiv 'is arm blown to a rag,
        'Ummin' 'Break the Noos to Mother,' w'ile 'e sucked a
            soothin' fag.

"Now, the British Tommy curses, an' the French does fancy
    stunts,
An' the Turk 'e 'owls to Aller, an' the Gurkha grins an' grunts;
    But our boys is singin', singin', while the blinded shells is
        flingin'
Mud an' death inter the trenches in them 'eavens called the
    Fronts.
    An' I guess their souls keep singin' when they gits the tip
        to go ..."
    So I gits it, straight frum Ginger; an' Gawstruth! 'e ort to
        know.

An' 'is letter gits me thinkin' when I read sich tales as these,
An' I takes a look around me at the paddicks an' the trees;
    When I 'ears the thrushes trillin', when I 'ear the magpies
        fillin'
All the air frum earth to 'eaven wiv their careless melerdies—
    It's the sunshine uv the country, caught an' turned to bonzer
        notes;
    It's the sunbeams changed to music pourin' frum a thousand
        throats.

Can a soljer 'elp 'is singin' when 'e's born in sich a land?
Wiv the sunshine an' the music pourin' out on ev'ry 'and,
    Where the very air is singin', an' each breeze that blows is
        bringin'
'Armony an' mirth an' music fit to beat the blazin' band.
    On the march, an' in the trenches, when a swingin' chorus
        starts,
    They are pourin' bottled sunshine of their 'Omeland frum
        their 'earts.

The Singing Soldiers

O I've 'eard it, Lord, I've 'eard it since the days when I wus
 young,
On the beach an' in the bar-room, in the bush I've 'eard it sung;
 "Belle Mahone" an' "Annie Laurie," "Sweet Marie" to
  "Tobermory,"
Common toons and common voices, but I've 'eard 'em when
 they rung
 Wiv full, 'appy 'earts be'ind 'em, careless as a thrush's song—
 Wiv me arm around me cliner, an' me notions fur frum
  wrong.

So they growed wiv 'earts a-singin' since the days uv careless
 kids;
Beefin' out an 'appy chorus jist when Mother Nacher bids;
 Singin', wiv their notes a-quiver, "Down upon the Swanee
  River,"
Them's sich times I'd not be sellin' fer a stack uv golden quids.
 An' they're singin', still they're singin', to the sound uv guns
  an' drums,
 As they sung one golden Springtime underneath the wavin'
  gums.

When they socked it to the *Southland* wiv our sunny boys
 aboard—
Them that stopped a dam torpeder, an' a knock-out punch wus
 scored;
 Tho' their 'ope o' life grew murky, wiv the ship 'ead over
  turkey,
Dread o' death an' fear o' drownin' wus jist trifles they ignored.
 They spat out the blarsted ocean, an' they filled 'emselves
  wiv air,
 An' they passed along the chorus of "Australia will be There."

Ginger Mick

Yes, they sung it in the water; an' a bloke aboard a ship
Sez 'e *knoo* they wus Australians be the way they give it lip—
   Sung it to the soothin' motion of the dam devourin' ocean
Like a crowd o' seaside trippers in to 'ave a little dip.
    When I 'eard that tale, I tell yeh, straight, I sort o' felt a
      choke;
    Fer I seemed to 'ear 'em singin', an' I know that sort o' bloke

Yes, I know 'im; so I seen 'im, barrackin' Eternity.
An' the land that 'e wus born in is the land that mothered me.
    Strike! I ain't no sniv'lin' blighter; but I own me eyes git
      brighter
When I see 'em pokin' mullock at the everlastin' sea:
    When I 'ear 'em mockin' terror wiv a merry slab o' mirth,
    'Ell! I'm proud I bin to *gaol* in sich a land as give 'em birth!

       . . . . . .

"When I'm sittin' in me dug-out wiv the bullets droppin' near,"
Writes ole Ginger; "an' a chorus smacks me in the flamin' ear:
   P'raps a song that Rickards billed, er p'raps a line o' 'Waltz
     Matilder',
Then I feel I'm in Australia, took an' shifted over 'ere.
    Till the music sort o' gits me, an' I lets me top notes roam
    While I treats the gentle foeman to a chunk uv ' 'Ome,
      Sweet 'Ome.' "

They wus singin' on the troopship, they wus singin' in the train;
When they left their land be'ind 'em they wus shoutin' a refrain,
   An' I'll bet they 'ave a chorus, gay an' glad in greetin' for us,
When their bit uv scrappin's over, an' they lob back 'ome
     again ...
    An' the blokes that ain't returnin'—blokes that's paid the
      biggest price,
    They go singin', singin', singin' to the Gates uv Paradise.

In Spadger's Lane

OLE Mother Moon 'oo yanks 'er beamin' dile
    Acrost the sky when we've grown sick o' day,
She's like some fat ole Jane 'oo loves to smile
    On all concerned, an' smooth our faults away;
An', like a woman, tries to 'ide again
The sores an' scars crool day 'as made too plain.

To all the earth she gives the soft glad-eye;
    She picks no fav'rits in this world o' men;
She peeps in nooks, where 'appy lovers sigh,
    To make their joy more bonzer still; an' then,
O'er Spadger's Lane she waves a podgy 'and,
An' turns the scowlin' slums to Fairyland.

Aw, strike! I'm gettin' soft in my ole age!
    I'm growin' mushy wiv the passin' years.
Me! that 'as called it weakness to ingage
    In sloppy thorts that coax the pearly tears.
But say, me state o' mind I can't ixplain
When I seen Rose lars' night in Spadger's Lane.

'Twas Spadger's Lane where Ginger Mick 'ung out
    Before 'e took to follerin' the Flag;
The Lane that echoed to 'is drunken shout
    When 'e lobbed 'omeward on a gaudy jag.
Now Spadger's Lane knows Ginger Mick no more,
Fer 'e's become an 'ero at the War.

Ginger Mick

A flamin' 'ero at the War, that's Mick.
  An' Rose—'is Rose, is waitin' in the Lane,
Nursin' 'er achin' 'eart, an' lookin' sick
  As she crawls out to work an' 'ome again,
Givin' the bird to blokes 'oo'd be 'er "friend,"
An' prayin', wiv the rest, fer wars to end.

Quite right; I'm growin' sloppy fer a cert;
  But I must git it orf me chest or bust.
So 'ere's a song about a grievin' skirt,
  An' love, an' Ginger Mick, an' maiden trust!
The choky sort o' song that fetches tears
When blokes is full o' sentiment—or beers.

Lars' night, when I sneaks down to taste again
  The sights an' sounds I used to know so well,
The moon wus shinin' over Spadger's Lane,
  Sof'nin' the sorrer where 'er kind light fell;
Sof'nin' an' soothin', like it wus 'er plan
To make ixcuses fer the sins uv man.

Frum shadder inter shadder, up the street,
  A prowlin' moll sneaks by, wiv eyes all 'ate,
Dodgin' some unseen John, 'oo's sure, slow feet
  Comes tappin' after, certin as 'er fate;
In some back crib, a shicker's loud 'owled verse
Stops sudden, wiv a crash, an' then a curse.

Low down, a splotch o' red, where 'angs a blind
  Before the winder uv a Chow caboose,
Shines in the dead black wall, an' frum be'ind,
  Like all the cats o' Chinertown broke loose,
A mad Chow fiddle wails a two-note toon ...
An' then I seen 'er, underneath the moon.

In Spadger's Lane

Rosie the Rip they calls 'er in the Lane;
    Fer she wus alwiz willin' wiv 'er 'an's,
An' uses 'em to make 'er meanin' plain
    In ways that Spadger's beauties understan's.
But when ole Ginger played to snare 'er 'eart,
Rosie the Rip wus jist the soft, weak tart.

'Igh in 'er winder she wus leanin' out,
    Swappin' remarks wiv fat ole Mother Moon.
The things around I clean fergot about—
    Fergot the fiddle an' its crook Chow toon;
I only seen one woman in the light
Achin' to learn 'er forchin frum the night.

Ole Ginger's Rose! To see 'er sittin' there,
    The moonlight shinin' fair into 'er face,
An' sort o' touchin' gentle on 'er 'air,
    It made me fair fergit the time an' place.
I feels I'm peepin' where I never ought,
An' tries 'arf not to 'ear the words I caught.

One soljer's sweet'eart, that wus wot I seen:
    One out o' thousands grievin' thro' the land.
A tart frum Spadger's or a weepin' queen—
    Wot's there between 'em, when yeh understand?
She 'olds fer Mick, wiv all 'is ugly chiv,
The best a lovin' woman 'as to give.

The best a woman 'as to give—Aw, 'Struth!
    When war, an' grief, an' trouble's on the land
Sometimes a bloke gits glimpses uv the truth
    An' sweats 'is soul to try an' understand ...
An' then the World, like some offishus John,
Shoves out a beefy 'and, an' moves 'im on.

Ginger Mick

So I seen Rose; an' so, on that same night
    I seen a million women grievin' there.
Ole Mother Moon she showed to me a sight
    She sees around the World, most everyw'ere.
Sneakin' beneath the shadder uv the wall
I seen, an' learned, an' understood it all.

An' as I looks at Rosie, dreamin' there,
    'Er 'ead drops on 'er arms ... I seems to wake;
I sees the moonlight streamin' on 'er 'air;
    I 'ears 'er sobbin' like 'er 'eart ud break.
An' me there, pryin' on 'er misery.
"Gawstruth!" I sez, "This ain't no place fer me!"

On my tip-toes I sneaks the way I came—
    (The crook Chow fiddle ain't done yowlin' yet)—
An' tho' I tells it to me bitter shame—
    I'm gittin' soft as 'ell—me eyes wus wet.
An' that stern John, as I go moochin' by
Serloots me wiv a cold, unfeelin' eye.

The fat ole Mother Moon she's got a 'eart.
    An' so I like to think, when she looks down
Wiv 'er soft gaze upon some weepin' tart
    In bonzer gardens or the slums o' town;
She soothes 'em, mother-like, wiv podgy 'ands,
An' makes 'em dream agen uv peaceful lands.

The Straight Griffin

"'EROES? Orright. You 'ave it 'ow yeh like.
    Throw up yer little 'at an' come the glad;
But not too much 'Three-'Earty-Cheers' fer Mike;
    There's other things that 'e'll be wantin' bad.
The boys won't 'ave them kid-stakes on their mind
Wivout there's somethin' solider be'ind."

Now that's the dinkum oil frum Ginger Mick,
    In 'orspital, somew'ere be'ind the front;
Plugged in the neck, an' lately pretty sick,
    But now right on the converlescent stunt.
"I'm on the mend," 'e writes, "an' nearly doo
To come the 'ero act agen—Scene two."

I'd sent some papers, knowin' 'ow time drags
    Wiv blokes in blankits, waitin' fer a cure.
"An' 'Struth!" Mick writes, "the way they et them rags
    Yeh'd think that they'd bin weaned on litrachure.
They wrestled thro' frum 'Births' to 'Lost and Found';
They even give the Leaders 'arf a round."

Mick spent a bonzer day propped up in bed,
    Soothin' 'is soul wiv ev'ry sportin' page;
But in the football noos the things 'e read
    Near sent 'im orf 'is top wiv 'oly rage;
The way 'is team 'as mucked it earned 'is curse;
But 'e jist swallered it—becos uv nurse.

Ginger Mick

An' then this 'eadline 'it 'im wiv bokays;
    "*Australian Heroes!*" is the song it makes.
Mick reads the boys them ringin' words o' praise;
    But they jist grins a bit an' sez "Kid stakes!"
Sez Mick to nurse, "You tumble wot I am?
A bloomin' little 'ero. Pass the jam!"

Mick don't say much uv nurse; but 'tween the lines—
    ('Im bein' not too strong on gushin' speech)—
I seem to see some tell-tale sort o' signs.
    Sez 'e, "Me nurse-girl is a bonzer peach."
An' then 'e 'as a line: " 'Er sad, sweet look."
'Struth! Ginger must 'a' got it from a book.

Say, I can see ole Ginger, plain as plain,
    Purrin' to feel the touch uv 'er cool 'and,
Grinnin' a bit to kid 'is wound don't pain,
    An' yappin' tork she don't 'arf understand,
That makes 'er wonder if, back where she lives,
They're all reel men be'ind them ugly chivs.

But that's orright. Ole Ginger ain't no flirt.
    "You tell my Rose," 'e writes, "she's still the sweet.
An' if Long Jim gits messin' round that skirt,
    When I come back I'll do 'im up a treat.
Tell 'im, if all me arms an' legs is lame
I'll *bite* the blighter if 'e comes that game!"

There's jealousy! But Ginger needn't fret.
    Rose is fer 'im, an' Jim ain't on 'er card;
An' since she spragged 'im last time that they met—
    Jim ain't inlisted—but 'e's thinkin' 'ard.
Mick wus 'er 'ero long before the war,
An' now 'e's sort o' chalked a double score.

That's all Sir Garneo. But Mick, 'e's vowed
    This " 'Ail the 'Ero" stunt gits on 'is nerves,
An' makes 'im peevish; tho' 'e owns 'is crowd
    Can mop up all the praises they deserves.
"But don't yeh spread the 'ero on too thick
If it's exhaustin' yeh," sez Ginger Mick.

"We ain't got no objections to the cheers;
    We're good an' tough, an' we can stand the noise;
But three 'oorays and five or six long beers
    An' loud remarks about 'Our Gallant Boys'
Sounds kind o' weak—if you'll ixcuse the word—
Beside the fightin' sounds we've lately 'eard.

"If you'll fergive our blushes, we can stand
    The 'earty cheerin' an' the songs o' praise.
The loud 'Osannas uv our native land
    Makes us feel good an' glad in many ways.
An' later, when we land back in a mob,
Per'aps we might be arstin' fer a job.

"I'd 'ate," sez Mick, "to 'ave you think us rude,
    Or take these few remarks as reel bad taste;
'Twould 'urt to 'ave it seem ingratichude,
    Wiv all them 'earty praises gone to waste.
We'll take yer word fer it, an' jist remark
This 'ero racket is a reel good lark.

"Once, when they caught me toppin' off a John,
    The Bench wus stern, an' torked uv dirty work;
But, 'Struth! it's bonzer 'ow me fame's come on
    Since when I took to toppin' off the Turk.
So, if it pleases, shout yer loud 'Bravoes,'
An' later—don't fergit there's me, an' Rose."

Ginger Mick

So Ginger writes. I gives it word fer word;
    An' if it ain't the nice perlite reply
That nice, perlite old gents would like to've 'eard
    'Oo've been 'ip-'ippin' 'im up to the sky—
Well, I dunno, I s'pose 'e's gotter learn
It's rude fer 'im to speak out uv 'is turn.

'Eroes. It sounds a bit uv reel orl-right—
    "Our Gallant 'Eroes uv Gallipoli."
But Ginger, when 'e's thinkin' there at night,
    Uv Rose, an' wot their luck is like to be
After the echo dies uv all this praise,
Well—'e ain't dazzled wiv three loud 'oorays.

A Letter to the Front

I 'AVE written Mick a letter in reply to one uv 'is.
Where 'e arsts 'ow things is goin' where the gums an' wattles is.
So I tries to buck 'im up a bit; to go fer Abdul's fez;
An' I ain't no nob at litrachure; but this is wot I sez:

I suppose you fellers dream, Mick, in between the scraps out
    there,
Uv the land yeh left be'ind yeh when yeh sailed to do yer share:
Uv Collins Street, or Rundle Street, or Pitt, or George, or Hay,
Uv the land beyond the Murray or along the Castlereagh.
An' I guess yeh dream of old days an' the things yeh used to do,
An' yeh wonder 'ow 'twill strike yeh when yeh've seen this
    business thro',
An' yeh try to count yer chances when yeh've finished wiv the
    Turk
An' swap the gaudy war game fer a spell o' plain, drab work.

Well, Mick, yeh know jist 'ow it is these early days o' Spring,
When the gildin' o' the wattle chucks a glow on ev'rything.
Them olden days, the golden days that you remember well,
In spite o' war an' worry, Mick, are wiv us fer a spell.
Fer the green is on the paddicks, an' the sap is in the trees,
An' the bush birds in the gullies sing the ole, sweet melerdies;
An' we're 'opin', as we 'ear 'em, that, when next the Springtime
    comes,
You'll be wiv us 'ere to listen to that bird tork in the gums.

Ginger Mick

It's much the same ole Springtime, Mick, yeh reckerlect uv yore,
Boronier an' dafferdils and wattle blooms once more
Sling sweetness over city streets, an' seem to put to shame
The rotten greed an' butchery that got you on this game—
The same ole sweet September days, an' much the same ole place;
Yet, there's a sort o' *somethin'*, Mick, upon each passin' face,
A sort o' look that's got me beat; a look that you put there,
The day yeh lobbed upon the beach an' charged at Sari Bair.

It isn't that we're boastin', lad; we've done wiv most o' that—
The froth, the cheers, the flappin' flags, the giddy wavin' 'at.
Sich things is childish memories; we blush to 'ave 'em told,
Fer we 'ave seen our wounded, Mick, an' it 'as made us old.
We ain't gowed soggy wiv regret, we ain't swelled out wiv pride;
But we 'ave seen it's up to us to lay our toys aside.
An' it wus you that taught us, Mick, we've growed too old fer play,
An' everlastin' picter shows, an' goin' down the Bay.

An', as a grown man dreams at times uv boy'ood days gone by,
So, when we're feelin' crook, I s'pose, we'll sometimes sit an' sigh.
But as a clean lad takes the ring wiv mind an' 'eart serene,
So I am 'opin' we will fight to make our man'ood clean.
When orl the stoushin's over, Mick, there's 'eaps o' work to do:
An' in the peaceful scraps to come we'll still be needin' you.
We will be needin' you the more fer wot yeh've seen an' done;
Fer you were born a Builder, lad, an' we 'ave jist begun.

There's bin a lot o' tork, ole mate, uv wot we owe to you,
An' wot yeh've braved an' done fer us, an' wot we mean to do.
We've 'ailed you boys as 'eroes, Mick, an' torked uv just reward
When you 'ave done the job yer at an' slung aside the sword.
I guess it makes yeh think a bit, an' weigh this gaudy praise;
Fer even 'eroes 'ave to eat, an'—there is other days:
The days to come when we don't need no bonzer boys to fight:
When the flamin's picnic's over an' the Leeuwin looms in sight.

A Letter to the Front

Then there's another fight to fight, an' you will find it tough
To sling the Kharki clobber fer the plain civilian stuff.
When orl the cheerin' dies away, an' 'ero-worship flops,
Yeh'll 'ave to face the ole tame life—'ard yakker or 'ard cops,
But, lad, yer land is wantin' yeh, an' wantin' each strong son
To fight the fight that never knows the firin' uv a gun:
The steady fight, when orl you boys will show wot you are worth.
An' punch a cow on Yarra Flats or drive a quill in Perth.

The gilt is on the wattle, Mick, young leaves is on the trees,
An' the bush birds in the gullies swap the ole sweet melerdies,
There's a good, green land awaitin' you when you come 'ome again
To swing a pick at Ballarat or ride Yarrowie Plain.
The streets is gay wiv dafferdils—but—haggard in the sun,
A wounded soljer passes; an' we know ole days is done.
Fer somew'ere down inside us, lad, is somethin' you put there
The day yeh swung a dirty left, fer us, at Sari Bair.

Rabbits

"AR! Gimme fights wiv foemen I kin see,
    To upper-cut an' wallop on the jor.
Life in a burrer ain't no good to me.
              'Struth! This ain't war!
Gimme a ding-dong go fer 'arf a round,
An' you kin 'ave this crawlin' underground.

"Gimme a ragin', 'owlin', tearin' scrap,
    Wiv room to swing me left, an' feel it land.
This 'idin', sneakin' racket makes a chap
              Feel secon'-'and.
Stuck in me dug-out 'ere, down in a 'ole,
I'm feelin' like I've growed a rabbit's soul."

Ole Ginger's left the 'orspital, it seems;
    'E's back at Anzac, cursin' at the game;
Fer this 'ere ain't the fightin' uv 'is dreams;
              It's too dead tame.
'E's got the oopizootics reely bad,
An' 'idin' in a burrer makes 'im mad.

'E sort o' takes it personal, yeh see.
    'E used to 'awk 'em for a crust, did Mick.
Now, makin' *'im* play rabbits seems to be
              A narsty trick.
To shove 'im like a bunny down a 'ole
It looks like chuckin' orf, an' sours 'is soul.

Rabbits

"Fair doos," 'e sez. "I joined the bloomin' ranks
    To git away frum rabbits: thinks I'm done
Wiv them Australian pests, an' 'ere's their thanks:
        They makes me one!
An' 'ere I'm squattin', scared to shift about;
Jist waitin' fer me little tail to sprout.

"Ar, strike me up a wattle! but it's tough!
    But 'ere's the dizzy limit, fer a cert—
To live this bunny's life is bad enough,
        But 'ere's reel dirt:
Some tart at 'ome 'as sent, wiv lovin' care,
A coat uv rabbit-skins fer me to wear!

"That's done it! Now I'm nibblin' at me food,
    An' if a dawg shows up I'll start to squeal.
I s'pose I orter melt wiv gratichude:
        'Tain't 'ow I feel.
She might 'a' fixed a note on wiv a pin:
'Please, Mister Rabbit, yeh fergot yer skin!'

"I sees me finish!... War? Why, this ain't war!
    It's ferritin'! An' I'm the bloomin' game.
Me skin alone is worth the 'untin' for—
        That tart's to blame!
Before we're done, I've got a silly scare,
Some trappin' Turk will catch me in a snare.

" 'E'll skin me, wiv the others 'e 'as there,
    An' shove us on a truck, an' bung us 'round
Constantinople at a bob a pair—
        'Orl fresh an' sound!
'Eads down, 'eels up, 'e'll 'awk us in a row
Around the 'arems, 'owlin' 'Rabbee-oh!'

"But, dead in earnest, it's a job I 'ate.
    We've got to do it, an' it's gittin' done;
But this soul-dopin' game uv sit-an'-wait
        It ain't no fun.
There's times I wish, if we weren't short uv men,
That I wus back in 'orspital again.

"Ar, 'orspital! There is the place to git.
    If I thort Paradise wus 'arf so snug
I'd shove me 'ead above the parapit
        An' stop a slug.
But one thing blocks me playin' sich a joke:
I want another scrap before I croak.

"I want it bad. I want to git right out
    An' plug some josser in the briskit—'ard.
I want to 'owl an' chuck me arms about,
        An' jab, an' guard,
An' swing, an' upper-cut, an' crool some pitch,
Or git passed out meself—I don't care w'ich.

"There's some blokes 'ere they've tumbled to a stunt
    Fer gittin' 'em the spell that they deserves.
They chews some cordite when life at the front
        Gits on their nerves.
It sends yer tempracher clean out uv sight,
An', if yeh strike a simple doc, yer right.

"I tries it once. Me soul 'ad got the sinks,
    Me thorts annoyed me, an' I 'ad the joes,
I feels like no one loves me, so I thinks,
        Well, Mick, 'ere goes!
I breaks a cartridge open, chews a bit,
Reports I'm sick, an' throws a fancy fit.

Rabbits

"Me lovin' sargint spreads the gloomy noos,
    I gits paraded; but, aw, 'Struth! me luck!
It weren't no baby doc I interviews,
        But some ole buck
Wiv gimblet eyes. 'Put out yer tongue!' 'e 'owls.
Then takes me temp, an' stares at me, an' growls.

" 'Well, well,' 'e sez. 'Wot is yer trouble, lad?'
    I grabs me tummy 'ard, an' sez I'm ill.
'You are,' sez 'e. 'Yeh got corditis, bad.
        Yeh need a pill.
Before yeh go to sleep,' 'e sez, 'to-night,
Swaller the bullet, son, an' you'll be right.'

" 'Ow's that fer rotten luck? But orl the same,
    I ain't complainin' when I thinks it out.
I seen it weren't no way to play the game,
        This pullin' out.
We're orl uv us in this to see it thro'.
An' bli'me, wot we've got to do, we'll do.

"But 'oles an' burrers! Strike! An' this is war!
    This is the bonzer scrappin' uv me dreams!
A willin' go is wot I bargained for,
        But 'ere it seems
I've died, someway, an' bin condemned to be
Me own Wile Rabbee fer eternity.

"But 'orspital! I tell yeh, square an' all,
    If I could meet the murderin' ole Turk
'Oo's bullet sent me there to loaf an' sprawl,
        An' dodge me work,
Lord! I'd shake 'an's wiv 'im, an' thank 'im well
Fer givin' me a reel ole bonzer spell.

Ginger Mick

" 'E might 'a' made it jist a wee bit worse.
    I'd stand a lot uv that before I'd scream.
The grub wus just the thing; an', say, me nurse!
        She wus a dream!
I used to treat them tony tarts wiv mirth;
But now I know why they wus put on earth.

"It treated me reel mean, that wound uv mine;
    It 'ealed too quick, considerin' me state.
An' 'ere I am, back in the firin' line
        Gamblin' wiv Fate.
It's like two-up: I'm 'eadin' 'em this trip;
But lookin', day be day, to pass the kip.

"You tell Doreen, yer wife, 'ow I am chock
    Full to the neck wiv thanks fer things she sends.
Each time I shoves me foot inside a sock
        I bless sich friends.
I'm bustin' wiv glad thorts fer things she did;
So tell 'er I serloots 'er, an' the kid.

"Make 'im a soljer, chum, when 'e gits old.
    Teach 'im the tale uv wot the Anzacs did.
Teach 'im 'e's got a land to love an' hold.
        Gawd bless the kid!
But I'm in 'opes when 'is turn comes around
They'll chuck this style uv rootin' underground.

"We're up agin it, mate; we know that well.
    There ain't a man among us wouldn't lob
Over the parapit an' charge like 'ell
        To end the job.
But this is war; an' discipline—well, lad,
We sez we 'ates it; but we ain't too bad.

Rabbits

"Glory an' gallant scraps is wot I dreamed,
    Ragin' around an' smashin' foeman flat;
But war, like other things, ain't wot it seems.
        So 'stid uv that,
I'm sittin' in me dug-out scrawlin' this,
An' thankin' Gawd when the shells go by—an' miss.

"I'm sittin' in me dug-out day be day—
    It narks us; but Australia's got a name
Fer doin' little jobs like blokes 'oo play
        A clean, straight game.
Wiv luck I might see scrappin' 'fore I'm done,
Or go where Craig 'as gone, an' miss the fun.

"But if I dodge, an' keep out uv the rain,
    An' don't toss in me alley 'fore we wins;
An' if I lobs back 'ome an' meets the Jane
        'Oo sent the skins—
These bunnies' overcoats I lives inside—
I'll squeal at 'er, an' run away an' 'ide.

"But, torkin' straight, the Janes 'as done their bit.
    I'd like to 'ug the lot, orl on me pat!
They warms us well, the things they've sewed an' knit:
        An' more than that—
I'd like to tell them dear Australian tarts
The spirit uv it warms Australian 'earts."

To the Boys Who Took the Count

SEE, I'm writin' to Mick as a bloke to a bloke—
    To a cobber o' mine at the front—
An' I'm gittin' full up uv the mullock they poke
    At the cove that is bearin' the brunt.
Fer 'e mus'n't do this an' 'e shouldn't do that,
    An' 'e's crook if 'e looks a bit shick,
An' 'e's gittin' too uppish, an' don't touch 'is 'at—
    But 'ere's 'ow I puts it to Mick.

Now, it's dickin to style if yer playin' the game,
    If it's marbles, or shinty, or war;
I've seen 'em lob 'ome 'ere, the 'alt an' the lame,
    That wus fine 'efty fellers before.
They wus toughs, they wus crooks, they wus ev'ry bad thing,
    But they mixed it as gentlemen should.
So 'ere's to the coot wiv 'is eye in a sling,
    An' a smile in the one that is good.

It wus playin' the game in the oval an' ring—
    An' playin' fer orl it wus worth—
That give 'em the knack uv a punch wiv a sting
    When they fought fer the land uv their birth.
They wus pebs, they wus narks, they wus reel naughty boys,
    But they didn't need no second 'int,
So ere's to the bloke wiv 'is swearin' an' noise,
    An' 'is foot in a fathom uv lint.

To the Boys Who Took the Count

There wus fellers I knoo in the soft days uv peace;
    An' I didn't know much to their good;
An' they give more 'ard graft to the overworked p'leece
    Than a reel puffick gentleman should.
They wus lookin' fer lash long before it wus doo;
    When it come, they wus into it, straight.
So 'ere's to the bloke wiv 'is shoulder shot thro'
    'Oo is cursin' the days 'e's to wait.

Ar, dickin to swank! when it comes to a mill,
    It's the bloke wiv a punch 'oo's yer friend.
An' a coarse, narsty man wiv the moniker Bill
    Earns the thanks uv the crowd in the end.
(An' when I sez "earns" I am 'opin' no stint
    Will be charged agin us by-an'-bye.)
So 'ere's to the boy wiv 'is arm in a splint
    An' a "don't-care-a-dam" in 'is eye.

'Cos the fightin's too far fer to give us a grip
    Of the 'ell full uv slaughter an' noise,
There's a breed that gives me the pertickler pip
    Be the way that they torks uv the boys.
O, they're coarse, an' they're rude, an' it's awful to live
    Wiv their cursin' an' shoutin' an' fuss.
Dam it! 'Ere's to the bloke wiv the bad-lookin' chiv
    That 'e poked inter trouble fer us!

O, it's dead agin etikit, dead agin style
    Fer to swear an' to swagger an' skite;
But a battle ain't won wiv a drorin'-room smile,
    An' yeh *'ave* to be rude in a fight.
An' it's bein' reel rude to enemy blokes
    That'll earn yeh that 'ero-like touch,
So 'ere's to the boy wiv 'is curses an' jokes
    'Oo is 'oppin' about on a crutch.

Ginger Mick

Now, the Turk is a gent, an' they greets 'im as such,
    An' they gives doo respect to 'is Nibs;
But 'e never 'eld orf to apolergise much
    When 'e slid 'is cold steel in their ribs.
An' our boys won the name that they give 'em of late
    'Cos they fought like a jugful uv crooks,
So 'ere's to the bloke wiv the swaggerin' gait
    An' a bullet mark spoilin' 'is looks.

So, the bloke wiv the scoff, an' the bloke wiv the sneer,
    An' the coot wiv the sensitive soul,
'E 'as got to sit back, an' jist change 'is idear
    Uv the stuffin' that makes a man whole.
Fer the polish an' gilt that's a win wiv the skirts
    It wears thin wiv the friction uv war.
So 'ere's to the cove 'oo is nursin' 'is 'urts
    Wiv an oath in the set uv 'is jor.

When yeh've stripped a cove clean an' got down to the buff
    Yeh come to the meat that's the man.
If yeh want to find grit an' sich similar stuff,
    Yeh've to strip on a similar plan.
Fer there's nothin' like scrappin' to bare a man's soul,
    If it's Billo, or Percy, or Gus.
So 'ere's to the bloke 'oo 'ops round on a pole
    An' 'owls songs goin' 'ome on the bus.

Spare me days! When a bloke takes the count in a scrap
    That 'e's fightin' fer you an' fer me,
Is it fair that a snob 'as the nerve fer to snout
    Any swad 'cos 'is manners is free?
They're deservin' our thanks, frum the best to the worst—
    An' there's some is reel rorty, I own—
But 'ere's to the coot wiv the 'ang-over thirst
    'Oo sprags a stray toff fer a loan.

To the Boys Who Took the Count

So I'm writin' to Mick; an' I'm feelin' reel wet
    Wiv the sort o' superior nark,
'Oo tilts up 'is conk an' gits orl the boys set,
    'Oo are out fer a bit uv a lark.
So I puts it to Mick, as I sez when I starts,
    An' I ends wiv the solemest toast:
'Ere's to 'im—(raise yer glass)—'oo left pride in our 'earts
    An' 'is bones on Gallipoli coast.

The Game

"HO! the sky's as blue as blazes an' the sun is shinin' bright,
    An' the dicky birds is singin' over'ead,
An' I'm 'ummin', softly 'ummin', w'ile I'm achin' for a fight,
    An' the chance to fill some blighter full o' lead.
An' the big guns they are boomin', an' the shells is screamin' past,
But I'm corperil—lance-corperil, an' found me game at last!"

I ixpects a note frum Ginger, fer the time wus gettin' ripe,
    An' I gits one thick wiv merry 'owls uv glee,
Fer they've gone an' made 'im corperil—they've given 'im a stripe,
    An' yeh'd think, to see 'is note, it wus V.C.
Fer 'e chortles like a nipper wiv a bran' noo Noer's Ark
Since Forchin she 'as smiled on 'im, an' life's no more a nark.

"Ho! the sky along the 'ill-tops, it is smudged wiv cannon smoke,
    An' the shells along the front is comin' fast,
But the 'eads 'ave 'ad the savvy fer to reckernise a bloke,
    An' permotion's gettin' common-sense at last.
An' they picked me fer me manners, w'ich wus snouted over 'ome,
But I've learned to be a soljer since I crossed the ragin' foam.

"They 'ave picked me 'cos they trust me; an' it's got me where I live,
    An' it's put me on me metal, square an' all.
I wusn't in the runnin' once when blokes 'ad trust to give,
    But over 'ere I answers to the call.
So some shrewd 'ead 'e marked me well, an' when the time was ripe,
'E took a chance on Ginger Mick, an' I 'ave snared me stripe.

The Game

"I know wot I wus born fer now, an' soljerin's me game,
    That's no furphy; but I never guessed it once;
Fer when I 'it things up at 'ome they said I wus to blame,
    An' foolish beaks they sent me up fer munce.
But 'ere—well, things is different to wot sich things wus then.
Fer me game is playin' soljers, an' me lurk is 'andlin' men.

"Me game is 'andlin' men, orl right, I seen it in the parst
    When I used to 'ead the pushes in the Lane.
An' ev'ry bloke among 'em then done everythin' I arst,
    Fer I never failed to make me meanin' plain.
Disturbers uv the peace we wus them days, but now I know
We wus aimin' to be soljers, but we never 'ad a show.

"We never 'ad no discipline, that's wot we wanted bad,
    It's discipline that gives the push its might.
But wot a time we could 'ave give the coppers if we 'ad,
    Lord! We'd 'ave capchered Melbourne in a night.
When I think uv things that might 'ave been I sometimes sit an' grin,
Fer I might be King uv Footscray if we'd 'ad more discipline.

"I've got a push to 'andle now wot makes a soljer proud.
    Yeh ort to see the boys uv my ole squad.
The willin'est, the cheeriest, don'-care-a-damest crowd
    An' the toughest ever seen outside o' quod.
I reckon that they gimme 'em becos they wus so meek,
But they know me, an' they understan' the lingo that I speak.

"So I'm a little corperil, wiv pretties on me arm,
    But yeh'd never guess it fer to see me now,
Fer me valet 'e's been careless an' me trooso's come to 'arm.
    An' me pants want creasin' badly I'll allow.
But to see me squad in action is a cure fer sandy blight,
They are shy on table manners, but they've notions 'ow ter fight.

"There's a little picnic promised that 'as long been overdoo,
   An' we're waitin' fer the order to advance;
An' me bones is fairly achin' fer to see my boys bung thro',
   Fer I know they're dancin' mad to git the chance.
An' there's some'll sure be missin' when we git into the game;
But if they lorst their corperil 'twould be a cryin' shame.

"We can't afford no corperils. But, some'ow, I dunno,
   I got a nervis feelin' in me chest,
That this 'ere bit uv fancy work might be me final go
   An' I won't be 'ome to dinner wiv the rest.
It's rot; but it keeps comin' back, that lonely kind o' mood.
That fills me up wiv mushy thorts that don't do any good.

"When it's gettin' near to evenin' an' the guns is slowin' down
   I fergits the playful 'abits uv our foes,
An' finds meself a-thinkin' thorts uv good ole Melbourne town.
   An' dreamin' dilly dreams about ole Rose.
O' course I'll see me girl again, an' give a clean, square deal,
When I come smilin' 'ome again ... But that ain't 'ow I feel.

"I feel ... I dunno 'ow I feel. I feel that things is done.
   I seem t've 'it the limit in some way.
Per'aps I'm orf me pannikin wiv sittin' in the sun,
   But I jist wrote to Rose the other day.
An' I wrote 'er sort o' mournful 'cos—I dunno 'ow it seems ...
Ar, I'm a gay galoot to go an' 'ave these dilly dreams!

"Wot price the bran' noo corperil, wiv sof'nin' uv the 'eart!
   If my pet lambs thort me a turtle dove
I'd 'ave to be reel stern wiv 'em, an' make another start
   To git 'em where I got 'em jist wiv love ...
But don't fergit, if you or your Doreen sees Rose about,
Jist tell 'er that I'm well an' strong, an' sure uv winnin' out.

"Ho! the sky's as blue as blazes, an' the sun is shinin' still,
  An' the dicky bird is perchin' on the twig,
An' the guns is pop, pop, poppin' frum the trenches on the 'ill,
  An' I'm lookin' bonny in me non-com's rig.
An' when yer writin' me again—don't think I want ter skite—
But don't fergit the 'Corperil'; an' mind yeh spells it right."

"A Gallant Gentleman"

A MONTH ago the world grew grey fer me;
    A month ago the light went out fer Rose.
To 'er they broke it gentle as might be;
    But fer 'is pal 'twus one uv them swift blows
That stops the 'eart-beat; fer to me it came
Jist, "Killed in Action," an', beneath, *'is* name.

'Ow many times 'ave I sat dreamin' 'ere
    An' seen the boys returnin', gay an' proud.
I've seen the greetin's, 'eard 'is rousin' cheer,
    An' watched ole Mick come stridin' thro' the crowd.
'Ow many times 'ave I sat in this chair
An' seen 'is 'ard chiv grinnin' over there.

'E's laughed, an' told me stories uv the war.
    Changed some 'e looked, but still the same ole Mick,
Keener an' cleaner than 'e wus before.
    'E's took me 'and, an' said 'e's in great nick.
Sich wus the dreamin's uv a fool 'oo tried
To jist crack 'ardy, an' 'old gloom aside.

An' now—well, wot's the odds? I'm only one:
    One out uv many 'oo 'as lost a friend.
Manlike, I'll bounce again, an' find me fun;
    But fer poor Rose it seems the bitter end.
Fer Rose, an' sich as Rose, when one man dies
It seems the world goes black before their eyes.

Fer Rose, an' sich as Rose, thro' orl the world,
    War piles the burdens wiv a 'eavy 'and.
Since bugles called an' banners were unfurled,
    A sister'ood 'as growed thro' orl the land—
A 'oly sister'ood that puts aside
Sham things, an' 'and takes 'and in grief—an' pride.

Ar, well; if Mick could 'ear me blither now,
    I know jist wot 'e'd say an' 'ow 'e'd look:
"Aw, cut it out, mate; chuck that silly row!
    There ain't no sense in takin' sich things crook.
I've took me gamble; an' there's none to blame
Becos I drew a blank; it's in the game."

A parson cove he broke the noos to Rose—
    A friend uv mine, a bloke wiv snowy 'air,
An' gentle, soothin' sort o' ways, 'oo goes
    Thro' life jist 'umpin' others' loads uv care.
Instid uv Mick—jist one rough soljer lad—
Yeh'd think 'e'd lost the dearest friend 'e 'ad.

But 'ow kin blows be sof'n'd sich as that?
    Rose took it as 'er sort must take sich things.
An' if the jolt uv it 'as knocked me flat,
    Well, 'oo is there to blame 'er if it brings
Black thorts that comes to women when they frets,
An' makes 'er tork wild tork an' foolish threats.

An' then there come the letter that wus sent
    To give the strength uv Ginger's passin' out—
A long, straight letter frum a bloke called Trent.
    'Tain't no use tellin' wot it's orl about.
There's things that's in it I kin see quite clear
Ole Ginger Mick ud be ashamed to 'ear.

Things praisin' 'im, that pore ole Mick ud say
    Wus comin' it too 'ot; fer, spare me days!
I well remember that 'e 'ad a way
    Uv curlin' up when 'e wus slung bokays.
An' Trent 'e seems to think that in some way
'E owes Mick somethin' that 'e can't repay.

Well, p'raps 'e does; an' in the note 'e sends
    'E arsts if Mick 'as people 'e kin find.
Fer Trent's an English toff wiv swanky friends,
    An' wants to 'elp wot Ginger's left be'ind.
'E sez strange things in this 'ere note 'e sends:
"He was a gallant gentleman," it ends.

A gallant gentleman! Well, I dunno.
    I 'ardly think that Mick ud like that name.
But this 'ere Trent's a toff, an' ort to know
    The breedin' uv the stock frum which 'e came.
Gallant an' game Mick might 'a' bin; but then—
Lord! Fancy 'im among the gentlemen!

'E wus a man; that's good enough fer me,
    'Oo wus 'is cobber many years before
'E writ it plain fer other blokes to see,
    An' proved it good an' plenty at the war.
'E wus a man; an', by the way 'e died,
'E wus a man 'is friend kin claim wiv pride.

The way 'e died ... Gawd! but it makes me proud
    I ever 'eld 'is 'and, to read that tale.
An' Trent is one uv that 'igh-steppin' crowd
    That don't sling praise around be ev'ry mail.
To 'im it seemed some great 'eroic lurk;
But Mick, I know, jist took it wiv 'is work.

"A Gallant Gentleman"

No matter wot 'e done. It's jist a thing
    I knoo 'e'd do if once 'e got the show.
An' it would never please 'im fer to sling
    Tall tork at 'im jist 'cos 'e acted so.
"Don't make a song uv it!" I 'ear 'im growl,
"I've done me limit, an' tossed in the tow'l."

This little job, 'e knoo—an' I know well—
    A thousand uv 'is cobbers would 'ave done.
Fer they are soljers; an' it's crook to tell
    A tale that marks fer praise a single one.
An' that's 'ow Mick would 'ave it, as I know;
An', as 'e'd 'ave it, so we'll let it go.

Trent tells 'ow, when they found 'im, near the end,
    'E starts a fag an' grins orl bright an' gay.
An' when they arsts fer messages to send
    To friends, 'is look goes dreamin' far away.
"Look after Rose," 'e sez, "when I move on.
Look after ... Rose ... Mafeesh!" An' e' wus gone.

"We buried 'im," sez Trent, "down by the beach.
    We put mimosa on the mound uv sand
Above 'im. 'Twus the nearest thing in reach
    To golden wattle uv 'is native land.
But never wus the fairest wattle wreath
More golden than the 'eart uv 'im beneath."

An' so—Mafeesh! as Mick 'ad learned to say.
    'E's finished; an' there's few 'as marked 'im go.
Only one soljer, outed in the fray,
    'Oo took 'is gamble, an' 'oo 'ad 'is show.
There's few to mourn 'im: an' the less they leave,
The less uv sorrer; fewer 'earts to grieve.

Ginger Mick

An' when I'm feelin' blue, an' mopin' 'ere
    About the pal I've lorst; Doreen, my wife,
She come an' takes my 'and, an' tells me, "Dear,
    There'd be more cause to mourn a wasted life.
'E proved 'imself a man; an' 'e's at rest."
An' so, I tries to think sich things is best.

A gallant gentleman ... Well, let it go.
    They sez they've put them words above 'is 'ead,
Out there where lonely graves stretch in a row;
    But Mick 'e'll never mind it now 'e's dead.
An' where 'e's gone, when they weigh praise an' blame,
P'raps gentlemen an' men is much the same.

They fights; an' orl the land is filled wiv cheers.
    They dies; an' 'ere an' there a 'eart is broke.
An' when I weighs it orl—the shouts, the tears—
    I sees it's well Mick wus a lonely bloke.
'E found a game 'e knoo, an' played it well;
An' now 'e's gone. Wot more is there to tell?

A month ago, fer me the world grew grey;
    A month ago the light went out fer Rose;
Becos one common soljer crossed the way,
    Leavin' a common message as 'e goes.
But ev'ry dyin' soljer's 'ope lies there:
"Look after Rose. Mafeesh!" Gawd! It's a pray'r!

That's wot it is; an' when yeh sort it out,
    Shuttin' yer ears to orl the sounds o' strife—
The shouts, the cheers, the curses—'oo kin doubt
    The claims uv women: mother, sweet'eart, wife?
An' 'oo's to 'ear our soljers' dyin' wish?
An' 'oo's to 'eed? ... "Look after Rose ... Mafeesh!"

DOREEN

FER 'er sweet sake I've gone an' chucked it clean:
The pubs an' schools an' all that leery game.
Fer when a bloke 'as come to know Doreen,
       It ain't the same.
There's 'igher things, she sez, fer blokes to do.
An' I am 'arf believin' that it's true.

            — THE SENTIMENTAL BLOKE

Washing Day

THE little gipsy vi'lits, they wus peepin' thro' the green
As she come walkin' in the grass, me little wife, Doreen.
The sun shone on the sassafras, where thrushes sung a bar.
—The 'ope an' worry uv our lives wus yellin' fer 'is Mar.—
I watched 'er comin' down the green; the sun wus on 'er 'air—
Jist the woman that I marri'd, when me luck wus 'eadin' fair.

I seen 'er walkin' in the sun that lit our little farm.
She 'ad three clothes-pegs in 'er mouth, an' washin' on 'er arm—
    Three clothes-pegs, fer I counted 'em, an' watched 'er as she
        come.
    "The stove-wood's low," she mumbles, "an' young Bill 'as cut
        'is thumb,"
Now, it weren't no giddy love-speech, but it seems to take me
    straight
Back to the time I kissed 'er first beside 'er mother's gate.

Six years uv wedded life we've 'ad, an' still me dreams is sweet ...
Aw, them bonzer little vi'lits, they wus smilin' round me feet.
    An' wot's a bit uv stove-wood count, wiv paddicks grinnin'
        green,
    When a bloke gits on to dreamin' uv the old days an'
        Doreen—
The days I thort I snared a saint; but since I've understood
I 'ave wed a dinkum woman, which is fifty times as good.

I 'ave wed a dinkum woman, an' she's give me eyes to see.
Oh, I ain't been mollycoddled, an' there ain't no fluff on me!
    But days when I wus down an' out she seemed so 'igh above;
    An' a saint is made fer worship, but a woman's made fer love.
An' a bloke is growin' richer as sich things 'e comes to know ...
(She pegs another sheet an' sez, "The stove-wood's gittin' low.")

Doreen

A bloke 'e learns a lot uv things in six years wiv a tart;
But thrushes in the sassafras ain't singin' like me 'eart.
   'Tis the thrushes 'oo 'ave tort me in their choonful sort o' way
   That it's best to take things singin' as yeh meet 'em day be
      day.
Fer I wed a reel, live woman, wiv a woman's 'appy knack
Uv torkin' reason inside out an' logic front to back.

An' I like it. 'Struth I like it! Fer a wax doll in a 'ome,
She'd give a man the flamin' pip an' longin's fer to roam.
   Aw, I ain't no silk-sock sonkie 'oo ab'ors the rood an' rough;
   Fer, city-born an' gutter-bred, me schoolin' it wus tough.
An' I like the dinkum woman 'oo ... (She jerks the clothes-prop, so,
An' sez, so sweet an' dangerous, "The stove-wood's gittin' low.")

See, I've studied men in cities, an' I've studied 'em out 'ere;
I've seen 'em 'ard thro' piety an' seen 'em kind thro' beer.
   I've seen the meanest doin' deeds to make the angels smile,
   An' watched the proudest playin' games that crooks 'ud
      reckon vile.
I 'ave studied 'em in bunches an' I've read 'em one be one,
An' there isn't much between 'em when the 'ole thing's said an'
   done.

An' I've sort o' studied wimmin—fer I've met a tidy few—
An' there's times, when I wus younger, when I kids meself I knew.
   But 'im 'oo 'opes to count the stars or measure up the sea,
   'E kin 'ave a shot at woman, fer she's fairly flummoxed me ...
("I'll 'ave to 'ave *some* wood," she sez, an' sez it most perlite
An' secret to a pair uv socks; an' jams a peg in, tight.)

Now, a woman, she's a woman. I 'ave fixed that fer a cert.
They're jist as like as rows uv peas from 'at to 'em uv skirt.
    An' then, they're all so different, yeh find, before yeh've
        done,
    The more yeh know uv all uv 'em the less yeh know uv one.
An' then, the more yeh know uv one ... (She gives 'er 'air a
        touch:
"The stove-wood's nearly done," she sez. "Not that it matters
        much.")

The little gipsy vi'lits, they wus smilin' round me feet.
An' this dreamin' dilly day-dreams on a Summer day wus sweet.
    I 'eaves me frame frum orf the fence, an' grabs me little axe;
    But, when I'm 'arf way to the shed, she stops me in me tracks.
"Yer lunch is ready. That ole wood kin easy wait a while."
Strike! I'm marri'd to a woman ... But she never seen me smile.

Logic and Spotted Dog

"UNLESS you *'ide* that axe," she sez, " 'E'll 'urt 'imself reel bad.
An' after all—Now, Bill, don't cry!—the trouble that I've 'ad
    Wiv 'im thro' croop an' whoopin' corf, 'e goes an' cuts 'imself!
    Why don't you 'ang it on the wall, or 'ide it on a shelf?
But there it wus, jist thrown about. You *ort* to take more care!
              You left it there!

"You left it there," she sez, "an' now..." I sez, " 'Old on a jiff.
Let's git the fac's all sorted out before we 'as a tiff.
    I'm mighty careful wiv that axe, an' never leaves it out.
    An' I'd be mad if that young imp got knockin' it about."
"Ole axe!" she sez. "Look at 'is *thumb!* A precious lot *you* care!
              You left it there!"

I am marri'd to a woman; which is nacheral an' right.
I sez that over to meself, fer safety, day an' night.
    Most times I sez it fond an' proud wiv gladness in me mind;
    But sometimes philosophic-like an' wot yeh'd call resigned.
"An axe as sharp as *that*," she sez. "It reely isn't fair!
              You left it there!

"The way you pet that axe," she sez—"the way it's ground an' filed,
The way you fairly fondle it, you'd think it wus a child!
    An' when I pick the ole thing up to cut a bit uv string
    Yeh rave an' shout..." "Wait on," I sez. "But ir'n's a different thing.
An' you wus choppin' fencin' wire!" She sez, "Well, I don't care.
              You *left* it there!"

Logic and Spotted Dog

I 'elps meself to spotted dog, an' chews, an' thinks a while.
"I'm reely sorry," I begins. Then, as I seen 'er smile,
    I plays 'er fer the fun uv it, an' sez, "But, all the same,
    If he gits foolin' wiv that axe 'e's got 'imself to blame."
'Er eyes spark up. "A child like that! Now, Bill, it isn't fair!
              You left it there!"

I cuts another slice an' sez, "This spotted dog's a treat.
Uv course, 'ooever left it there," I sez, "wus—indiscreet."
    "Careless!" she sez. "You *know* you are! 'E might 'a' cut 'is
        face!
    An axe as sharp as that," she sez, "should be kep' in its place."
"Quite right," I sez. "An' not," she sez, "jist thrown round anywhere.
              You left it *there*!"

An' then I lets 'er 'ave it, an' I sez, "Now, think a bit.
I put that axe away last night when all the wood wus split."
    "Well, that's enough about it now," she sez. I seen 'er wince,
    An' sez, "I put that axe away, *an' 'aven't used it since*;
But someone else wus usin' it this mornin', I kin swear,
              An' left it there."

"Well, never mind ... Poor Bill!" she sez. "Was 'is poor thumb
    all 'urt?"
(Oh, it's entertainin' sometimes fer to argue wiv a skirt.)
    "There's someone else," I sez, an' grins, an' kids I'm doin fine,
    "Wus usin' it this mornin' fer to cut a bit uv pine.
So now," I sez, "apolergise! I've beat you fair an' square!
              You left it there!"

Fer 'arf a mo she pets young Bill, an' would'nt meet me eye.
Thinkin' she wus—I knew she wus. An' then she lets it fly:
    "If you 'ad cut that wood," she sez, "an I implored you to,
    There wouldn't be no need fer me to 'ave such things to do!
It ain't right fer a woman ..." " 'Ere!" I sez. "Now, I don't care
              'Oo left it there!"

Doreen

"Uv course you don't!" she gits me back. "You never care a bit!
An' it ain't right fer a woman to 'ave kin'lin' wood to split;
    While there's a man about the 'ouse!" I sees the tears is near,
    An' pats 'er 'air. "Now, let it drop," I sez. "Don't worry, dear."
" 'Ow can I let it drop?" she sobs. "You said you didn't care
                  'Oo left it there."

"I do!" I yells. "I mean—I don't—I . . ." Oh, Gaw spare me days!
When you argue wiv a woman she 'as got you either ways!
    You *'ave* to do it in the end; an' so I licks the dirt,
    An' sez, "Dear, I apolergise. I'm—sorry—if I 'urt."
Yes, I'm marri'd to a woman. An' she smiles, an' strokes me 'air,
                  An'—leaves it there.

Vi'lits

I wus pickin' gipsy vi'lits fer to try an' square Doreen.
We 'ad words ... about pianners—fer she wants one awful
    keen—
    'Igh words, about 'igh-toned idears—an', like a love-sick
        fool,
    'Ere I'm pickin' gipsy vi'lits when the kid come 'ome frum
        school.
'E started school a month ago, an' ain't got very far;
But, judgin' be the scraps 'e 'as, 'e's takin' after Par.

I tips there's somethin' wrong, the way 'e sneaks around the
    'ouse.
An' then I seen 'is eye. Oh, strike! 'E 'ad a bonzer mouse!—
    A reel black-eye, that, in me day, I would 'a' worn wiv pride.
    But I'm a father now, an' sez, " 'Ere, son, you git inside
An' show yer mother that there eye. 'Ow did it come about?"
Sez 'e, "A big bloke gimme that. I knocked the beggar out!"

I looks fer 'arf a second at the fambily disgrace,
Then I picks another vi'lit so 'e couldn't see me face.
    I wus grinnin' most unfatherlike, an' feelin' good inside.
    "You show yer Mar that eye uv yours. I'm 'shamed uv you!"
        I lied.
I watch 'im creep inside the 'ouse, an' 'ear 'is mother's yell.
An' then I straightens up me face an' goes inside as well.

'Twus raw beef-steak an' vinegar, an' tears, before she's done.
An' the sort uv look she gimme sez, "Yeh see 'ow 'e's begun!"
    I don't disturb the rites excep' to give some kind advice.
    In younger days I've caught black-eyes, an' give 'em once or
        twice.
"That big boy should be punished," sez Doreen, " 'oo 'it our Bill."
I pats the 'ero's bandages, an' answers 'er, " 'E will."

That ev'nin, down be'ind the shed, near where the scrub grows dense,
I gives young Bill a lesson in the art uv self-defence.
    I teaches 'im an uppercut that Ginger Mick tort me
    In ole days, down in Spadger's Lane. I gits down on me knee
To show 'im 'ow to time 'is 'it. 'E sneaks beneath me guard
Quite sudden, while I'm yappin', an' 'e cracks me one reel 'ard.

Did it please me? Wot do *you* think? Strike! That kid 'as got the knack!
An' it pleased me all to pieces 'ow the ole game all came back:
    Left-swings an' jolts an' short-arm jabs—the 'ole dash box uv tricks,
    Sich as we used down in the Lane when we wus short uv bricks.
I'm showin' 'im a fancy 'it, a reel ole ding-dong clout,
When the murderin' young savage tries to knock me front teeth out!

Uv course, 'e 'urt 'is little 'and, an' fetches out a yell
That brings Doreen down double quick. An' then—'twus merry 'ell.
    She grabs the kid up in 'er arms, an' gives me sich a look
    As I ain't seen since years ago, when I done—somethin' crook.
"You'll 'ave 'im like *you* wus!" she cries. "I'd sooner see 'im dead!
You want to make 'im ..." "Don't," I sez. "We'll take the rest as said."

It 'urt to see 'er shieldin' 'im as tho' I wus a plague.
An' ain't 'e mine as much as 'ers? Yet, I seen, sort o' vague,
    The woman's way she looked at it, the picters that she 'ad
    Uv young Bill goin' to the pack, an' follerin' 'is dad.
I tries me 'ardest to ixplain, an' made some fool ixcuse;
But I'm marri'd to a woman, an'—Aw, wot's the flamin' use?

Vi'lits

I tells 'er if we'd 'ave young Bill keep up 'is end at school
'E will 'ave to use 'is flippers; but I sez it like a fool.
    I sez it like I wus ashamed to 'ave 'im learn to fight,
      When all the time, down in me 'eart, I knoo that I wus right.
She just gives me another look, an' goes in wiv the kid.
An' me? I picks them vi'lits up, not knowin' *wot* I did.

I 'as them fool things in me 'and when I lobs in the 'ouse,
An' makes bets wiv meself about the chances that she'll rouse.
    But 'er, she comes the calm an' cold. Think's I, " 'Ere's where I fall
    Fer a forty-quid pianner, if I want to square it all.
Goo'-bye to forty lovely quid—time-paymint, fifty-three—
Then all at once she smiles an' sez, "Did you pick *those* fer me?"

"Did you pick those fer *me*," she sez. "Oh, Bill!" 'an then, "Oh, *Bill*!"
I 'ints I 'ad idears to leave 'em to 'er in me will.
    She grabs them dilly vi'lits, an' she 'olds 'em to 'er nose.
    "Oh, Bill!" she smiles, "You alwus knoo 'ow fond I wus uv those!
Oh, Bill! You *dear*!" She 'ugs me then, jist in the same ole way.
'Struth! I'm marri'd to a woman, an' ... I'll learn young Bill some day!

Possum

JIST *'ere* it gripped me, on a sudden, like a red-'ot knife.
I wus diggin' in the garden, talkin' pleasant to me wife,
   When it got me good an' solid, an' I fetches out a yell,
    An' curses soft down in me neck, an' breathes 'ard fer a spell.
Then, when I tries to straighten up, it stabs me ten times worse.
I thinks per'aps I'm dyin', an' chokes back a reel 'ot curse.

"I've worked too fast," I tells Doreen. "Me back-bone's runnin' 'ot.
I'm sick! I've got—Oo, 'oly wars! I dunno *wot* I've got!
   Jist 'ere—*Don't touch!*—Jist round back 'ere, a blazin' little pain
Is clawin' up me spinal cord an' slidin' down again."
"You come inside," she sez. "Per'aps it's stoopin' in the sun.
Does it 'urt much?" I sez, "Oh, no; I'm 'avin' lots o' fun."

Then, cooin' to me, woman-like, she pilots me inside.
It stabs me every step I takes; I thort I would 'a' died.
   "There now," she sez. "Men can't stand pain, it's alwus understood."
   "Stand pain?" I 'owls. Then, Jumpin' Jakes! It gits me reely good!
So I gets to bed in sections, fer it give me beans to bend,
An' shuts me eyes, an' groans again, an' jist waits fer the end.

"Now, you lie still," she orders me, "until I think wot's best.
Per'aps 'ot bran, or poultices. You jist lie still, an' rest,"
   Rest? 'Oly Gosh! I clinched me teeth, an' clawed the bloomin' bunk;
    Fer a red-'ot poker jabbed me ev'ry time I much as wunk.
I couldn't corf, I couldn't move, I couldn't git me breath.
"Look after Bill," I tells Doreen. "I feels that ... this is ... death."

"Death, fiddlesticks," she laughs at me. "You jist turn over now."
I 'owls, " 'Ere! Don't you *touch* me, or there'll be a blazin' row!
   I want to die jist as I am," She sez, "Now, Bill, 'ave sense.
   This 'as to go on while it's 'ot." I groans, "I've no defence."
An' so she 'as 'er way wiv me. An', tho' I'm suff'rin' bad,
I couldn't 'elp but noticin' the gentle touch she 'ad.

That ev'nin', when the doctor come, sez 'e, "Ah! 'Urtin' much?
Where is the trouble?" I sez, "Where you ain't allowed to touch!"
   'E mauls an' prods me while I 'owls to beat the bloomin' band.
   Gawbli'me! I'd 'a' cracked 'im if I'd strength to lift me 'and.
"Discribe yer symtims now," sez 'e. I fills meself wiv wind,
An' slung 'im out a catalog while 'e jist stood an' grinned.

"Ar, har!" 'e sez. "Sciatiker! Oh, we'll soon 'ave yeh well."
"Sciatiker?" sez I. "Yer sure yeh don't mean Jumpin' 'Ell?
   It ain't no privit devil wiv a little jagged knife?"
   "Tut, tut," 'e grins. "You'll soon be right. I leaves yeh to yer wife."
I looks at 'er she smiles at me, an' when I seen that smile:
"Aw, poultices!" I groans. An' she enjoys it all the while!

But I'm marri'd to a woman; an', I gives yeh my straight tip,
It makes a man feel glad uv it when sickness gits a grip.
   'Er looks is full uv tenderness, 'er ways is full uv love,
   An' 'er touch is like a blessin' as she gently bends above.
'Er speech is firm, but motherin'; 'er manners strict, but mild:
Yer 'er 'usban', an' 'er patient, an' 'er little orphin child.

When yer marri'd to a woman an' yer feelin' well an right;
When yer frame is full uv ginger an' yer mouth is full uv skite,
   Then yeh tork about the "missus" in an 'orf'and sort uv way;
   She's 'andy in the 'ouse if she don't 'ave too much to say.
But when Ole Man Sciatiker, 'e does yeh up reel neat,
Then she's yer own reel mate, she is, an' all yer 'ands an' feet.

Doreen

An' so Doreen, she nurses me while I lie there an' grouch;
Fer I'm snarky when I tumble that it ain't me dyin' couch.
    I barks at 'er, an' snarls at 'er, an' orders 'er about,
    An' nearly wears the feet orf 'er wiv trottin' in an' out.
An' while Ole Man Sciatiker, 'e 'as me in 'is sway
Doreen, she jist gives in to me—an' alwus gits 'er way.

Three solid days I 'as uv it, an' then the pain lets out.
I'm feelin' fit fer graft again, an' wants to git about.
    It's then she lets me see 'er 'and, an' orders, "You stay there
    Until yeh gits yer 'ealth an' strength to sit up in a chair."
"But there's that stove-wood," I begins. Sez she, "Now, don't
    you fret.
I'm very sparin' wiv it, an' there's tons an' tons there yet."

Tell yeh straight; I got to like it. It's a crook thing to confess,
But to 'ave 'er fussin' round me give me chunks uv 'appiness.
    So I gits out in the garden wiv an arm-chair an' a rug,
    An' I comes the floppin' invaleed, an' makes meself reel snug.
I droops me eyes an' 'angs me 'ands, an' looks dead crook an' ill;
An' wriggles ev'ry time she sez, "Wot would yeh like now, Bill?"

An' then, one day, I 'ears the axe down there be'ind the 'ouse;
An' I sees meself a loafer, an' me conscience starts to rouse.
    I 'eaves me frame out uv the chair, an' wanders down the yard.
    She's beltin' at a knotty log, an' beltin' good an' 'ard.
I grabs the axe. "Give up," I sez. "I ain't no shattered wreck.
This 'ere's my job." An' then, Gawstruth! I gits it in the neck!

"Am I yer wife?" she asks me straight. "Why can't yeh trust me,
    Bill?
Am I not fit to see to things when you are weak an' ill?"
    I tries to say I'm possumin', an' reely well an' strong;
    But ev'ry time I starts to tork she's got me in the wrong.
"Yeh can't deceive me, Bill," she sez. "Yer 'ealth is fur frum good.
Yeh jist can't trust yer wife to chop a little bit uv wood!

"Yeh got to come out in the cold," she sez, "wivout yer wraps.
An' now I'll 'ave yeh on me 'ands for days wiv a relapse!"
    "I been pretendin'," I ixplains. She sez, "Am I yer wife?
    Yet sooner than yeh'd trust to me yeh go an' risk yer life,"
Well, I'm marri'd to a woman, an'—it might seem sort uv
    meek—
I goes back into bed again ... an' *'ates* it ... fer a week!

DIGGER SMITH

TO THE A.I.F.

Before the War

"BEFORE the war," she sighs. "Before the war."
    Then blinks 'er eyes, an' tries to work a smile.
"Ole scenes," she sez, "don't look the same no more.
    Ole ways," she sez, "seems to 'ave changed their style,
    The pleasures that we 'ad don't seem worth while—
Them simple joys that passed an hour away—
    An' troubles, that we used to so revile,
'Ow small they look," she sez. " 'Ow small to-day.

"This war!" sighs ole Mar Flood. An' when I seen
    The ole girl sittin' in our parlour there,
Tellin' 'er troubles to my wife, Doreen,
    As though the talkin' eased 'er load uv care,
    I thinks uv mothers, 'ere an' everywhere,
Smilin' a bit while they are grievin' sore
    For grown-up babies, fightin' Over There;
An' then I 'ears 'em sigh, "Before the war."

My wife 'as took the social 'abit bad.
    I ain't averse—one more new word I've learned—
Averse to tea, when tea is to be 'ad;
    An' when it comes I reckon that it's earned.
    It's jist a drink, as fur as I'm concerned,
Good for a bloke that's toilin' on the land;
    But when a caller comes, 'ere I am turned
Into a social butterfly, off-'and.

Digger Smith

Then drinkin' tea becomes an 'oly rite.
    So's I won't bring the fam'ly to disgrace
I gits a bit uv coachin' overnight
    On ridin' winners in this bun-fed race.
    I 'ave to change me shirt, an' wash me face,
An' look reel neat, from me waist up at least,
    An' sling remarks in at the proper place,
An' not makes noises drinkin', like a beast.

" 'Ave some more cake. Another slice, now do.
    An' won't yeh 'ave a second cup uv tea?
'Ow is the children?" Ar, it makes me blue!
    This boodoor 'abit ain't no good to me.
    I likes to take me tucker plain an' free:
Tea an' a chunk out on the job for choice,
    So I can stoke with no one there to see.
Besides, I 'aven't got no comp'ny voice.

Uv course, I've 'ad it all out with the wife.
    I argues that there's work that must be done,
An' tells 'er that I 'ates this tony life.
    She sez there's jooties that we must not shun.
    You bet that ends it; so I joins the fun,
An' puts 'em all at ease with silly grins—
    Slings bits uv rerpartee like " 'Ave a bun,"
An' passes bread an ' butter, for me sins.

Since I've been marri'd, say, I've chucked some things,
    An' learned a whole lot more to fill the space.
I've slung all slang; crook words 'ave taken wings,
    An' I 'ave learned to entertain with grace.
    But when ole Missus Flood comes round our place
I don't object to 'er, for all 'er sighs;
    Becos I likes 'er ways, I likes 'er face,
An', most uv all, she 'as them mother's eyes.

Before the War

"Before the war," she sighs, the poor ole girl.
    'Er talk it gets me thinkin' in between,
While I'm assistin' at this social whirl....
    She comes across for comfort to Doreen,
    To talk about the things that might 'ave been
If Syd 'ad not been killed at Suvla Bay,
    Or Jim not done a bunk at seventeen,
An' not been 'eard uv since 'e went away.

They 'ave a little farm right next to us—
    'Er an' 'er 'usband—where they live alone.
Spite uv 'er cares, she ain't the sort to fuss
    Or serve up sudden tears an' sob an' moan,
    An' since I've known 'er some'ow I 'ave grown
To see in 'er, an' all the grief she's bore,
    A million brave ole mothers 'oo 'ave known
Deep sorrer since them days before the war.

"Before the war," she sez. "Yeh mind our Syd?
    Poor lad.... But then, yeh never met young Jim—
'Im 'oo was charged with things 'e never did.
    Ah, both uv you'd 'ave been reel chums with 'im.
    'Igh-spirited 'e was, a perfect limb.
It's six long years now since 'e went away—
    Ay, drove away." 'Er poor ole eyes git dim.
"That was," she sighs, "that was me blackest day.

"Me blackest day! Wot am I sayin' now?
    There was the day the parson come to tell
The news about our Syd.... An', yet, some'ow....
    My little Jim!" She pauses for a spell....
    "Your 'olly'ocks is doin' reely well,"
She sez, an' battles 'ard to brighten up.
    "An' them there pinks uv yours, 'ow sweet they smell.
An'—Thanks! I think I *will* 'ave one more cup."

As fur as I can get the strength uv it,
  Them Floods 'ave 'ad a reel tough row to hoe.
First off, young Jim, 'oo plays it 'igh a bit,
  Narks the ole man a treat, an' slings the show.
  Then come the war, an' Syd 'e 'as to go.
'E run 'is final up at Suvla Bay—
  One uv the Aussies I was proud to know.
An' Jim's cracked 'ardy since 'e went away.

'Er Jim! These mothers! Lord, they're all the same.
  I wonders if Doreen will be that kind.
Syd was the son 'oo played the reel man's game;
  But Jim 'oo sloped an' left no word be'ind,
  His is the picter shinin' in 'er mind.
'Igh-spirited! I've 'eard that tale before.
  I sometimes think she'd take it rather kind
To 'ear that 'is 'igh spirits run to war.

"Before the war," she sez. "Ah, times was good.
  The little farm out there, an' jist us four
Workin' to make a decent liveli'ood.
  Our Syd an' Jim!... Poor Jim! It grieves me sore;
  For Dad won't 'ave 'im mentioned 'ome no more.
'E's 'urt, I know, cos 'e thinks Jim 'urt me.
  As if 'e could, the bonny boy I bore....
But I must off 'ome now, an' git Dad's tea."

I seen 'er to the gate. (Take it frum me,
  I'm some perlite.) She sez, "Yeh mustn't mind
Me talkin' so uv Jim, but when I see
  Your face it brings 'im back; 'e's jist your kind.
  Not quite so 'an'some, p'r'aps, nor so refined.
I've got some toys uv 'is," she sez, "But there—
  This is ole woman's talk, an' you be'ind
With all yer work, an' little time to spare."

Before the War

She gives me 'and a squeeze an' turns away,
    Sobbin', I thort; but when she looks be'ind,
Smilin', an' wavin', like she felt reel gay,
    I wonders 'ow the women works that blind,
    An' jist waves back; then goes inside to find
A lookin'-glass, an' takes a reel good look....
    " 'Not quite so 'an'some, p'r'aps, nor so refined!'
Gawd 'elp yeh, Jim," I thinks. "Yeh must be crook."

Dummy Bridge

"IF I'd 'a' played me Jack on that there Ten,"
    Sez Peter Begg, "I might 'a' made the lot."
" 'Ow could yeh?" barks ole Poole. " 'Ow could yeh, when
    I 'ad me Queen be'ind?" Sez Begg, "Wot rot!
I slung away me King to take that trick."
"*Which* one! Say, ain't yer 'ead a trifle thick?"

"Now, don't yeh see that when I plays me King
    I give yer Queen a chance, an' lost the slam."
But Poole, 'e sez 'e don't see no sich thing,
    So Begg gits 'ot, an' starts to loose a "Damn."
'E twigs the missus jist in time to check,
An' makes it "Dash," an' gits red down 'is neck.

There's me an' Peter Begg, an' ole man Poole—
    Neighbours uv mine, that farm a bit close by—
Jist once a week or so we makes a school,
    An' gives this game uv Dummy Bridge a fly.
Doreen, she 'as 'er sewin' be the fire,
The kid's in bed; an' 'ere's me 'eart's desire.

'Ome-comfort, peace, the picter uv me wife
    'Appy at work, me neighbours gathered round
All friendly-like—wot more is there in life?
    I've searched a bit, but better I ain't found.
Doreen, she seems content, but in 'er eye
I've seen reel pity when the talk gits 'igh.

Dummy Bridge

This ev'nin' we 'ad started off reel 'ot:
    Two little slams, an' Poole, without a score,
Still lookin' sore about the cards 'e'd got—
    When, sudden-like, a knock comes to the door.
"A visitor," growls Begg, "to crool our game."
An' looks at me, as though I was to blame.

Jist as Doreen goes out, I seen 'er grin.
    "Deal 'em up quick!" I whispers. "Grab yer 'and,
An' look reel occupied when they comes in.
    Per'aps they'll 'ave the sense to understand.
If it's a man, maybe 'e'll make a four;
But if"—Then Missus Flood comes in the door.

'Twas ole Mar Flood, 'er face wrapped in a smile.
    "Now, boys," she sez, "don't let me spoil yer game.
I'll jist chat with Doreen a little while;
    But if yeh stop I'll be ashamed I came."
An' then she waves a letter in 'er 'and.
Sez she, "Our Jim's a soldier! Ain't it grand?"

"Good boy," sez Poole. "Let's see. I make it 'earts."
    "Doubled!" shouts Begg.... "An' 'e's been in a fight,"
Sez Missus Flood, "out in them furrin' parts.
    French, I suppose. I can't pronounce it right.
'E's been once wounded, somewhere in the leg...."
" 'Ere, Bill! Yeh gone to sleep?" asks Peter Begg.

I plays me Queen uv Spades; an' plays 'er bad.
    Begg snorts.... "My boy," sighs Missus Flood. "My Jim." ...
"King 'ere," laughs Poole. "That's the last Spade I 'ad." ...
    Doreen she smiles: "I'm glad yeh've 'eard from 'im." ...
"We're done," groans Begg. "Why did yeh nurse yer Ace?" ...
"My Jim!" An' there was sunlight in 'er face.

"I always thought a lot uv Jim, I did,"
    Sez Begg. " 'E does yeh credit. 'Ere, your deal."
"That's so," sez Poole. " 'E was an all-right kid.
    No trumps? I'm sorry that's the way yeh feel.
'Twill take yeh all yer time to make the book." ...
An' then Doreen sends me a wireless look.

I gets the S.O.S.; but Begg is keen.
    "My deal," 'e yaps. "Wot rotten cards I get."
Ole Missus Flood sits closer to Doreen.
    "The best," she whispers, "I ain't told yeh yet."
I strains me ears, an' leads me King uv Trumps.
"Ace 'ere!" grins Begg. Poole throws 'is Queen—an' thumps.

"That saves me Jack!" 'owls Begg. "Tough luck, ole sport." ...
    Sez Missus Flood, "Jim's won a medal too
For doin' somethin' brave at Bullycourt." ...
    "Play on, play on," growls Begg. "It's up to you."
Then I reneges, an' trumps me partner's Ace,
An' Poole gets sudden murder in 'is face.

"I'm sick uv this 'ere game," 'e grunts. "It's tame."
    "Righto," I chips. "Suppose we toss it in?"
Begg don't say nothin'; so we sling the game.
    On my wife's face I twigs a tiny grin.
"Finished? sez she, su'prised. "Well, p'r'aps it's right.
It looks to me like *'earts* was trumps to-night."

An' so they was. An', say, the game was grand.
    Two hours we sat while that ole mother told
About 'er Jim, 'is letter in 'er 'and,
    An', on 'er face, a glowin' look that rolled
The miles all up that lie 'twixt France an' 'ere,
An' found 'er son, an' brought 'im very near.

Dummy Bridge

A game uv Bridge it was, with 'earts for trumps.
    We was the dummies, sittin' silent there.
I knoo the men, like me, was feelin' chumps:
    Foolin' with cards while this was in the air.
It took Doreen to shove us in our place;
An' mother 'eld the lot, right from the Ace.

She told us 'ow 'e said 'e'd writ before,
    An' 'ow the letters must 'ave gone astray;
An' 'ow the stern ole father still was sore,
    But looked like 'e'd be soft'nin', day by day;
'Ow pride in Jim peeps out be'ind 'is frown,
An' 'ow the ole fool 'opes to 'ide it down.

"I knoo," she sez. "I never doubted Jim.
    But wot could any mother say or do
When pryin' folks asked wot become uv 'im,
    But drop 'er eyes an' say she never knoo.
Now I can lift me 'ead to that sly glance,
An' say, 'Jim's fightin', with the rest, in France.' "

An' when she's gone, us four we don't require
    No gossipin' to keep us in imploy.
Ole Poole sits starin' 'ard into the fire.
    I guessed that 'e was thinkin' uv 'is boy,
'Oo's been right in it from the very start;
An' Poole was thinkin' uv a father's part.

An' then 'e speaks: "This war 'as turned us 'ard.
    Suppose, four years ago, yeh said to me
That I'd sit 'eedless, starin' at a card
    While that ole mother told—Good Lord!" sez 'e
"It takes the women for to put us wise
To playin' games in war-time," an' 'e sighs.

An' 'ere Doreen sets out to put 'im right.
  "There's games an' games," she sez. "When women starts
A hand at Bridge like she 'as played to-night
  It's Nature teachin' 'em to make it 'earts.
The other suits are yours," she sez; "but then,
That's as it should be, seein' you are men."

"Maybe," sez Poole; an' both gits up to go.
  I stands beside the door when they are gone,
Watchin' their lantern swingin' to an' fro,
  An' 'ears Begg's voice as they goes trudgin' on:
"If you 'ad led that Queen we might 'ave made...."
"Rubbidge!" shouts Poole. "You mucked it with yer Spade!"

Dad

I'VE knowed ole Flood this last five year or more;
I knoo 'im when 'is Syd went to the war.
   A proud ole man 'e was. But I've watched 'im,
   An' seen 'is look when people spoke uv Jim:
As sour a look as most coves want to see.
It made me glad that this 'ere Jim weren't me.

I sized up Flood the first day that we met—
Stubborn as blazes when 'is mind is set.
   Ole-fashioned in 'is looks an' in 'is ways,
   Believin' it is honesty that pays;
An' still dead set, in spite uv bumps 'e's got,
To keep on honest if it pays or not.

Poor ole Dad Flood, 'e is too old to fight
By close on thirty year; but, if I'm right
   About 'is doin's an' about 'is grit.
   'E's done a fair bit over 'is fair bit.
They are too old to fight, but, all the same,
'Is kind's quite young enough to play the game.

I've 'eard it called, this war—an' it's the truth—
I've 'eard it called the sacrifice uv youth.
   An' all this land 'as reckernized it too,
   An' gives the boys the praises that is doo.
I've 'eard the cheers for ev'ry fightin' lad;
But, up to now, I ain't 'eard none for Dad.

Digger Smith

Ole Flood, an' all 'is kind throughout the land,
They ain't been 'eralded with no brass band,
    Or been much thought about; but, take my tip,
    The war 'as found 'em with a stiffened lip,
'Umpin' a load they thought they'd dropped for good,
Crackin' reel 'ardy, an'—jist sawin' wood.

Dad Flood, 'is back is bent, 'is strength is gone;
'E'd done 'is bit before this war come on.
    At sixty-five 'e thought 'is work was done;
    'E gave the farmin' over to 'is son,
An' jist sat back in peace, with 'is ole wife,
To spend content the ev'nin' uv 'is life.

Then come the war. An' when Syd 'esitates
Between the ole folk an' 'is fightin' mates,
    The ole man goes outside an' grabs a hoe.
    Sez 'e, "Yeh want to, an' yeh ought to go.
Wot's stoppin' yeh?" 'E straightens 'is ole frame.
"Ain't I farmed long enough to know the game?"

There weren't no more to say. An' Syd went—West:
Into the sunset with ole Aussie's best.
    But no one ever 'eard no groans from Dad.
    Though all 'is pride an' 'ope was in that lad
'E showed no sign excep' to grow more grim.
'Is son was gone—an' it was up to 'im.

One day last month when I was down at Flood's
I seen 'im strugglin' with a bag uv spuds.
    "Look 'ere," I sez, "you let me spell yeh, Dad.
    You 'umpin' loads like that's a bit too bad."
'E gives a grunt that's more than 'arf a groan.
"Wot's up?" 'e snaps. "Got no work uv yer own?"

That's 'im. But I've been tippin' that the pace
Would tell; an' when 'is wife comes to our place,
   An' sez that Dad is ill an' took to bed,
   Flat out with work—though that ain't wot she said—
I ain't su'prised; an' tells 'er when I'm thro'
I'll come across an' see wot I can do.

I went across, an'—I come back again.
Strike me! it's no use reas'nin' with some men.
   Stubborn ole cows! I'm sick uv them ole fools.
   The way 'e yells, "Keep yer 'ands off my tools!"
Yeh'd think I was a thief. 'Is missus said
I'd better slope, or 'e'd be out uv bed.

'E 'eard us talkin' through the open door.
" 'Oo's that?" 'e croaks, altho' 'e tries to roar.
   An' when 'is wife ixplains it's only me
   To 'elp a bit: "I want no charity!"
'E barks. "I'll do me work meself, yeh 'ear?"
An' then 'e gits so snarky that I clear.

But 'e'll do me. I like the ole boy's nerve.
We don't do nothin' that 'e don't deserve;
   But me an' Peter Begg an' ole man Poole,
   We fairly 'as our work cut out to fool
The sly ole fox, when we sneaks down each day
An' works a while to keep things under way.

We digs a bit, an' ploughs a bit, an' chops
The wood, an' does the needful to 'is crops.
   We does it soft, an' when 'e 'ears a row
   'Is missus tells 'im it's the dog or cow.
'E sez that it's queer noises for a pup.
An'—there'll be ructions when ole Flood gits up.

It ain't all overwork that's laid 'im out.
Ole Pride in 'im is 'avin' scraps with Doubt.
    To-day 'is wife sez, "Somethin's strange in 'im,
  For in 'is sleep sometimes 'e calls for Jim.
It's six long years," she sez, an' stops to shake
'Er 'ead. "But 'e don't mention 'im awake."

Dad Flood. I thought 'im jist a stiff-necked fool
Before the war; but, as I sez to Poole,
    This war 'as tested more than fightin' men.
  But, say, 'e is an 'oly terror when
Friends try to 'elp 'im earn a bite an' sup.
Oh, there'll be 'Ell to pay when 'e gits up!

Digger Smith

'E CALLS me Digger; that's 'ow 'e begins.
'E sez 'es' only arf a man; an' grins.
   Judged be 'is nerve, I'd say 'e was worth two
               Uv me an' you.
Then 'e digs 'arf a fag out uv 'is vest,
Borrers me matches, an' I gives 'im best.

The first I 'eard about it Poole told me.
"There is a bloke called Smith at Flood's," sez 'e;
   Come there this mornin', sez 'e's come to stay,
               An' won't go 'way.
Sez 'e was sent there be a pal named Flood;
An' talks uv contracts sealed with Flanders mud.

"No matter wot they say, 'e only grins,"
Sez Poole. " 'E's rather wobbly on 'is pins.
   Seems like a soldier bloke. An' Peter Begg
               'E sez one leg
Works be machinery, but I dunno.
I only know 'e's there an' 'e won't go.

" 'E grins," sez Poole, "at ev'rything they say.
Dad Flood 'as nearly 'ad a fit to-day.
   'E's cursed, an' ordered 'im clean off the place;
               But this cove's face
Jist goes on grinnin', an' 'e sez, quite carm,
'E's come to do a bit around the farm."

The tale don't sound too good to me at all.
"If 'e's a crook," I sez, " 'e wants a fall.
   Maybe 'e's dilly. I'll go down an' see.
            'E'll grin at me
When I 'ave done, if 'e needs dealin' with."
So I goes down to interview this Smith.

'E 'ad a fork out in the tater patch.
Sez 'e, "Why 'ello, Digger. Got a match?"
   "Digger?" I sez. "Well, you ain't digger 'ere.
           You better clear.
You ought to know that you can't dig them spuds.
They don't belong to you; they're ole Dad Flood's."

"Can't I?" 'e grins. "I'll do the best I can,
Considerin' I'm only 'arf a man.
   Give us a light. I can't get none from Flood,
           An' mine is dud."
I parts; an' 'e stands grinnin' at me still;
An' then 'e sez, " 'Ave yeh fergot me, Bill?"

I looks, an' seen a tough bloke, short an' thin.
Then, Lord! I recomembers that ole grin.
   "It's little Smith!" I 'owls, "uv Collin'wood.
           Lad, this is good!
Last time I seen yeh, you an' Ginger Mick
Was 'owling rags, out on yer final kick."

"Yer on to it," 'e sez. "Nex' day we sailed.
Now 'arf uv me's back 'ome, an' 'arf they nailed.
   An' Mick.... Ar, well, Fritz took me down a peg."
           'E waves 'is leg.
"It ain't too bad," 'e sez, with 'is ole smile;
"But when I starts to dig it cramps me style.

"But I ain't grouchin'. It was worth the fun.
We 'ad some picnic stoushin' Brother 'Un—
    The only fight I've 'ad that some John 'Op
               Don't come an' stop.
They pulled me leg a treat, but, all the same,
There's nothin' over 'ere to beat the game.

"An' now," 'e sez, "I'm 'ere to do a job
I promised, if it was me luck to lob
    Back 'ome before me mate," 'e sez, an' then,
               'E grins again.
"As clear as mud," I sez. "But I can't work
Me brains to 'old yer pace. Say, wot's the lurk?"

So then 'e puts me wise. It seems that 'im
An' this 'ere Flood—I tips it must be Jim—
    Was cobbers up in France, an' things occurred.
               (I got 'is word
Things did occur up there). But, anyway,
Seems Flood done somethin' good for 'im one day.

Then Smith 'e promised if 'e came back 'ome
Before 'is cobber o'er the flamin' foam,
    'E'd see the ole folks 'ere, an' 'e agreed,
               If there was need,
'E'd stay an' do a bit around the farm
So long as 'e 'ad one sound, dinkum arm.

"So, 'ere I am," 'e sez, an' grins again.
"A promise is a promise 'mong us men."
    Sez I, "You come along up to the 'ouse.
               Ole Dad won't rouse
When once 'e's got yer strength, an' as for Mar,
She'll kiss yeh when she finds out 'oo yeh are."

So we goes up, an' finds 'em both fair dazed
About this little Smith; they think 'e's crazed.
   I tells the tale in words they understand;
               Then it was grand
To see Dad grab Smith's 'and an' pump it good,
An' Mar, she kissed 'im, like I said she would.

Mar sez 'e must be starved, an' right away
The kettle's on, she's busy with a tray.
   An', when I left, this Digger Smith 'e looked
              Like 'e was booked
For keeps, with tea an' bread an' beef inside.
"Our little Willie's 'ome," 'e grins, "an' dried."

West

"I'VE seen so much uv dirt an' grime
 I'm mad to 'ave things clean.
I've seen so much uv death," 'e said—
"So many cobbers lyin' dead—
    You won't know wot I mean;
But, lad, I've 'ad so much uv strife
I want things straightened in my life.

"I've seen so much uv 'ate," 'e said—
    "Mad 'ate an' silly rage—
"I'm yearnin' for clear thoughts," said 'e.
"Kindness an' love seem good to me.
    I want a new, white page
To start all over, clean an' good,
An' live me life as reel men should."

We're sittin' talkin' by the fence,
    The sun's jist goin' down,
Paintin' the sky all gold an' pink.
Said 'e, "When it's like that, I think—"
    An' then 'e stops to frown.
Said 'e, "I think, when it's jist so,
Uv .... God or somethin': I dunno.

"I ain't seen much uv God," said 'e;
    "Not 'ere nor Over There;
But, partly wot I've seen an' read,
An' partly wot the padre said,
    It gits me when I stare
Out West when it's like that is now.
There must be somethin' else—some'ow.

Digger Smith

"I've thought a lot," said Digger Smith—
   "Out There I thought a lot.
I thought uv death, an' all the rest,
An' uv me mates, good mates gone West;
   An' it ain't much I've got;
But things get movin' in me 'ead
When I look over there," 'e said.

'E's got me beat, 'as little Smith.
   I knoo 'im years ago:
I knoo 'im as a reel tough boy
'Oo roughed it up with 'oly joy;
   But now, well, I dunno.
An' when I ask Mar Flood she sighs—
An' sez 'e's got the Anzac eyes.

She sez 'e's got them soldier's eyes
   That makes 'er own eyes wet.
An' we must give 'im wholesome food
An' lead 'is thoughts to somethin' good
   An' never let 'im fret.
But 'e ain't frettin', seems to me;
More—puzzled, fur as I can see.

The clouds above the hills was tore
   Apart, until, some'ow,
It seemed like some big, shinin' gate.
Said 'e, "Why, lad, I tell yeh straight,
   I feel like startin' now,
An' walkin on, an' on, an' thro',
Dead game an'—Ain't it so to you?

"I've seen enough uv pain," 'e said,
    "An' cursin', killin' 'ordes.
I ain't the man to smooge with God
To get to 'Eaven on the nod,
    Or 'owl 'ymns for rewards.
But this believin'? Why—Oh, 'Struth!
This never 'it me in me youth.

"They talk uv love 'twixt men," said 'e.
    "That sounds dead crook to you.
But lately I 'ave come to see." ...
" 'Old on," I said; "it seems to me
    There's love uv women too.
An you?" 'E turns away 'is 'ead.
"I'm only 'arf a man," 'e said.

"I've seen so much uv death," said 'e,
    "Me mind is in a whirl.
I've 'ad so many thoughts uv late." ...
Said I, "Now, tell me, tell me straight,
    Own up; ain't there a girl?"
Said 'e, "I've done the best I can.
Wot does she want with 'arf a man?"

It weren't no use. 'E wouldn't talk
    Uv nothin' but the sky.
Said 'e "Now, dinkum, talkin' square,
When you git gazin' over there
    Don't you 'arf want to cry?
I wouldn't be su'prised to see
An angel comin' out," said 'e.

"Gone West!" said Digger Smith. "Ah, lad,
    I've seen 'em goin' West,
An' often wonder, when I look,
If they 'ave 'ad it dealt 'em crook,
    Or if they've got the rest
They earned twice over by the spell
They spent down in that dinkum 'Ell."

The gold was creepin' up, the sun
    Was 'arf be'ind the range.
It don't seem strange a man should cry
To see that glory in the sky—
    To me it don't seem strange.
"Digger!" said 'e. "Look at it now!
There *must* be somethin' else—some'ow."

Over the Fence

'TAINT my idea uv argument to call a man a fool,
An' I ain't lookin' round for bricks to 'eave at ole man
   Poole;
   But when 'e gets disruptin' 'e's inclined to lose 'is 'ead.
   It ain't so much 'is choice uv words as 'ow the words is said.

'E's sich a coot for takin' sides, as I sez to Doreen.
Sez she, " 'Ow can 'e, by 'imself?" Wotever that may mean.
   My wife sez little things sometimes that nearly git me riled.
   I knoo she meant more than she said be that soft way she
      smiled.

To-day, when I was 'arrowin', Poole comes down to the fence
To get the loan uv my long spade' an' uses that pretence
   To 'ave a bit uv friendly talk, an' one word leads to more,
   As is the way with ole man Poole, as I've remarked before.

The spade reminds 'im 'ow 'e done some diggin' in 'is day,
An' diggin' brings the talk to earth, an' earth leads on to clay,
   Then clay quite natural reminds a thinkin' bloke uv bricks,
   An' mortar brings up mud, an' then, uv course, it's politics.

Now, Poole sticks be 'is Party, an' I don't deny 'is right;
But when 'e starts abusin' mine 'e's lookin' for a fight.
   So I delivers good 'ome truths about 'is crowd; then Poole
   Wags 'is ole beard across the fence an' tells me I'm a fool.

Now, that's the dizzy limit; so I lays aside the reins,
An' starts to prove 'e's storin' mud where most blokes keeps their
      brains.
   'E decorates 'is answers, an' we're goin' it ding-dong,
   When this returned bloke, Digger Smith, comes sauntering
      along.

Digger Smith

Poole's gripped the fence as though 'e means to tear the rails in two,
An' eyes my waggin' finger like 'e wants to 'ave a chew.
    Then Digger Smith 'e grins at Poole, an' then 'e looks at me,
    An' sez, quite soft an' friendly-like, "Winnin' the war?" sez 'e.

Now, Poole deserves it, an' I'm pleased the lad give 'im that jolt.
'E goes fair mad in argument when once 'e gets a holt.
    "Yeh make me sad," sez Digger Smith; "the both uv you," sez 'e.
    "The both uv us! Gawstruth!" sez I. "You ain't includin' me?"

"Well, it takes two to make a row," sez little Digger Smith.
"A bloke can't argue 'less 'e 'as a bloke to argue with.
    I've come 'ome from a dinkum scrap to find this land uv light
    Is chasin' its own tail around an' callin' it a fight.

"We've seen a thing or two, us blokes 'oo've fought on many fronts;
An' we've 'ad time to think a bit between the fightin' stunts.
    We've seen big things, an' thought big things, an' all the silly fuss,
    That used to get us rattled once, seems very small to us.

"An' when a bloke's fought for a land an' gets laid on the shelf
It pains 'im to come 'ome an' find it scrappin' with itself;
    An' scrappin' all for nothin', or for things that look so small—
    To us, 'oo've been in bigger things, they don't seem reel at all.

"P'r'aps we 'ave 'ad some skite knocked out, an' p'r'aps we seen more clear,
But seems to us there's plenty cleanin'-up to do round 'ere.
    We've learnt a little thing or two, an' we 'ave unlearnt 'eaps,
    An' silly partisans, with us, is counted out for keeps.

"This takin' sides jist for the sake uv takin' sides—Aw, 'Struth!
I used to do them things one time, back in me foolish youth.
    Out There, when I remembered things, I've kicked meself reel
        good.
    In football days I barracked once red 'ot for Collin'wood.

"I didn't want to see a game, nor see no justice done.
It never mattered wot occurred as long as my side won.
    The other side was narks an' cows an' rotters to a man;
    But mine was reel bonzer chaps. I was a partisan.

"It might sound like swelled-'ead," sez Smith. "But show me, if
        yeh can." ...
"'Old 'ard," sez Poole. "Jist tell me this: wot is a partisan?"
    Then Digger Smith starts to ixplain; Poole interrupts straight
        out;
    An' I wades in to give my views, an' as to nearly shout.

We battles on for one good hour. My team sleeps where it stands;
An' Poole 'as tossed the spade away to talk with both 'is 'ands;
    An' Smith 'as dropped the maul 'e 'ad. Then I looks round
        to see
    Doreen quite close. She smiles at us. "Winnin' the war?"
        sez she.

A Digger's Tale

"'MY oath!' the Duchess sez. 'You'd not ixpect
  Sich things as that. Yeh don't mean kangaroos?
Go hon!' she sez, or words to that effect—
  (It's 'ard to imitate the speech they use)
I tells 'er, 'Straight; I drives 'em four-in-'and
                'Ome in my land.'

"You 'ear a lot," sez little Digger Smith,
   "About 'ow English swells is so stand-off.
Don't yeh believe it; it's a silly myth.
   I've been reel cobbers with the British toff
While I'm on leaf; for Blighty liked our crowd,
                An' done us proud.

"Us Aussies was the goods in London town
   When I was there. If they jist twigged yer 'at
The Dooks would ask yeh could yeh keep one down,
   An' Earls would 'ang out 'Welcome' on the mat,
An' sling yeh invites to their stately 'alls
                For fancy balls.

"This Duchess—I ain't quite sure uv 'er rank;
   She might uv been a Peeress. I dunno.
I meets 'er 'usband first. 'E owns a bank,
   I 'eard, an' 'arf a dozen mints or so.
A dinkum toff. 'E sez, 'Come 'ome with me
                An' 'ave some tea.'

"That's 'ow I met this Duchess Wot's'-'er-name—
    Or Countess—never mind er moniker;
I ain't no 'and at this 'ere title game—
    An' right away, I was reel pals with 'er.
'Now, tell me all about yer 'ome,' sez she,
                An' smiles at me.

"That knocks me out. I know it ain't no good
    Paintin' word-picters uv the things I done
Out 'ome 'ere, barrackin' for Collin'wood,
    Or puntin' on the flat at Flemin'ton.
I know this Baroness uv Wot-yeh-call
                Wants somethin' tall.

"I thinks reel 'ard; an' then I lets it go.
    I tell 'er, out at Richmond, on me Run—
A little place uv ten square mile or so—
    I'm breedin' boomerangs; which is reel fun,
When I ain't troubled by the wild Jonops
                That eats me crops.

"I talks about the wondrous Boshter Bird
    That builds 'er nest up in the Cobber Tree,
An' 'atches out 'er young on May the third,
    Stric' to the minute, jist at 'arf pas' three.
'Er eyes get big. She sez, 'Can it be true?'
                'Er eyes was blue.

"An' then I speaks uv sport, an' tells 'er 'ow
    In 'untin' our wild Wowsers we imploy
Large packs uv Barrackers, an' 'ow their row
    Wakes echoes in the forests uv Fitzroy,
Where lurks the deadly Shicker Snake 'oo's breath
                Is certain death.

"I'm goin' on to talk uv kangaroos,
    An' 'ow I used to drive 'em four-in-'and.
'Wot?' sez the Marchioness. 'Them things in Zoos
    That 'ops about? I've seen 'em in the Strand
In double 'arness; but I ain't seen four.
                Tell me some more.'

"I baulks a bit at that; an' she sez, 'Well,
    There ain't no cause at all for you to feel
Modest about the things you 'ave to tell;
    An' wot yeh says sounds wonderfully reel.
Your talk'—an' 'ere I seen 'er eyelids flick—
                'Makes me 'omesick.

" 'I reckerlect,' she sez—'Now, let me see—
    In Gippsland, long ago, when I was young,
I 'ad a little pet Corroboree,'
    (I sits up in me chair like I was stung.)
'On its 'ind legs,' she sez, 'it used to stand.
                Fed from me 'and.'

"Uv course, I threw me alley in right there.
    This Princess was a dinkum Aussie girl.
I can't do nothin' else but sit an' stare,
    Thinkin' so rapid that me 'air roots curl.
But 'er? She sez, 'I ain't 'eard talk so good
                Since my child'ood.

" 'I wish,' sez she, 'I could be back again
    Beneath the wattle an' that great blue sky.
It's like a breath uv 'ome to meet you men.
    You've done reel well,' she sez. 'Don't you be shy.
When yer in Blighty once again,' sez she,
                'Come an' see me.'

"I don't see 'er no more; 'cos I stopped one.
    But, 'fore I sails, I gits a billy doo
Which sez, 'Give my love to the dear ole Sun,
    An' take an exile's blessin' 'ome with you.
An' if you 'ave some boomerangs to spare,
                Save me a pair.

" 'I'd like to see 'em play about,' she wrote,
    'Out on me lawn, an' stroke their pretty fur.
God bless yeh, boy.' An' then she ends 'er note,
    'Yer dinkum cobber,' an' 'er moniker.
A sport? You bet! She's marri'd to an Earl—
                An Aussie girl."

Jim's Girl

"'OO is that girl," sez Digger Smith,
"That never seems to bother with
No blokes: the bint with curly 'air?
    I've often seen 'er over there
Talkin' to Missus Flood, an' she
Seems like a reel ripe peach to me.

"Not that I'm askin' " ... 'Ere 'is eyes
Goes sort uv swiv'ly, an' 'e sighs.
    "Not that I'm askin' with idears
    Uv love an' marridge; 'ave no fears.
I've chucked the matrimony plan,"
'E sez. "I'm only 'arf a man."

This Digger Smith 'as fairly got
Me rampin' with 'is " 'arf man" rot.
    'E 'as a timber leg, it's true;
    But 'e can do the work uv two.
Besides, the things 'e's done Out There
Makes 'im one man an' some to spare.

I knoo 'is question was jist kid.
'E'd met this girl; I know 'e did.
    'E knoo Jim Flood an' 'er was booked
    For double when the 'Un was cooked.
But, seein' 'er, it used to start
'Im thinkin' uv another tart.

Jim's Girl

"Oh, 'er?" sez I. "She is a pearl.
I've 'eard she used to be Jim's girl;
    But she was jist a child when Jim
    Got out. She 'as forgotten 'im."
I knows jist wot was in 'is mind.
An' sez, "Wade in, if you're inclined."

'E give me sich a narsty look
I thought 'e meant to answer crook;
    But, "I ain't out for jokes," sez 'e
    "Yeh needn't sling that stuff to me.
I only was jist thinkin'—p'r'aps ...
There's some," 'e sez, "that sticks to chaps.

"Some girls," sez 'e, "keeps true to chaps,
An' wed 'em when they've done with scraps,
    An' come 'ome whole. Yeh don't ixpec'
    No tart to tie up to a wreck?
Besides," 'e sez.... "Well, any'ow,
That girl's all right; I know it now.

"I know," sez Smith. "I got it right.
Jim used to talk to me at night
    About a little girl 'e tracked.
    'Er name is Flo. Ain't that a fact?
That's 'er. I know she writes to 'im
Each mail. She ain't forgotten Jim.

"I'd like to swap my luck for Jim's
If 'e comes 'ome with all 'is limbs.
    An' if 'e don't—well, I dunno.
    I've taken notice uv this Flo,
An' wonder if"—'e stares at me—
"If there is more like 'er" sez 'e.

Digger Smith

Now, Digger Smith 'as learned a lot
Out fightin' there, but 'e ain't got
    The cunnin' for to 'ide 'is 'eart.
    'E's too dam honest, for a start;
'Is mind's dead simple to a friend.
I've read 'im through from end to end.

I've learned from things 'e 'asn't said
Jist wot's been runnin in 'is 'ead.
    I know there is a girl, somewhere:
    Some one 'oo 'ad the 'eart to care
For 'im when 'e went to the war.
I know all that, an' somethin' more.

I know that since 'e came back 'ere
'E 'asn't seen that girl for fear
    She'd turn 'im down—give 'im the bird,
    An' 'and 'im out the frozen word,
Because 'e's left a leg in France;
An' 'e's afraid to take a chance.

Well, not afraid, per'aps, but—shook.
It's jist the form 'is nerves 'ave took.
    Now 'e's been watchin' Flo an' seen
    'Er style an' 'ow she's always keen
For news uv Jim. Then 'e starts out
To 'ope, an' 'esitate, an' doubt.

'E wonders if 'is own girl spoke
Jist this same way about 'er bloke.
    'E wonders if in 'is girl's eyes
    That same look came; an' then 'e sighs,
An' dulls 'is senses with the dope
That 'arf a man ain't got no 'ope.

'E makes me tired. But, all the same,
I tries to work a little game.
    "Look 'ere," I sez. "About this Flo.
    Jim mightn't come back 'ome, yeh know.
You 'ave a fly; yeh're sure to score;
Besides, all's fair in love an' war."

"Sling that!" 'e sez; but I goes on:
"Ole Jim won't blame yeh when she's gone.
    'E knows, the same as me an' you,
    These silly tarts, they can't keep true."
I piles it on until I've got
'Im where I want 'im—jumpin' 'ot.

An' then 'e sez, " 'Ere, sling that talk!
I might be groggy in me walk;
    But if yeh say them things to me
    I'm man enough to crack yeh; see?"
"Righto," sez I. "That was me plan.
Now wot about this 'arf a man?"

'E stares at me, an' then sez, slow,
"Wot is yer game? Wot do yeh know?"
    "Nothin'," I tells 'im, "only this:
    When there's a waitin' tart to kiss
Yeh're only 'arf a man; but when
There's blokes to fight, yeh're twenty men."

"Wot tart?" 'e asks. "Yeh mean this Flo?"
"P'r'aps not," I sez. "You ought to know." . . .
    I waits to let me words sink in.
    An' then—'e beats me with that grin.
"Match-makin', Bill?" 'e laughs. "Oh, 'Ell!
You take up knittin' for a spell."

The Boys Out There

"WHY do they do it? I dunno,"
    Sez Digger Smith. "Yeh got me beat.
Some uv the yarns yeh 'ear is true,
An' some is rather umptydoo,
    An' some is—indiscreet.
But them that don't get to the crowd,
Them is the ones would make yeh proud."

With Digger Smith an' other blokes
    'Oo 'ave returned it's much the same:
They'll talk uv wot they've seen an' done
When they've been out to 'ave their fun;
    But no word uv the game.
On fights an' all the tale uv blood
Their talk, as they remark, is dud.

It's so with soldiers, I 'ave 'eard,
    All times. The things that they 'ave done,
War-mad, with blood before their eyes,
An' in their ears wild fightin' cries,
    They ever after shun.
P'r'aps they forget; or find it well
Not to recall too much uv 'Ell.

An' when they won't loose up their talk
    It's 'ard for us to understand
'Ow all those boys we used to know,
Ole Billo, Jim an' Tom an' Joe,
    Done things to beat the band.
We knoo they'd fight; but they've became
'Ead ringers at the fightin' game.

The Boys Out There

Well, wot I've 'eard from Digger Smith
    An' other soldier blokes like 'im
I've put together bit by bit,
An' chewed a long time over it;
    An' now I've got a dim
An' 'azy notion in me 'ead
Why they is battlers, born an' bred.

Wot did they know uv war first off,
    When they joined up? Wot did I know
When I was tossed out on me neck
As if I was a shattered wreck
    The time I tried to go?
Flat feet! Me feet 'as len'th an' brea'th
Enough to kick a 'Un to death!

They don't know nothin', bein' reared
    Out 'ere where war 'as never spread—
"A land by bloodless conquest won,"
As some son uv a writin' gun
    Sez in a book I read—
They don't know nix but wot they're told
At school; an' that sticks till they're old.

Yeh've got to take the kid at school,
    Gettin' 'is 'ist'ry lesson learned—
Then tales uv Nelson an' uv Drake,
Uv Wellin'ton an' Fightin' Blake.
    'Is little 'eart 'as burned
To get right out an' 'ave a go,
An' sock it into some base foe.

Nothin' but glory fills 'is mind;
    The British charge is somethin' grand;
The soldier that 'e reads about
Don't 'ave no time for fear an' doubt;
    'E's the 'eroic brand.
So, when that boy gets in the game,
'E jist wades in an' does the same.

Not bein' old 'ands at the stunt,
    They simply does as they are told;
But, bein' Aussies—Spare me days!—
They never thinks uv other ways,
    But does it brave an' bold.
That's 'arf; an' for the other part
Yeh got to go back to the start.

Yeh've got to go right back to Dad,
    To Gran'dad and the pioneers,
'Oo packed up all their bag uv tricks
An' come out 'ere in sixty-six,
    An' battled thro' the years;
Our Gran'dads; *and their women, too,*
That 'ad the grit to face the new.

It's that old stock; and, more than that,
    It's Bill an' Jim an' ev'ry son
Gettin' three good meat meals a day
An' 'eaps uv chance to go an' play
    Out in the bonzer sun.
It's partly that; but, don't forget,
When it's all said, there's somethin' yet.

The Boys Out There

There's somethin' yet; an' there I'm beat.
    Crowds uv these lads I've known, but then,
They 'ave got somethin' from this war,
Somethin' they never 'ad before,
    That makes 'em better men.
Better? There's no word I can get
To name it right. There's somethin' yet.

We 'ear a lot about reward;
    We praise, an' sling the cheers about;
But there was debts we can't repay
Piled up on us one single day—
    When that first list come out.
There ain't no way to pay that debt.
Do wot we can—there's somethin' yet.

Half A Man

"I WASH me 'ands uv 'im," I tells 'em, straight.
  "You women can do wot yeh dash well like.
I leave this 'arf a man to 'is own fate;
  I've done me bit, an' now I'm gone on strike.
Do wot yet please; but don't arsk 'elp from me;
'E's give me nerves; so now I'll let 'im be."

Doreen an' ole Mar Flood 'as got a scheme.
  They've been conspirin' for a week or more
About this Digger Smith, an' now they dream
  They've got 'is fucher waitin' in cool store
To 'and 'im out, an' fix 'im up for life.
But they've got Buckley's, as I tells me wife.

I've seen 'em whisperin' up in our room.
  Now they wants me to join in the debate;
But, "Nix," I tells 'em. "I ain't in the boom,
  An' Digger Smith ain't risin' to me bait;
'E's fur too fly a fish for me to catch,
An' two designin' women ain't 'is match."

I puts me foot down firm, an' tells 'em, No!
  Their silly plan's a thing I wouldn't touch.
An' then me wife, for 'arf an hour or so,
  Talks to me confident, of nothin' much;
Then, 'fore I know it, I am all red 'ot
Into the scheme, an' leader uv the plot.

Half A Man

'Twas Mar Flood starts it. She got 'old uv 'im—
    You know the way they 'ave with poor, weak men—
She drops a tear or two concernin' Jim;
    Tells 'im wot women 'ave to bear; an' then
She got 'im talkin', like a woman can.
'E never would 'ave squeaked to any man.

She leads 'im on—It's crook the way they scheme—
    To talk about this girl 'e's left be'ind.
Not that she's pryin'! Why, she wouldn't dream!—
    But speakin' uv it might jist ease 'is mind.
Then, 'fore 'e knows, 'e's told, to 'is su'prise,
Name an' address—an' colour uv 'er eyes!

An' then she's off 'ere plottin' with Doreen—
    Bustin' a confidence, I tells 'em, flat.
But all me roustin' leaves 'em both serene:
    Women don't see a little thing like that.
An' I ain't cooled off yet before they've got
Me workin' for 'em in this crooked plot.

Nex' day Mar Flood she takes 'er Sund'y dress
    An' 'er best little bonnet up to town.
'Er game's to see the girl at this address
    An' word 'er in regard to comin' down
To take Smith be su'prise. My part's to fix
A meetin' so there won't be any mix.

I tips, some'ow, that girl won't 'esitate.
    She don't. She comes right back with Mar nex' day,
All uv a fluster. When I seen 'er state
    I thinks I'd best see Digger straight away;
'Cos, if I don't, 'e's bound to 'ear the row,
With 'er: "Where is 'e? Can't I see 'im now?"

I finds 'im in the paddick down at Flood's.
    I 'ums an' 'ars a bit about the crops.
'E don't say nothin': goes on baggin' spuds.
    " 'Ow would yeh like," I sez to 'im, an' stops.
" 'Ow would it be" ... 'E stands an' looks at me:
"Now, wot the 'Ell's got into you?" sez 'e.

That don't restore me confidence a bit.
    The drarmer isn't goin' as I tipped.
I corfs, an' makes another shot at it;
    While 'e looks at me like 'e thinks I'm dipped.
"Well—jist suppose," I sez; an' then I turn
An' see 'er standin' there among the fern.

She don't want no prelimin'ries, this tart;
    She's broke away before they rung the bell;
She's beat the gun, an' got a flyin' start.
    Smith makes a funny noise, an' I sez, " 'Ell!"
Because I tumbles that I'm out uv place.
But, as I went, I caught sight uv 'er face.

That's all I want to know. An', as I ran,
    I 'ears 'er cry, "My man! Man an' a 'arf!
Don't fool me with yer talk uv 'arf a man!"....
    An' then I 'ears ole Digger start to larf.
It was a funny larf, so 'elp me bob:
Fair in the middle uv it come a sob....

I don't see Digger till the other night.
    "Well, 'Arf-a-man," I sez. " 'Ow goes it now?"
"Yes, 'arf a man," sez 'e. "Yeh got it right;
    I can't change that, alone, not any'ow.
But she is mendin' things." 'E starts to larf.
"Some day," 'e sez, "she'll be the better 'arf."

Sawin' Wood

I wondered wot was doin'. First I seen
Ole Missus Flood wave signals to Doreen.
    I'm in the paddick slashin' down some ferns;
    She's comin' up the road; an' if she turns
An 'andspring I won't be su'prised a bit,
The way she's caperin', an' goin' it.

She yells out some remark when she gets near,
Which I don't catch, I'm too fur off to 'ear.
    An' then Doreen comes prancin' to our door,
    An' Missus Flood she sprints, an' yells some more;
My wife runs to the gate an' waves 'er arms....
But I lays low; I'm used to these alarms.

A marri'd bloke, in time, 'e learns a bit;
An' 'e ain't over keen to throw a fit
    Each time the women calls the fire-reel out.
    It's jist a trifle 'e'll know all about
When things get normal. That's a point I learn;
So I saws wood, an' keeps on cuttin' fern.

At least, I cut a few. I got to give
Reel fac's, an' own I was inquisitive;
    An' these 'ere fireworks get me fair perplexed.
    I watch the 'ouse to see wot 'appens next;
But nothin's doin'. They jist goes on in,
An' leaves me wonderin' wot's caused the din.

I stands it for a full 'arf-hour or more;
Then gets dead sick uv starin' at the door.
    I goes down to the 'ouse an' 'unts about
    To find some 'baccer, which I 'ave no doubt
Is in me trousers pocket all the while.
When I goes in, the talk stops, an' they smile.

I sez I've lost me smoke, an' search a bit,
An' ask Doreen wot 'as became uv it,
    An' turns the mantelshelf all upside-down,
    An' looks inside the teapot, with a frown;
Then gives it up, an' owns I'd like a drink;
When Missus Flood sez, "Bill, *wot do you think?*"

Now, ain't that like a woman? Spare me days,
I'll never get resigned to all their ways.
    When they 'as news to tell they smile, an' wink,
    An' bottle it, an' ask yeh wot yeh think.
It's jist a silly game uv theirs, an' so,
I gives the countersign: "Wot? I dunno."

"Then guess," she sez. Well, I'm a patient bloke,
So I sits down an' starts to cut a smoke.
    (To play this game yeh've got to persevere.)
    "Couldn't," I sez, "if I guessed for a year";
Then lights me pipe, an' waits for 'er to speak.
At last she sez, "*Jim's comin' back next week!*"

"Go on," sez I; an' puffs away awhile
Quite unconcerned. But for to see 'er smile
    Was jist a treat: 'er eyes was shinin' bright,
    An' she'd grow'd ten years younger in a night.
Jist 'ere, Doreen she sez to me, "Good Lor,
Wot do yeh want *two* plugs uv 'baccer for?"

Sawin' Wood

I takes me pipe out uv me mouth an' stares,
An' stammers, "Must 'ave found a piece—somewheres."
   But, by the way she smiles—so extra sweet—
   I know she twigs me game, an' I am beat.
"Fancy," she sez. "Yeh're absent-minded, dear.
Sure there was nothin' else yeh wanted 'ere?"

"Nothin'," I sez, an' feels a first-prize fool;
An' goes outside, an' grabs the nearest tool.
   It was the crosscut; so I works like mad
   To keep me self-respeck from goin' bad.
"This game," I tells meself, "will do yeh good.
You ain't proficient, yet, at sawin' wood."

Jim

"Now, be the Hokey Fly!" sez Peter Begg.
"Suppose 'e comes 'ome with a wooden leg.
　Suppose 'e isn't fit to darnce at all,
　Then, ain't we 'asty fixin' up this ball?
A little tournament at Bridge is my
Idear," sez Peter. "Be the Hokey Fly!"

Ole Peter Begg is gettin' on in years.
'E owns a reel good farm; an' all 'e fears
　Is that some girl will land 'im, by an' by,
　An' share it with 'im—be the Hokey Fly.
That's 'is pet swear-word, an' I dunno wot
'E's meanin', but 'e uses it a lot.

"Darncin'!" growls Begg. We're fixin' up the 'all
With bits uv green stuff for a little ball
　To welcome Jim, 'oo's comin' 'ome nex' day.
　We're 'angin' flags around to make things gay.
An' shiftin' chairs, an' candle-greasin' floors,
As is our way when blokes come 'ome from wars.

"A little game uv Bridge," sez Peter Begg,
"Would be more decent like, an' p'r'aps a keg
　Uv somethin' if the 'ero's feelin' dry.
　But this 'ere darncin'! Be the Hokey Fly,
These selfish women never thinks at all
About the guest; they only wants the ball.

Jim

"Now, cards," sez Begg, "amuses ev'ry one.
An' then our soldier guest could 'ave 'is fun
    If 'e'd lost *both* 'is legs. It makes me sick—
    'Ere! Don't yeh spread that candle-grease too thick.
Yeh're wastin' it; an' us men 'as to buy
Enough for nonsense, be the Hokey Fly!"

Begg, 'e ain't never keen on wastin' much.
"Peter," I sez "it's you that need a crutch.
    Why don't yeh get a wife, an' settle down?"
    'E looks reel fierce, an' answers, with a frown,
"Do you think I am goin' to be rooked
For 'arf me tucker, jist to get it cooked?"

I lets it go at that, an' does me job;
An' when a little later on I lob
    Along the 'omeward track, down by Flood's gate
    I meet ole Digger Smith, an' stops to state
Me views about the weather an' the war....
'E tells me Jim gets 'ere nex' day, at four.

An' as we talk, I sees along the road
A strange bloke 'umpin some queer sort uv load.
    I points 'im out to Smith an' sez, " 'Oo's that?
    Looks like a soldier, don't 'e, be 'is 'at?"
"Stranger," sez Digger, "be the cut uv 'im."
But, trust a mother's eyes.... "*It's Jim! My Jim!*

My Jim" I 'ears; an', scootin' up the track
Come Missus Flood, with Flo close at 'er back.
    It was a race, for lover an' for son;
    They finished neck an' neck; but mother won,
For it was 'er that got the first good 'ug.
(I'm so took back I stands there like a mug.)

Then come Flo's turn; an' Jim an' Digger they
Shake 'ands without no fancy, gran'-stand play.
    Yeh'd think they parted yesterd'y, them two,
    For all the wild 'eroics that they do.
"Yeh done it, lad," sez Jim. "I knoo yeh would."
"You bet," sez Smith; "but I'm all to the good."

Then, uv a sudden, all their tongues is loosed.
They finds me there an' I am intrajuiced;
    An' Jim tells 'ow it was 'e come to land
    So soon, while Mar an' Flo each 'olds a 'and.
But, jist as sudden, they all stop an' stare
Down to the 'ouse, at Dad Flood standin' there.

'E's got 'is 'and up shadin' off the sun.
Then 'e starts up to them; but Dad don't run:
    'E isn't 'owlin' for 'is lost boy's kiss;
    'E's got 'is own sweet way in things like this.
'E wanders up, an' stands an' looks at Jim.
An', spare me days, that look was extra grim!

I seen the mother pluckin' at 'er dress;
I seen the girl's white face an' 'er distress.
    An' Digger Smith, 'e looks reel queer to me:
    Grinnin' inside 'imself 'e seemed to be.
At last Dad sez—oh, 'e's a tough ole gun!—
"Well, are yeh sorry now for wot yeh done?"

Jim gives a start; but answers with a grin,
"Well, Dad, I 'ave been learnin' discipline.
    An' tho' I ain't quite sure wot did occur
    Way back"—'e's grinnin' worse—"I'm sorry, sir."
(It beats me, that, about these soldier blokes:
They're always grinnin', like all things was jokes.)

Jim

P'r'aps Dad is gettin' dull in 'is ole age;
But 'e don't seem to see Jim's cammyflage.
    P'r'aps 'e don't want to; for, in 'is ole eye,
    I seen a twinkle as 'e give reply.
"Nex' week," 'e sez, "we will begin to cart
The taters. Yeh can make another start."

But then 'e grabs Jim's 'and. I seen the joy
In mother's eyes. "Now, welcome 'ome, me boy,"
    Sez Dad; an' then 'e adds, "Yeh've made me proud;"
    That's all. An' 'e don't add it none too loud.
Dad don't express 'is feelin's in a shout;
It cost 'im somethin' to git that much out.

       .   .   .   .   .   .

We 'ad the darnce. An', spite uv all Begg's fears,
Jim darnced like 'e could keep it up for years;
    Mostly with Flo. We don't let up till three;
    An' then ole Peter Begg, Doreen an' me
We walk together 'ome, an' on the way,
Doreen 'as quite a lot uv things to say.

"Did you see Flo?" sez she. "Don't she look grand?
That Jim's the luckiest in all the land—
    An' little Smith—that girl uv 'is, I'm sure,
    She'll bring 'im 'appiness that will endure."
She 'ugs my arm, then sez, " 'Usband or wife,
If it's the right one, is the wealth uv life."

I sneaks a look at Begg, an' answers, "Yes,
Yeh're right, ole girl; that's the reel 'appiness.
    An' if ole, lonely growlers was to know
    The worth uv 'appy marridge 'ere below,
They'd swap their bank-books for a wife," sez I.
Sez Peter Begg, "*Well! Be the—Hokey—Fly!*"

A Square Deal

"DREAMIN'?" I sez to Digger Smith.
    "Buck up, ole sport, an' smile.
Ain't there enough uv joy to-day
To drive the bogey man away
    An' make reel things worth while?
A bloke would think, to see you stare,
There's visions on the 'ill-tops there."

"Dreamin'," sez Digger Smith. "Why not?
    An' there is visions too.
An' when I get 'em sorted out,
An' strafe that little bogey, Doubt,
    I'll start me life all new.
Oh, I ain't crook; but packed in 'ere
Is thoughts enough to last a year.

"I'm thinkin' things," sez Digger Smith.
    "I'm thinkin' big an' fine
Uv Life an' Love an' all the rest,
An' wot is right an' wot is best,
    An' 'ow much will be mine.
Not that I'm wantin' overmuch:
Some work, some play, an' food an' such."

"See 'ere," I sez. "You 'ark to me.
    I've done some thinkin' too.
An' this 'ere land, for wot yeh did,
Owes some few million solid quid
    To fightin' blokes like you.
So don't be too dam modest or
Yeh'll git less than yeh're lookin' for."

A Square Deal

"Money?" sez Digger. "Loot?" sez 'e
    "Aw, give that talk a rest!
I'm sick uv it. I didn't say
That I was thinkin' all uv pay,
    But wot was right an' best.
An' that ain't in the crazy game
Uv grabbin' wealth an' chasin' fame.

"Do you think us blokes Over There,
    When things was going' strong,
Was keepin' ledgers day be day
An' reck'nin' wot the crowd would pay?
    Pull off! Yeh got it wrong.
Do you think all the boys gone West
Wants great swank 'ead-stones on their chest?

"You coots at 'ome 'as small ideer
    Uv wot we think an' feel.
We done our bit an' seen it thro',
An' all that we are askin' you
    Is jist a fair, square deal.
We want this land we battled for
To settle up—an' somethin more.

"We want the land we battled for
    To be a land worth while.
We're sick uv greed, an' 'ate, an' strife,
An' all the mess that's made uv life." ...
    'E stopped a bit to smile.
"I got these thoughts Out There becos
We learnt wot mateship reely was."

. . . . . .

The hills be'ind the orchard trees
    Was showin' misty blue.
The ev'nin' light was growin' dim;
An' down I sat 'longside uv 'im,
    An' done some dreamin' too.
I dreams uv war; an' wot is paid
By blokes that went an' blokes that stayed.

I dreams uv honour an' reward,
    An' ow to pay a debt.
For partin' cash, an' buyin' farms,
An' fittin' chaps with legs an' arms
    Ain't all—there's somethin' yet.
There's still a solid balance due;
An' now it's up to me an' you.

There's men I know ain't yet woke up,
    Or reckernized that debt—
Proud men 'oo wouldn't take yeh down
Or owe their grocer 'arf-a-crown—
    They ain't considered, yet,
There's somethin' owin'—to the dead,
An' Diggers live for more than bread.

"*We* learnt wot mateship was," 'e sez.
    Us Diggers found the good
That's hid away somewhere in chaps,
An' ain't searched for enough, per'aps,
    Or prized, or understood.
But all this game uv grab an' greed
An' silly 'ate —— Why, where's the need?"

The hills be'ind the orchard trees
    Jist caught the settin' sun.
A bloke might easy think that there,
'Way back be'ind the range somewhere,
    Where streaks uv sunlight run,
There was a land, swep' clear uv doubt,
When men finds wot they dreams about.

        . . . . . .

"Beauty," sez Digger, sudden-like,
    "An' love, an' kindliness;
The chance to live a clean, straight life,
A dinkum deal for kids an' wife:
    A man needs nothin' less. . . .
Maybe they'll get it when I go
To push up daisies, I dunno."

"Dreamin'," sez Digger Smith. "Why not?
    There's visions on the hill." . . .
Then I gets up an' steals away,
An' leaves 'im with the dyin' day,
    Dreamin' an' doubtin' still. . . .
Cobber, it's up to me an' you
To see that 'arf is dream comes true.

Armistice

To His Dead Cobber from The Sentimental Bloke

I'm Sittin' 'ere, Mick—sittin' 'ere today,
   Feelin' 'arf glum, 'arf sorter—reverent,
Thinkin' strange, crooked thorts of 'ow they say:
   "The 'eads is bowed thro' all a continent";
An' wond'rin'—wond'rin' in a kind of doubt
   If other coves is feelin' like I do,
Tryin' to figure wot it's all about,
     An'—if it's meanin' anythin' to you.

Silence ... The hour strikes soon thro' all the land
An' 'eads bend low. Old mate, give me your 'and.
   Silence—for you, Mick, an' for blokes like you
   To mark the Day—the Day you never knoo.

The Day you never knoo, nor we forget ...
   I can't tell why I'm sittin' 'ere this way,
Scrawlin' a message that you'll never get—
   Or will you? I dunno. It's 'ard to say.
P'raps you'll know about it, where you are,
   An' think, "Ah, well, they ain't too bad a lot."
An' tell them other digs up on your star
   That now, or nevermore, they ain't fergot.

Silence ... Not 'ere alone, Mick—everywhere—
In city an' in country 'eads are bare.
   An', in this room, it seems as if I knoo
   Some friend 'oo came—Ole cobber! Is it you?

Me 'eart is full, Mick ... 'Struth! I ain't the bloke,
   As you well know, to go all soft an' wet.
Fair's fair, lad. Times I've known when you 'ave spoke
   Like you was tough an' 'ard as 'ell—an' yet

Armistice

Somethin' be'ind your bluff an' swagger bold
    Showed all them narsty sentiments was kid.
It was that thing inside yeh, lad, wot told.
    It made you go an' do the thing you did.

Silence ... There's mothers, Mick. You never knoo
No mother. But they're prayin' for you too.
    In every heart—The Boys! The Boys are there,
    The Boys ... That very name, lad, is a pray'r.

The Boys! Old Cobber, I can see 'em still:
    The drums are rollin' an' the sunlight gleams
On bay'nits. Men are marchin' with a will
    On to the glory of their boy'ood's dreams.
Glory? You never found it that, too much.
    But, lad, you stuck it—stuck it with the rest,
An' if your bearin' 'ad no soulful touch,
    "Twas for *OUR* souls that you went marchin'—West.

Silence ... The children too, Mick—little kids,
Are standin'. Not becos their teacher bids:
    They've knoo no war; but they 'ave stopped their play
    Becos they know, they feel it is The Day.

So may it be thro' all the comin' years.
    But sorrow's gone, lad. It's not that we know.
The sobbin's passed, 'ole cobber, an' the tears,
    An' well we un'erstand you'd 'ave it so.
But somethin' deeper far than that 'as come,
    Somethin' a mind can't get within its bound,
Somethin' I can't explain. A man is dumb
    When 'e thinks ... Listen ! 'Ear the bugles sound!

Silence

        . . . . .

Armistice

Well, Mick, ole cock, I dunno why I've wrote,
    It's just to ease a thing inside wot says
"Sit down, you sloppy coot, an' write a note
    To that ole cobber of the olden days.
'E'll know—for sure 'e'll know". "So, lad, it's done,
    Work's waitin', an' a man can't get in wrong:
Our goal is still ahead. But yours is won:
    That's the one thing we know, lad, an'—So long.

Silence ... It's over, Mick; so there you are.
I know you're 'appy up there on yer star.
    Believe us, lad; that star shall never fall
    While one is left to say, "Gawd keep 'em all!"

ROSE OF
SPADGERS

Introduction

I've crawled; I've eaten dirt; I've lied a treat;
I've dodged the cops an' led a double life;
I've readied up wild tales to tell me wife,
W'ich afterwards I've 'ad to take an' eat
Red raw. Aw, I been goin' it to beat
A big massed band: mixin' with sin an' strife,
Gettin' me bellers punchered with a knife
An' all but endin' up in Russell Street.

I've mixed it—with the blessin' uv the church—
Down there in Spadgers, fightin' mad, an' blind
With 'oly rage. I've 'ad full leaf to smirch
Me tongue with sich rude words as come to mind,
Becos I 'ated leavin' in the lurch
Wot Ginger Mick, me cobber, left be'ind.

Don't git me wrong. I never went an' planned
No gory all-in scraps or double deals.
But one thing follered on another 'eels,
Jist like they do in life, until I land
Flop in the soup—su'prised, you un'erstand,
But not averse; jist like a feller feels
'Oo reaches fer the water-jug at meals
An' finds a dinkum gargle in 'is 'and.

Su'prised but not averse. That puts it right
An', if Fate 'as these things all fixed before,
Well, wot's a bloke to do, to 'oo a fight
Was not unwelkim in the days of yore?
Pertickler when 'e knows 'is cause is right
An' 'as a gorspil spruiker to ongcore.

Regardin' morils, I was on a cert;
Fer if I'd missed the step an' fell frum grace
By rudely pushin' in me brother's face
Without no just ixcuse, it might uv 'urt.
But this Spike Wegg—the narsty little squirt!—
Collected 'is becos ther' was no trace
Uv virchoo in the cow. 'Is aims was base
When 'e laid out to tempt a honest skirt.

An' so me arm was strong becoz me cause
Was on the square, an' I don't 'esitate.
The parson bloke, 'e sez all moril laws
They justified me act .... But, anyrate,
Before I crools this yarn we better pause
Till I gives you the dope an' git it straight.

Now, Ginger Mick, me cobber, went to war,
An' on Gallipoli, 'e wandered West.
Per'aps, less said about 'is life the best;
It was 'is death that shoved along 'is score.
But that tale's old; an' Ginger ain't no more.
E's done 'is bit an' faded, like the rest
'Oo fought an' fell an' left wot they loved best
In 'opes they'd be dealt fair by pals of yore.

An' all Mick left was Rose. "Look after Rose.
Mafeesh!" 'e sez when 'e was on the brink.
An' there was thousan's like 'im, I suppose.
I ain't no moralizer fer to think
Wot others ort to do; I only knows
I 'ad me job, frum w'ich I durstn't shrink.

Introduction

Unless you 'ave a beat down Spadgers way
I don't ixpect you ever met with Rose.
She don't move in yer circle, I suppose,
Or call to bite a bun upon yer Day.
An' if yeh got a intro, I dare say
Yeh'd take it snifty an' turn up yer nose.
Now that we don't need Micks to fight our foes
Them an' their Roses 'as to fade away.

They 'ave to simmer down an' not ubtrude,
Now we are safe an' finished with the war.
We don't intend to be unkind or rude
Or crayfish on the things we said before
Uv our brave boys. An', as fer gratichood,
Well, there's a Guv'mint, ain't there? Wot's it for?

But Mick buzzed orf too quick to wed a bride
An' leave a widder doo fer Guv'mint aid.
Spite uv ole Spadgers, Rose was still a maid;
An' spite uv Spadgers, she still 'as 'er pride
That wouldn't let 'er whimper if she tried,
Or profit by 'er misery, an' trade
On Mick's departin' an' the noise it made.
I know 'er. An' I know she'd sooner died.

I know 'er. But to them that never knows,
An' never tries to know the 'earts an' ways
Uv common folk, there was n't much to Rose
That called fer any speshul loud 'Oorays—
Nothin' 'eroic. She's jist "one uv those"—
One uv the ruck that don't attract our gaze.

Rose of Spadgers

I guess you was n't born down Spadgers way,
Or spent yer child'ood in the gutter there
Jist runnin' wild, or dragged up be the 'air
Till you was fit to earn a bit of pay
By honest toil or—any other way.
You never 'ad to battle to keep square,
Or learn, first 'and, uv every trap an' snare
That life 'as waitin' for yeh day by day.

But I 'ave read about a flower that grows
Once in a while upon a 'eap uv muck.
It ain't the flower's own choosin', I suppose,
An' bein' sweet an' pure is jist its luck.
There's 'uman blooms I've knowed the like uv those,
Strugglin' in weeds; an' 'struth! I like their pluck.

Don't make no error. I ain't givin' Rose
The 'igh-bred manners uv some soshul queen.
She were n't no shrinkin', simperin', girleen,
With modest glances droopin' to 'er toes.
She'd smash a prowlin' male acrost the nose
As quick as any tart I ever seen.
But, bli'me, she was straight an' she was clean,
As more than one mauled lady-killer knows.

Straight as a die! An jist as clean an' sweet
An' thorny as the bloom 'oose name she bears.
To cling on to 'er virchoo weren't no feat
With 'er; she simply kep' it unawares
An' natchril, like people trust their feet,
An, don't turn silly 'and-springs on the stairs.

Introduction

That's 'ow Mick found, an' left 'er—straight an' clean.
She seen the good in 'im long years before
'E proved it good an' plenty at the war.
She loved an' mothered 'im becos she seen
The big, soft-'earted boy 'e'd alwiz been
Be'ind 'is leery ways an' fightin' jor,
An' all 'is little mix-ups with the Lor.
She knoo 'e weren't the man to treat 'er mean.

They was a proper match. But Mick, 'e goes
An' slips 'is wind, there, on Gallipoli;
Jist pausin' to remark, "Look after Rose."
An', if them partin' words weren't meant fer me,
Well, I'm the gay angora, I suppose,
In this divertin' slab uv 'istory.

It ain't no soft romance, with pale pink bows,
This common little tale I 'ave to tell
Concernin' common folk, an' wot befell
When me an' my ole parson cobber goes
An' does our bit in lookin' after Rose.
The Church admits I done my part reel well;
An' there won't be no need to ring a bell
Or call the cops in when the langwidge flows.

So, 'ere's a go. If my remarks is plain
An' short uv frills, they soots me tale; an' so,
I 'opes the rood boorjosie will refrain
Frum vulger chuckin'-orf; fer well I know
Ladies an' gentlemen uv Spadgers Lane
Won't fail to un'erstand. So, 'ere's a go.

                        THE SENTIMENTAL BLOKE.

The Faltering Knight

IT knocks me can in, this 'ere game uv life,
　A bloke gets born, grows up, looks round fer fun,
Dreams dilly dreams, then wakes to find a wife
　　An' fambly round 'im—all 'is young days done.
An', gazin' back, sees in 'is youth a man
Scarce reckernised. It fair knocks in me can!

Ther's me. I never seemed to make no change
　　As I mooched on through life frum year to year;
An' yet, at times it seems to me dead strange
　　That me, uv old, is me, 'oo's sittin' 'ere.
Per'aps it ain't. 'E was a crook young coot,
While I'm a sturdy farmer, growin' froot.

But, all the same, *'e* would n't back an' fill,
　　An' argue with 'imself, an' 'esitate,
Once 'e 'ad seen the way. 'E'd find the will
　　To go an' do the thing 'e 'ad to, straight.
That's 'ow I was; an' now—Ar, strike a light!
Life gits so mixed I can't git nothin' right.

But wot's the use? A bloke 'as got to own,
　　When once 'e 'as responsibility,
Ther's certin games is better left alone
　　Wot might be done if 'e was only free.
Ther's certin things—Oh, wot's the flamin' good?
A 'usband alwiz gits misun'erstood!

The Faltering Knight

It's no use hintin'. If yeh want it straight,
   Me an' me wife ain't seein' eye to eye:
All ain't been peace an' 'armony uv late,
   An' clouds is comin' up in our clear sky.
I ain't to blame, an' yet, no more's Doreen.
It's jist 'ard Fate 'as shoved 'is oar between.

All marrid blokes will un'erstand me well.
   I ain't addressin' no remarks to those
'Oove learnt but 'arf uv life. The things I tell
   Is fer the ears uv fellermen that *knows*:
Them symperthetic 'usbands 'oo 'ave 'eard
The fog-'orn soundin' in the wifely word.

Fer when stern jooty grips a 'usband's 'eart
   (That's me) an' eggs 'im on to start a scene
That's like to tear two 'appy lives apart,
   In spite uv all 'er carin' (That's Doreen)
Why, there you 'ave a story that would make
A bonzer movie—with a bit uv fake.

But 'ere's the plot. When my pal, Ginger Mick,
   Chucked in' is alley in this war we won,
'E left things tangled; fer 'e went too quick
   Fer makin' last requests uv anyone.
'E jist sez to the world, when last 'e spoke,
"Look after Rose!" ... 'E was a trustful bloke.

Rose lives in Spadgers Lane. She lived, them days,
   Fer Mick's returnin'. When 'e never came,
If she lost 'old, an' took to careless ways,
   Well, I ain't sayin' she was much to blame.
An' I don't worry, till I 'ear she's took,
Or thinks uv takin' on to ways that's crook.

Rose of Spadgers

Although I'm vegetatin' on a farm,
    I gets a city whisper now an' then.
An' when I 'ear she's like to come to 'arm
    Amongst a push uv naughty spieler men,
I gets the wind up. This is all I see:
Mick was my cobber; so it's up to me.

That's all I see, quite clear, with my two eyes.
    But marrid blokes will understand once more,
When I remarks that marrid blokes is wise
    'Oo 'ave the sense to take a squint through four.
Four eyes is needed in reviewin' plans—
Their vision's broader than a single man's.

But when them four eyes sees two ways at once—
    Gets crossed—Ar, well, ther's things in marrid life
For which a hint's enough fer any dunce.
    Ther's certin things between a man an' wife
That can't be quite—But take this fer a fack:
Don't start things uv a mornin'. It ain't tack.

That was me first bad break. I should 'ave seen
    The supper things washed up, an' 'elped a bit,
An' then 'ave broke it gently to Doreen,
    Promiscus, like I jist 'ad thought uv it.
But I done worse. I blurts wot I'd to say
Upon the mornin' uv a *washin'* day!

There's gumption fer yeh. Eights years I been hitched—
    Eight years uv trainin', an' I fall down flat!
Like some poor, love-sick softy 'oo gets switched
    Fer tellin' "sweetie" 'e don't like 'er 'at,
When she's jist come frum 'avin' rows no end
About it's trimmin' with 'er dearest friend.

The Faltering Knight

I own's me ta'tic's crook. But, all the same,
    Ther' were n't no need fer certin things she said.
Wantin' to do good acts don't call fer blame,
    Even on tackless 'usban's, eight years wed.
A bloke 'oo jist suggests a 'armless plan
Don't need remindin' 'e's a *marrid* man.

'Struth! Don't I know it? Can I well ferget
    While I still 'ave two 'ealthy ears to 'ark?
Not that she torks an' mags a lot; but yet
    Ther's somethin' in 'er choice uv a remark
That gets there, worse than yappin' all day long,
An' makes me pure intentions look dead wrong.

It seems it ain't right fer a marrid bloke
    To rescue maids. I starts to answer back;
But got took up before I 'ardly spoke,
    An' innercent designs is painted black.
I calls attention to the knights uv old;
But tin knights, an' romance jist leaves 'er cold.

I read 'er meaning' plain in 'er cool eye.
    Aw, strike! I ain't *admirin'* Rose!... Wot?... Me!
But when 'er look sez "Rats!" where's the reply
    A man can give, an' keep 'is dignity?
It can't be done. When they git on that lay,
Wise coves adjourns the meet, an' fades away.

That's wot I done. I gits out uv the 'ouse
    All dignified. An', jist to show 'er 'ow
Reel unconcerned I am, I starts to rouse
    Me neighbour, Wally Free, about 'is cow
Wot's got in to me cabbages, an' et
Close on a row uv 'em. I'll shoot 'er yet!

Rose of Spadgers

(A batchelor 'e is, this Wally Free—
    A soljer bloke that come this way last year
An' took the little farm nex' door to me.)
    When I gets mad, 'e grins frum ear to ear,
An' sez, "cool orf," 'e sez. "It's plain your wool
'As been pulled 'ard this mornin'." 'E's a fool!

If 'e don't mend that fence ... Ar, wot's the good?
    I lets 'im go, an' sneaks be'ind the shed,
An' sits there broodin' on a pile uv wood ....
    Ther's certin things she might 'ave left unsaid.
Ther' was n't nothin' fer to make 'er go
An' dig up chance remarks uv years ago.

Me problem's this: Either I 'urts Doreen,
    By doin' things with which she don't agree,
Or lets Rose slide, an' treats me cobber mean—
    Ole Ginger Mick, 'oo 'ad no friend but me.
I ain't a ringtail; but, by gum, it's tough.
I loves me wife too much to treat 'er rough.

If I was single .... 'Struth! 'Oo wants to be?
    Fool batchelers can larf their silly larf,
An' kid theirselves they got a pull on me.
    I'm out uv sorts, that's all; an' more than 'arf
Inclined to give some coot a crack, right now:
Fer pref'rince, some insultin' single cow!

Termarter Sorce

IT was n't kid stakes. I 'ad no crook lurk
   To act deceivin', or to treat 'er mean.
I'm old enough to know them games don't work—
   Not with Doreen.
Besides, deceit ain't in me bag uv tricks.
I got a few; but there is some that sticks.

Sticks in me gizzard. Some blokes sees no wrong
   In workin' points, an' thinks it bonzer sport
To trifle with a wife's belief, so long
   As they ain't cort.
But, when yeh play the game on dead straight lines,
It 'urts to be accused uv base designs.

It starts this mornin'. I wake with a tooth
   That's squirmin' like a basketful uv snakes.
Per'haps I groan a bit, to tell the truth;
   An' then she wakes,
An' arsts me wot I'm makin' faces for.
I glare at 'er, an' nurse me achin' jor.

That was no very 'appy mornin' song.
   I ain't excusin' my end uv the joke;
But, after that, things seem to go all wrong.
   She never spoke
One narsty word; but, while the chops she serves,
'Er shrieks uv silence fair got on me nerves.

Rose of Spadgers

She might 'ave arst wot ailed me. Spare me days!
    She seen that I was crook. She seen me face
Swelled like a poisoned pup's. She only says,
    "Please to say grace."
I mumbles ... Then, in tones that wakes brute force,
She twitters, "Will yeh take termarter sorce?"

I could n't eat no breakfast. Just the sight
    Uv sweet things give me tooth a new, worse ache.
Sez she: "You seem to lost yer apetite.
    'Ave some seed cake."
Seed cake! Gawstruth! I'm there in agerny,
An' she, 'oo swore to love, sits mockin' me.

At last, when our small son gits orf to school,
    I goes an' sits down sulkin' on a couch.
" *'Ave* you a toothache, Bill?" sez she, quite cool,
    "Or jist plain grouch?
Yer face looks funny. P'raps yer gittin' fat."
I glare at 'er an' answer, "Huh!" .. like that.

That one word, "Huh," said in a certain way,—
    'Eart-felt an' with intention—it can well
Make the beginnin's uv a perfick day
    A perfick 'ell.
So I sez "Huh!" .... an' then done my ole trick
(A low-down lurk) uv gittin' orf-stage quick.

It was a slap-up day. The wattle's gold
    'Ad jist began to peep among the green;
An dafferdils, commencin' to unfold,
    They make the scene
A pitcher that—'Struth! 'Ow that tooth did ache!
An' cravin' symperthy, I git—seed cake!

It was a bonzer day! The thrush's song
    Rose like a nymn. A touch uv queer remorse
Gits me fer 'arf-a-mo', then goes all wrong.
    Ter-marter sorce!
Women *don't* understand, it's all too plain.
Termarter sorce, she sez, an' me in pain!

I dunno 'ow the mornin' muddled through.
    That naggin' tooth was gittin' reel red-'ot.
I 'ad a 'arf a dozen things to do,
    An' slummed the lot.
Then, jist before I goes fer mornin' tea,
I start another row with Wally Free.

I tells 'im if that fence ain't mended—now—
    I'll summons 'im. But 'e jist stands 'an grins.
'E's always grinnin'. Silly lookin' cow!
    An' fer two pins
I'd go acrost an' give 'is eye a poke.
'E's far too 'appy—fer a single bloke.

While I am boilin' 'ot, Doreen comes out
    To call me fer me mornin' cup o' tea.
I turn an' answer with a savage shout.
    "Dear me!" sez she.
"You seem to be put out this mornin', Bill.
'E'll mend the fence, all right. I'm sure 'e will."

"Aw! It ain't that," I sez .... Then I let go,
    When once we git inside, an' ease me mind
By tellin' 'er some things she ought to know.
    I seemed to find
A lot uv things that 'elped to make me sore;
An' they remind me uv a 'ole lot more.

Rose of Spadgers

I tells 'er that no wife, 'oo was n't blind,
    Would treat 'er 'usban' like a block uv wood.
I sez I could n't un'erstand 'er mind—
    Blowed if I could!
I tells 'er that no woman with a brain
An' 'eart would smile to see a man in pain.

I sez some wives—*some* sorts uv wives, uv course,
    If you was lyin' dead, no more to wake,
Would arst yeh if yeh liked termarter sorse,
    Or else seed cake.
I sez I don't look for no fond caress,
But symperthy, an' un'erstandin'? *Yes*!

I sez, sarcastic, that I 'ave no doubt
    Some wives might think termarters an' seed cake
Was 'andy sorts uv things to 'ave about
    To stop toothache.
But wot *I* liked in wives, once in a while,
Was commin-sense. (An' 'ere, I seen 'er smile).

An' *then* I sez: "Gorbli' me! Ain't I worked
    Me fingers to the bone, an' toiled an' slaved?
Some fellers, if their wives 'ad smiled an' smirked
    An' so be'aved" . . . .
(She pours the tea, an' 'ands acrost my cup)
"Would lose their tempers, yes, an' smash things up!"

I sez—Oh, other things in that same strain
    I ain't got any fancy to recall.
(That tooth jist 'ad me jumpin' mad with pain)
    But through it all,
With them fool speeches bubblin' in me throat,
I saw meself a bleatin', babblin' goat.

Termarter Sorce

I gulps me tea; already 'arf ashamed
    Uv more than 'arf I'd said. But is me wife
All 'umble, like a woman 'oo's been blamed?
    Not on yer life!
She answers me as if she was me mar.
"There, there," she sez. "Wot a big kid you are!"

I gulps more tea; an' tells 'er, anyway,
    Me toothache ain't a thing to joke about;
An' I will 'ave to go to town to-day
    An' 'ave it out.
At that, she looks at me with 'er calm eyes
Searchin' me through an' through 'fore she replies.

Then, "Bill," sez she, "tell me the honest truth:
    Does your tooth ache, or is this an excuse?
Why, yesterd'y you 'ad no achin' tooth." ....
    Aw, wot's the use!
"Excuse! Wot for?" I yells. But she sez, "Oh,
If it's that bad I s'pose you'll 'ave to go."

"Excuse!" I sez. "I know wot's in yer mind.
    Yeh think I can't read women's thoughts, I s'pose.
Yeh think that I planned this so I could find
    Wot's 'appened Rose.
Yeh think I've come the double, lied an' schemed
About a thing I never even dreamed!

"Yeh think—" "There, there!" she sez to me again,
    Soothin' an' soft, still like a patient mar.
"It's plain you'll never un'erstand, you men,
    Wot women are,
Their thorts, their feelin's, 'ow they fear an' doubt.
Why, Bill, it's only you I think about."

Rose of Spadgers

I knoo. Somewhere inside me silly nob
    I knoo wot thort it is she won't explain.
She feared, if I got with the old, crook mob
    In Spadgers Lane
That I might miss the step. I've never queered
The pitch in eight long years; an' yet she feared.

"I'll promise you—" I starts. But she sez, "Don't!
    Don't promise wot you might regret some day.
I trust you, Bill; an' well I know you won't
    Choose the wrong way.
Women are silly sometimes. Let's ferget
All that was said .... Is that tooth achin' yet?"

I gives it up! ... It's fairly got me beat,
    The twists an' turin' uv a woman's mind.
Nex' thing, she's smilin' up at me so sweet,
    So soft an' kind
That I—with things still in me mind to tell—
I melts—jist like I always do. Ah, well!

It was a snodger day! ... The apple trees
    Was white with bloom. All things seemed good to me.
(Except that tooth). Then by the fence I sees
    Poor Wally Free,
Pretendin' to be happy, with 'is plough.
Poor lonely coot! I pity 'im, some'ow.

A Holy War

"YOUNG friend!" .... I tries to duck, but miss the bus.
   'E sees me first, an' 'as me by the 'and.
"Young friend!" 'e sez; an' starts to make a fuss
    At meetin' me. "Why, this," 'e sez, "is grand!
    Events is workin' better than I planned.
It's Providence that I should meet you thus.
      You're jist the man," 'e sez, "to make a stand,
        An' strive for us.

"Young friend," 'e sez, "allow me to explain ... "
    But wot 'e 'as to say too well I knows.
I got the stren'th uv it in Spadgers Lane
    Not 'arf an hour before 'and, when I goes
    To see if I could pick up news uv Rose,
After that dentist let me off the chain.
    ("Painless" 'e's labled. So 'e is, I s'pose.
      I 'ad the pain.)

"Young friend," 'e sez. I let 'im 'ave 'is say;
   Though I'm already wise to all 'e said—
The queer ole parson, with 'is gentle way—
    ('E tied Doreen an' me when we was wed).
    I likes 'im, from 'is ole soft, snowy 'ead
Down to 'is boots. 'E ain't the sort to pray
      When folks needs bread.

Yeh'd think that 'e was simple as a child;
    An' so 'e is, some ways; but, by and by,
While 'e is talkin' churchy-like an' mild,
    Yeh catch a tiny twinkle in 'is eye
    Which gives the office that 'e's pretty fly
To cunnin' lurks. 'E ain't to be beguiled
    With fairy tales. An' when I've seen 'em try
        'E's only smiled.

But, all the same, I did n't want to meet
    'Is 'oly nibs jist then; fer well I knoo,
When I fell up against 'im in the street,
    'E 'ad a little job fer me to do.
    Fer I 'ad gathered up a tip or two
In Spadgers, where 'is rev'rince 'as 'is beat,
    Tryin' to make that Gorfergotten crew
        'Olesome an' sweet.

"Young friend," 'e sez, "I am beset by foes.
    The Church," 'e sez, "is in a quandary."
An' then 'e takes an' spills out all 'is woes,
    An' 'ints that this 'ere job is up to me.
    "Yer aid—per'aps yer strong right arm," sez 'e,
"Is needed if we are to rescue Rose
    From wot base schemes an' wot iniquity
        Gawd only knows."

This is the sorry tale. Rose, sick, an' low
    In funds an' frien's, an' far too proud to beg,
Is gittin' sorely tempted fer to go
    Into the spielin' trade by one Spike Wegg.
    I knoo this Spike uv old; a reel bad egg,
'Oo's easy livin' is to git in tow
    Some country mug, an' pull 'is little leg
        Fer all 'is dough.

A Holy War

A crooked crook is Spike amongst the crooks,
   A rat, 'oo'd come the double on 'is friends;
Flash in 'is ways, but innercint in looks
   Which 'e works well fer 'is un'oly ends.
   "It's 'ard to know," sez Snowy, "why Fate sends
Sich men among us, or why Justice brooks
   Their evil ways, which they but seldom mends—
      Except in books.

"Young friend," 'e sez, "You're known in Spadgers Lane.
   You know their ways. We must seek out this man.
With 'er, pray'r an' persuasion 'ave been vain.
   I've pleaded, but she's bound to 'is vile plan.
   I'd 'ave you treat 'im gently, if you can;
But if you can't, well—I need not explain."
   ('E twinkles 'ere) "I'm growin' partisan;
      I must refrain."

"Do you mean stoush?" I sez. "Fer if yeh do
   I warn yeh that a scrap might put me queer."
"Young friend," sez 'e, "I leave the means to you.
   Far be it from the Church to interfere
   With noble works." But I sez, "Now, look 'ere,
I got a wife at 'ome; you know 'er too.
   Ther's certin things I never could make clear
      If once she knoo.

"I got a wife," I sez, "an' loves 'er well,
   Like I loves peace an' quite. An' if I goes
Down into Spadgers, raisin' merry 'ell,
   Breakin' the peace an' things account uv Rose,
   Where that might land me goodness only knows.
'Ow women sees these things no man can tell.
   I've done with stoush," I sez. " 'Ard knocks an' blows
      'Ave took a spell.

Rose of Spadgers

"I've done with stoush," I sez. But in some place
    Deep in me 'eart a voice begun to sing;
A lurin' little voice, with motives base . . . .
    It's ten long years since I was in a ring,
    Ten years since I gave that left 'ook a swing,
Ten weary years since I pushed in a face;
    An' 'ere's a chance to 'ave a little fling
        With no disgrace.

"Stoush? Stoush, young friend?" 'e sez. "Where 'ave I 'eard
    That term? I gather it refers to strife.
But there," 'e sez, "why quarrel with a word?
    As you 'ave said, indeed I know yer wife;
    An' should she 'ear you went where vice is rife
To battle fer the right—But it's absurd
    To look fer gallantry in modrin life.
        It's a rare bird.

"Young friend," 'e sez. An' quicker than a wink
    'Is twinklin' eyes grew sudden very grave.
"Young friend," 'e sez, "I know jist wot yeh think
    Uv 'ow us parsons blather an' be'ave.
    But I 'ave 'ere a woman's soul to save—
A lonely woman, tremblin' on the brink
    Uv black perdition, blacker than the grave.
        An' she must sink.

"Yes, she must sink," 'e sez. "For I 'ave done
    All that a man uv my poor parts can do.
An' I 'ave failed! There was not anyone
    That I could turn to, till I met with you.
    But now *that* 'ope 'as gone—an' 'er 'ope too."
" 'Old on," I sez. "Just let me think for one
    Brief 'arf-a-mo. I'd love a crack or two
        At this flash gun."

A Holy War

I thinks that fast I feels me brain-cells whirl,
    An' reckons up me chances in the game.
I thinks uv Ginger Mick, an' uv 'is girl
    'Eadin' for 'ell—an' I am part to blame.
    I thinks about Doreen an' uv me shame
When I git 'ome .... "Aw, give the game a twirl!"
    Sez that small voice inside. "Don't be a tame,
        Unsportin' churl!"

"Righto," I sez (an' turns me back on doubt)
    "I'm with yeh, parson. I go down to-night
To Spadgers, an' jist looks this Spike Wegg out."
    "Young friend," 'e sez, "be sure you've chosen right.
    Remember, I do not desire a fight.
But if——" "Now don't you fret" I sez, "about
    No vi'lince. If I'm forced, it will be quite
        A friendly clout."

"Young friend" 'e sez, "if you go, I go too.
    Maybe, by counsel, I may yet injuce
This evil man——" "It ain't no game for you,"
    I argues with 'im. But it ain't no use.
    "I go!" 'e sez, an' won't take no ixcuse.
So that's all fixed. An' us crusaders two
    Goes down to-night to Spadgers, to cut loose
        Till all is blue.

'Ow can Doreen make trouble or git sore?
    (Already I can 'ear 'er scold an' sob)
But this ain't stoushin'. It's a 'oly war!
    The blessin' uv the Church is on the job.
    I'm a church-worker, with full leaf to lob
A sacrid left on Spike Wegg's wicked jor.
    Jist let me! Once! An' after, s'elp me bob,
        Never no more!

Nocturne

I'M standin' at the corner uv the Lane—
   The Lane called Spadgers—waiting fer 'is jills.
The night's come chilly, an' a drizzlin' rain
    Falls steady where a near-by street lamp spills
A gashly yeller light on stones all wet,
An' makes the darkest corners darker yet.

Them darkest corners! 'Struth! Wot ain't I 'eard
    Uv dark deeds done there in the olden days,
When crooks inticed some silly sozzled bird
    Upstage, an' dealt with 'im in unkind ways—
Bashed 'im with bottles, woodened 'im with boots.
Spadgers was rood to flush an' festive coots.

If you are flush in Spadgers, 'tain't good form
    To git too festive, if you valyer thrift.
To flash yer gilt an' go the pace too warm
    Might make the Lane regard yeh as a gift.
Ther's nothin' loose they're likely to ferget;
An' all yeh've left is 'eadache an' regret.

Lestwise, that's 'ow it used to be. They say
    The Lane's reformed, an' took to honest trade.
An' so yeh'd think, to see it uv a day,
    All prim an' proper. But when ev'nin's shade
Comes down, an' fools as stacks uv beans to spill,
Why, 'umin nacher's 'umin nacher still.

Nocturne

Don't git me wrong. An' jist in case you might
    Misjudge the gents 'oo plys their callin' there,
In Spadgers darkest corners uv a night,
    Wot time a shikkered mug 'as gonce to spare,
I'd jist ixplain they takes their point uv view
Frum diff'rint angles to sich birds as you.

F'rinstance, s'posin' blokes like me an' you
    ('Oo *is* raspectabil, I 'ope) should see
Some prodigal all 'eadin' fer to do
    A one-ack "Road to Ruin" tragedy,
Would we jist let 'im flop before our eyes
Or, bein' decint 'umins, put 'im wise?

Would we not try to 'alt the wayward feet
    Uv this 'ere errin' brother with a word
Before 'is moril knock-out was complete?
    O' course we would. Advice is cheap, I've 'eard.
When sinners miss the step ther's few men ain't
Itchin' like 'ell to preach, an' be a saint.

Well, s'pose again, the Lane should see a bloke
    Dead keen to splash around 'is surplis wealth
On rapid livin' till 'e's bust an' broke
    An' rooned in repitation an' in 'ealth,
Do they tork empty words, an' let 'im go,
Jist for a chance to say, "I tole yeh so!"

Not them. They say, " 'Ere is a wasteful coot
    'Oo will be sorry ere tamorrer's sun."
Per meejim, then, uv bottle or uv boot
    They learn 'im wisdom, an' 'is sinful fun
Is ended. An', for quick results, their style
'As all yer preachin' beaten be a mile.

Rose of Spadgers

Quick-action missionaries, you might say.
    When they sees some stray sheep inclined to roam
An' chuck 'is 'ealth an' character away,
    They takes stern measures for to lead 'im 'ome.
An', if they reaps some profits at the game,
Well, 'oo are me an' you to sling 'em blame?

I'm standin' at the corner uv the Lane
    Toyin' with sich thorts idly, when I spys
A furtive coot come sloushin' through the rain
    An' stop to size me up with sidelong eyes.
An' then 'e chats me, with the punkest tale
That ever got a bad man into jail.

I s'pose me face ain't clear in that 'arf-dark,
    Or else 'e was near-sighted. An' I s'pose
I mighter seemed to 'im a easy mark—
    Me in me farmer's 'at an' country clo'es.
But, strike, it 'urt me pride to think that 'e
Would try to ring that old, old dope on me.

On me! 'Is make-up fairly yelled 'is trade,
    Brandin' 'im plain a low-down city gun.
The simple country mug was never made
    'Oo'd wear sich duds. It was all overdone:
'Is moleskin pants, 'is carpet-bag, 'is beard—
Like some cheap stage comeejin 'e appeared.

"Hey, mate," 'e w'ispers. "Could yeh do a bloke
    A little favor? Listen—on the square—
I've done me tin. I'm bottle-green, dead broke,
    An' can't git 'ome. I 'aven't got me fare.
But 'ere's me watch—reel gold—belong to Dad.
Lend us a fiver on it, will yeh, lad?"

A reel gold watch! Oh, 'elp! They worked that lay
    When I was jist a barefoot kid. 'Twas old
When cheap-Jacks sweated for their 'ard-earned pay
    At country shows. I knoo the sort of gold—
Priced in the brumy shops four an' a zac;
An' 'fore you git' 'em 'ome the gold's gone black.

"Send I may live!" I sez. "You got a nerve!
    That tale's got w'iskers longer than your own.
A slice of cold, 'ard quod's wot you deserve
    For springin' duds like that! Lea' me alone;
An' try some kindergarten with that lurk.
A man's a right to crack you! Aw, git work!"

But 'e won't take a 'int nor 'old 'is jaw,
    This amacher in crime with brums to sell,
But breasts right up to me an' starts to paw.
    Now, likewise, that's a game I know too well:
Pawin' with one 'and while the other dips
Into yer—"Back!" I yell, an' come to grips.

I grab 'im be the throat an' shake 'im good,
    Ixpectin' 'is fake w'iskers to come loose.
"A rotten way to earn yer livli'ood!"
    I growl ... 'E grunts ... 'Is face is goin' puce.
"You imitation crook!" I sez agen.
"Wot do yeh mean by swin'lin' honest men?"

I shake 'im 'ard once more. "The first John 'Op
    That comes," I sez, "can 'ave you for a gift!"
Me late idears uv thugs 'as all gone flop:
    Me point uv view, some'ow,' 'as seemed to shift;
'Tain't philosophic, like it used to be,
Now someone's took a fly at thuggin' me.

'E's gurglin' nicely—clawin' at the air.
    "You pest!" I sez. "You scum! You sewer rat!
Why can't yeh earn yer livin' on the square,
    An' be raspectabil?" I'm gettin' that
Right-thinkin' I am all one virchus glow.
"Leg-gug-" 'e gurgles, musical. "Leggo!"

We made a pretty pitcher standin' there—
    Nocturne, as artists sez. I felt, some'ow,
That, underneath the yeller lamp-light's glare,
    'Is upturned face (It's gittin' purple now)
Was sumpthin' painters would admire no end ....
Then a sharp voice be'ind me yelps, "Young friend!"

"Young friend," 'e sez, su'prised, "wot—wot's amiss?
    Yes; my ole parson friend. I drops the crook.
"You are mistook, young friend," 'e sez; "for this
    Is not the man for 'oo we've come to look."
Then 'e stares closer at the gaspin' gun.
"Why! Bless me 'eart!" 'e chirps. "It's Daniel Dunn!"

"It's Mister Dunn," 'e sez, "from Bungaroo!
    My farmer friend!" ('Ere was a flamin' mess!)
"Is this 'ere coot," I arsts, "well knowed to you?"
    The parson takes another gig. "Why, yes.
You're Mister Dunn?" An' Whiskers answers, "Ick!"
I notice then that Daniel's partly shick.

A dinkum farmer! Strike! I'm in all wrong!
    "Sorry," I sez. "My fault. 'Ow could I tell?
I acted nervis when 'e come along.
    But, if you're sure, it might be jist as well
To intrajuice us, 'coz it would appear
Ther's been some slight misun'erstandin' 'ere."

Then Snowy twinkles, an' pufforms the rite.
   (W'iskers 'as got 'is wind back with the spell)
" 'Appy to meet yeh, sir," 'e sez, perlite.
   "Don't mention it," sez me. "I 'ope you're well?"
"Not bad, consid'rin'," 'e remarks (an' takes
Me 'and) "the narsty weather." So we shakes.

Then I ixplain; an' W'iskers spills 'is tale—
   The old yarn uv the mug 'oo puts 'is trust
In nice new city frien's uv 'is 'oo fail
   To keep appointments, an' 'e wakes up bust.
We spring a overdraft, an' leave 'im there,
Bristlin' with gratichood in every 'air.

"Jist goes to show," I sez to Snowy then.
   "If I 'ad not—well, not detained yer friend,
'E mighter fallen in with reel rough men
   An' ended up all narsty in the end.
I feel to-night, some'ow, me luck's dead in,
An' I could give some crook a rotten spin."

"Young friend," sez Snowy, solemn, "should we meet
   This man we seek to-night—this feller Wegg,
Try to be diplermatic an' discreet;
   Reason with 'im; no vi'lince, friend, I beg."
"Wot? Vi'lince? Me?" I chirps. (I'm bublin' now)
"Wot do yeh know 'bout that? I'll *kiss* the cow!"

The Crusaders

"PETER the 'Ermit was a 'oly bloke,"
    The parson sez, "wot chivvied coves to war."
"Too right," I chips. "I've 'eard that yarn before."
"Brave knights sprung straight to arms where'er 'e spoke."
"Sure thing," sez I. "It muster been no joke
    Tinnin' yer frame in them dead days uv yore
    Before yeh starts to tap a foeman's gore."

"Peter the 'Ermit was a man inspired,"
    The parson sez. We're moochin' up the Lane,
    Snoopin' around for news we might obtain
Uv this Spike Wegg, the man 'oo I am 'ired
To snatch by 'ook or crook, jist as required
    By circs, frum out the sev'ril sins wot stain
    'Is wicked soul. I 'ope me meanin's plain.

"Peter the 'Ermit," says the parson, "saw
    No 'arm in vi'lince when the cause was just.
    While 'e deplored, no doubt, the fightin' lust,
'E preached——" " 'Old on," I sez. " 'Ere comes the Law:
'Ere's Brannigan, the cop. Pos'pone the jaw
    Till we confer. I got idears 'e must
    Keep track uv Spike; if 'e toils fer 'is crust."

"Spike Wegg?" growls Brannigan. "I know that bloke;
    An' 'e's the one sweet soul I long to see.
    That shrinkin' vi'lit 'ates publicity
Jist now," sez Brannigan. "Spike Wegg's in smoke.
Oh, jist concerns a cove 'e tried to croak.
    'E's snug in some joint round about, maybe.
    If you should meet, remember 'im to me."

The Crusaders

The cop passed on. "Peter the 'Ermit was
    A ri'chus man" the parson sez, "wot knoo——"
    " 'Old 'ard! I begs. "Jist for a hour or two
I wouldn't go an' nurse sich thorts, becoz
Too much soul-ferritin' might put the moz
    On this 'ere expedition. I'll 'elp you
    To search our conscience when the job is through.

"I know yer doubts," I sez, "an' 'ow you 'ate
    The thorts uv stoush, an' 'old 'ard blows in dread.
    But Pete the 'Ermit's been a long time dead.
'E'll keep. But we are in the 'ands uv Fate,
An' 'oly spruikers uv a ancient date
    Don't 'elp. I quite agrees with all you've said
    But——" "Say no more," 'e answers. "Lead ahead."

"But, all the same," 'e sez, "I want no fight."
    "Right 'ere, be'ind this 'oardin'," I replies,
    "A two-up school's in session. If we spies
About a bit, there is a chance we might
Git news——" Jist then the spotter comes to light.
    I word 'im gentle, with some 'asty lies:
    I'm seekin' Spike. See? Can 'e put me wise?

"Spike Wegg?" (At first 'e only twigs meself)
    " 'E's gone——" ('E spots the parson standin' by)
    A cold, 'ard glimmer comes in 'is fish eye:
" 'Ere! Wot's the game? 'e yelps. "Are you a shelf?"
" 'Ave sense!" I larfs. "I got a bit uv pelf,
    An' thort I'd like to take a little fly——"
    "Buzz orf!" 'e orders. So we done a guy.

"Blank number one," I sez. The parson sighed.
    "Joshuer fought, an' never seemed to shrink——"
"Now, look," I tells 'im. "Honest. Don't you think
Them Bible blokes 'oo've 'ad their day an' died
Is best fergot until we're 'ome an' dried?
    Now, up the street 'ere, is a little sink
    Uv sin that does a traffic in strong drink."

"Sly grog?" 'e arsts. But I sez, " 'Ush! This place
    Is kep' by Mother Weems, 'oo's sof', blue eye
    An' snow white 'air would make yeh 'shamed an' shy
To brand 'er name with any sich disgrace.
'Er kind, sweet smile, 'er innercint ole face
    Beams like a blessin'. Still, we'll 'ave a try
    To word the dear ole dame, an' pump 'er dry.

'Is nibs stands in the shadders while I knock.
    Mother unlocks the door, an' smiles, an' peers
    Into me face. She wears 'er three score years
Reel sweet in lacy cap an' neat black frock.
Then: "Bill;" she cries. "You've give me quite a shock!
    Why, dearie, I ain't seen you for long years.
    Come in." 'Er kind ole eyes seem close to tears.

"Dearie, come in," she chirps. But I pretend
    I'm on reel urgent biz. I got to 'aste.
    "Jist for ole times," she pleads. "One little taste."
"I can't," I sez. "I'm lookin' for a friend,
Spike Wegg, for 'oo I've certin news no end
    Important; an' I got no time to waste."
    "Wot? Spike?" she sez. "I 'ear 'e's bein' chased.

" 'E's bein' chased," she sez, "by D's, I've 'eard."
   "Too true," I owns. " 'E's got no time to lose."
   "Well, maybe, if you was to try Ah Foo's—
The privit room——" Then, as 'is rev'rince stirred,
She seen 'is choker. " 'Oo the 'ell's this bird?
   Is this a frame?" she shrieks.... Without adoos,
   We slap the pavemint with four 'asty shoes.

But, as along the sloppy lane we race,
   'Er 'ot words tumble after in a flood:
   "You pimps! You dirty swine! I'll 'ave yer blood!"
" 'Eavings!" the parson gasps. "With that sweet face!"
" 'Er words," I answer, "do seem outer place."
   "Vile words, that I 'ave scarce 'arf understud."
   Sez Snowy, sloshin' in a pool uv mud.

We reach Ah Foo's. "Now, 'ere," I sez, "is where
   You stop outside. Twice you 'ave put me queer
   It's a lone 'and I mean to play in 'ere.
You 'ang around an' breathe the 'olesome air."
"Young friend," 'e sez. "I go with you in there.
   I've led you into this. Why should I fear
   The danger? 'Tis me jooty to be near."

Snowy's a game un! I lob in the shop,
   The parson paddin' after on the floor.
   Ah Foo looks up. "Not there!" 'e squeaks. "Wha' for?"
But we sail past the Chow without a stop,
Straight for the little crib up near the top
   That I knoo well in sinful days uv yore....
   I turn the knob; an' sling aside the door.

Beside a table, fearin' 'arm from none,
    Spike an' another bloke is teet-ah-teet.
    Quick on the knock, Spike Wegg jumps to 'is feet
An' jerks a 'and be'ind 'im for 'is gun.
I rush 'im, grab a chair up as I run,
    A' swing it with a aim that ain't too neat.
    Spike ducks aside; an', with a bump, we meet.

An' then we mix it. Strife an' merry 'ell
    Breaks loose a treat, an' things git movin' fast.
    An', as a Chinee jar goes crashin' past,
'Igh o'er the din I 'ears the parson's yell:
"Hit! Hit 'im 'ard, young friend! Chastise 'im well!
    Hit 'im!" ... The 'oly war is in full blast;
    An' Pete the 'Ermit's come to light at last.

"'Ave a 'Eart!"

"'ERE! 'Ave a 'eart!" 'e sez. "Why, love a duck!
   A 'uman bein' ain't a choppin' block!
There ain't no call fer you to go an' chuck
   A man about when 'e 'as took the knock.
Gaw! Do yeh want to bust 'im all apart?
              'Ere! 'Ave a 'eart!

"Aw, 'ave a 'eart!" 'e weeps. "A fight's a fight;
   But, strike me bandy, this is bloody war!
It's murder! An' you got no blasted right
   To arst a 'uman man to come fer more.
'E 'ad no chance with you right frum the start.
              Aw, 'ave a 'eart!

"Yeh've pulped 'is dile," 'e whines; "yeh've pinched 'is gun;
   Yeh've bunged 'is eye 'an bashed in 'arf 'is teeth.
'Struth! Ain't yeh satisfied with wot yeh've done?
   Or are you out to fit 'im fer a wreath?
The man's 'arf dead a'ready! Wot's yer dart?
              Say, 'ave a 'eart!"

I never did 'ear sich a bloke to squeal
   About a trifle. This 'ere pal uv Spike's
Don't seem to 'ave the stummick fer a deal
   Uv solid stoush: rough work don't soot 'is likes.
'E ain't done much but blather frum the start,
            " 'Ere 'ave a 'eart!"

Rose of Spadgers

A rat-face coot 'e is, with rat-like nerves
    That's got all jangled with ixceedin' fright,
While I am 'andin' Spike wot 'e deserves.
    But twice 'e tried to trip me in the fight,
The little skunk, now sobbing like a tart,
        "Aw, 'ave a 'eart!"

This 'ere's the pretty pitcher in Ah Foo's
    Back privit room: Spike Wegg, well on the floor,
Is bleedin' pretty, with a bonzer bruise
    Paintin' one eye, an' 'arf 'is clobber tore.
While me, the conq'rin 'ero, stan's above
        'Owlin' me love.

The rat-face mutt is dancin' up and down;
    Ah Foo is singin' jazz in raw Chinee;
The parson's starin' at me with a frown,
    As if 'e thort sich things could never be;
An' I'm some bloke 'e's but 'arf rekernised.
        'E's 'ipnertised.

Foo's furniture is scattered any'ow,
    Artistic like, in bits about the floor.
An' 'arf a dozen blokes, drawn by the row,
    Nosey but nervis, 'overs near the door.
I ain't no pitcher orf no chocklit box.
        I've took some knocks.

I ain't no pitcher. But—O Glory!—*But*
    Ther's dicky-birds awarblin' in me soul!
To think that I ain't lost that upper-cut!
    An' my left-'ook's still with me, good an' whole.
I feared me punch was dead; but I was wrong.
        Me 'eart's all song!

"'Ave a 'Eart!"

Then, as Spike makes a move, I raise me mits
    Fearin' a foul; an' Rat-face does 'is block.
'E loosens up a string uv epi-tits
    That seem to jolt the parson with a shock.
Filthy an' free they was, make no mistakes.
        Then Snowy wakes.

All through the fight 'e 'ad seemed kind uv dazed,
    Ubsorbin' it like some saint in a dream.
But now 'e straightened up, 'is ole eyes blazed
    An', as the filth flowed in a red-'ot stream,
'Is voice blew in like cool winds frum the south:
        "Shut that foul mouth!"

"Shut your vile mouth, or, by the Lord!—" 'Is 'and
    Went up, an' there was anger on 'is face.
But Rat-face ducked. 'E weren't the man to stand
    Agin that figger uv avengin' grace.
Ducked, or 'e might uv stopped one 'oly smite
        Frum Snowy's right.

"Young friend," 'E turns to me. An' then I 'ear
    A yell: "The cops! The cops is in the Lane!"
"Parson," I sez, "we are de tropp, I fear.
    Mid 'appier scenes I'll vencher to ixplain.
'Ang to me 'and, 'an wave no fond farewell;
        But run like 'ell!"

Some say wrong livin' reaps no good reward.
    Well, I dunno. If I 'ad not cut loose
In Spadgers, in them days long, long deplored,
    'Ow could I knowed the run uv Foo's caboose?
That back-way entrance, used fer Chiner's friends'
        Un'oly ends.

Rose of Spadgers

Out by a green door; down a flight uv stairs;
    Along a passige; up another flight;
Through 'arf a dozen rooms, broadcastin' scares
    To twenty yellow men, pea-green with fright;
Me an' the parson, through that 'eathen land,
            Trips 'and in 'and.

Out uv dark corners, voices 'ere an' there
    Break sudden with a jabberin' sing-song,
Like magpies flutin' on the mornin' air.
    We pays no 'eed to them, but plug along,
Twistin' an' turnin' through them secret ways,
            Like in a maze.

I bust a bolted door. The parson gasps:
    The air inside is 'eavy with the drug.
A fat Chow goggles at the broken hasps;
    Another dreams un'eedin' on a rug.
Out by the other door—past piles uv fruit—
            'Ow we did scoot!

Red lanterns—lacquer-work—brass pots—strange smells—
    Silk curtains—slippers—baskets—ginger-jars—
A squealin' Chinee fiddle—tinklin' bells—
    Queer works uv art—filth—fowls—ducks—iron bars
To winders—All pass by us in a stream,
            Like 'twuz a dream.

Down to a cellar; up agen, an' out—
    Bananers—brandy jars—we rush pell-mell,
Turnin' to left, to right, then round about
    (The parson, after, said it seemed like 'ell)
Through one last orful pong, then up a stair
            Into clean air.

"'Ave a 'Eart!"

We're in a little yard; no thing to stop
    Our flight to freedom but a fence. "Now, jump!"
I grab 'is rev'rince, 'eaves 'im to the top,
    An' bungs me own frame over with a bump.
"Dam!" sez the parson—or it sounded so.
        But I dunno.

Seems that 'is coat got 'itched up on a nail.
    'E jerks it free an' gently comes to earth.
"Peter the 'ermit's 'home!" I sez. "All 'ail!"
    An' makes punk noises indicatin' mirth.
The parson, 'e walks on, as still as death.
        Seems out o' breath.

I walk beside 'im; but 'e sez no word.
    To put it straight, I'm feelin' pretty mean—
Feelin' a bit ashamed uv wot's occurred—
    But still, I never planned to 'ave no scene
With Spike. I did n't start the flamin' row,
        Not any'ow.

I tells 'im so. But still 'e never spoke.
    I arsts 'im 'ow else could the thing be done.
I tells 'im straight I'd let no flamin' bloke
    Take pot shots at me with no flamin' gun.
'E stops, an' pats me shoulder with 'is 'and:
        "I understand.

"Young friend." 'Is face is orful stern an' grave.
    "The brawl was not your seekin', we'll suppose.
But does it 'elp this girl we wish to save?
    'Ow can sich mad brutality serve Rose?
May be, in anger, you fergot, young friend,
        Our Christian end?"

Rose of Spadgers

"Not on yer life!" I tells 'im. "Spike's in soak,
    Whether the cops 'ave got 'im now or not.
An' that removes one interferin' bloke
    Wot 'ad a mind to queer our 'oly plot.
Tomorrer we'll find Rose, an' work good works
              With gentler lurks."

"Gentler?" 'e sez. "I 'ope so." Still 'e's grave.
    The ways uv 'Eaven's strange," 'e sez, "an' yours
Is stranger still. Yet all may work to save
    One strugglin' soul, if 'Eaven's grace endures."
'E's dreadful solemn. "I must own I feel
              Grieved a great deal.

"Your face," 'e sez, "is very badly cut—"
    "Now, look," I chips. " 'Old on. Let's git this right.
'Oo was it tried to stoush that rat-face mutt?
    'Oo was it barracked for me in the fight?
'Oo was it used that word uv evul sense
              Up on that fence?"

"Young friend!" . . . Indignant? 'Struth! I see 'im try
    To keep reel stern. But soon I rekernise
The little twinkle stealin' in 'is eye,
    That won't keep out, no matter 'ow 'e tries.
An' then—'is twitchin' lips smile wide apart:
              "Aw, 'ave a 'eart!"

Rose

"AH, wot's the use?" she sez. "Lea' me alone!
  Why can't I go to 'ell in my own way?
I never arst you 'ere to mag an' moan,
    Nor yet," she sez, "to pray.
I'll take wot's comin' an' whine no excuse.
    So wot's the use?

"Me life's me own!" she sez. "You got a nerve—
    You two—to interfere in my affairs.
Git out an' give advise where it may serve:
    Stay 'ome an' bleat yer pray'rs.
Did I come pleadin' for yer pity? No!
    Well, why not go?"

Pride! Dilly pride an' down-an'-out despair:
    When them two meet there's somethin' got to break.
I got that way, to see 'er sittin' there,
    I felt like I could take
That 'arf-starved frame uv 'er's by might an' main,
    An' shake 'er sane.

That's 'ow it is when me an' parson roam
    Down to the paradise wot Spadgers knows,
To find the 'ovel that she calls 'er 'ome,
    An' 'ave a word with Rose.
Ingagin' 'igh-strung cliners in dispute
    Ain't my long suit.

Rose of Spadgers

"Huh! Rescue work!" she sneers. 'Er eyes is bright;
    'Er voice is 'ard. "I'm a deservin' case.
Me? Fancy! Don't I look a pretty sight
    To come to savin' grace?
Pity the sinner—Aw, don't come that trick!
        It makes me sick!"

'Isterical she was, or nearly so:
    Too little grub, an' too much time to fret—
Ingrowin' grouch sich as few women know,
    Or want to know—an' yet,
When I glance at the parson, there I see
        Raw misery.

I've knowed ole Snowy since the days uv old;
    Yet never 'ad I got so close to see
A world-wise man 'oo's 'eart is all pure gold
    An' 'uman charity.
For, all that girl was suff'rin', well I knoo,
        'E suffered too.

"My child," 'e sez, "I don't come 'ere to preach.
    You're a good girl; an' when—" " 'Oo sez I ain't?
'Oo sez I ain't?" 'Er voice is near a screech.
    "I'm no hymn-singin' saint;
But you're a bit too previous given' me
        This third degree."

An' then she starts to laugh. I'd 'ate to see
    A woman laugh or look like that again.
She's in the dinkum 'igh-strikes now; to me
    That's showin' pretty plain.
She's like a torchered thing—'arf crazy—wild ....
        "Take thort, my child.

Rose

"Take thort," the parson sez. "I only ask
    Before you risk all for a life uv crime
You'll 'esitate. Is that too 'ard to task?
    May there not come a time—"
"Time? Yes," I chips. "You'll git *that* fer yer pains.
        Ar, brush yer brains!"

The parson sighs. "This man," 'e sez, "this Wegg
    'Oo dazzles you with tork uv gains frum sin—
Is 'e dependable? Think well, I beg—"
    "Beg nothin'," I chips in.
"To beg decoy ducks ain't the proper tack.
        She wants a smack!"

The parson groans. "I've offered you," 'e starts.
    "Offer 'er nothin'! Can't you pick 'er like?
No dinkum 'elp is any good to tarts
    'Oo'd fall fer sich as Spike.
She's short uv grit to battle on 'er own.
        An' stand alone."

That done it. If I'd let the parson gone
    An' come the mild an' gentle, sure enough,
She'd 'ad the willies. When the dames take on,
    The game's to treat 'em rough.
That's wot I 'eard. It woke Rose up, all right,
        An' full uv fight.

"Alone?" she sez. "I've stood alone, Gawd knows!
    Alone an' honest, battlin' on the square.
An' now—Oh, damn your charity! I've chose!
    I'm down; an' I don't care.
I'm fer the easy life an' pretty clo'es.
        That's that!" sez Rose.

Rose of Spadgers

The cause looks blue. Wot more was to be said?
    An' then, all on me own, I weaves right there
The bright idear wot after bowed me 'ead
    In sorrer an' despair.
I didn't ort to be let out alone.
        That much I own.

"Ah, well," I sez, resigned, "if that's the life,
    It's no use sayin' wot I come to say.
Which was," I sez, "a message frum me wife
    Arstin' you 'ome to stay."
"Your wife?" I nods. "If you 'ad cared to come."
        She seems struck dumb.

"Your wife?" she sez. "Wot does she know uv me?"
    Then pride an' 'er suspicions makes 'er flare:
"Is this more pretty schemes fer charity?
    Why should she arst me there?"
"Why? Well, you ort to know," I answer, quick.
        "Account uv Mick."

Down on 'er folded arms 'er 'ead went, flop.
    At larst our 'oly cause is won, I know.
She sobbed until I thort she'd never stop:
    It 'urt to see 'er so;
Yet I felt glad the way I'd worked me nob—
        An' let 'er sob.

"That's tore it," I remarks be'ind me 'and.
    The parson nods. 'E's smilin' now all gay.
Ten minutes later, an' the 'ole thing's planned
    Fer Rose's 'oliday.
We put the acid on, an' scold an' tease
        Till she agrees.

Once we're outside the parson takes me 'and.
    "Without your 'elp, your wit, we would 'ave failed."
"Aw, easy work," I answer, feelin' grand,
    Like some ole knight, tin-mailed.
Then, sudden, like a load uv punchered tyres,
        Me pride ixpires.

"Young friend," 'e starts.... "No, not too young; but old—
    Old with the cares," I sez, "uv fambly life.
This might 'ave been dead right when knights was bold;
    But wot about me wife?
She don't know nothin'! I 'ave done me dash
        Through actin' rash."

"A trifle!" sez 'is rev'rince. "Tut!" sez 'e.
    "I'll promise you fair sailin' with Doreen."
" 'Tain't that so much," I sez, "wot troubles me."
    "Trouble? Wot you mean?"
I grins at 'im. "Me conscience," I reply.
        "I've tole a lie!"

The Knight's Return

THE conq'rin' 'ero! Me? Yes, I don't think.
   This mornin' when I catch the train fer 'ome,
It's far more like a walloped pup I slink
   To kennel, with resolves no more to roam.
Crusades is orf. I'm fer the simple life,
    'Ome with me trustin' wife
        All safe frum strife.

I've read uv knights returnin' full uv gyp,
   Back to the bewchus lady in the tower.
They never seemed to git dumestic pip
   In them brave days when knight'ood was in flower.
But times is changed; an' 'usbands 'as to 'eed;
    Fer knight'ood's run to seed;
        It 'as indeed.

Snowy, the parson, came to say farewell.
   "Young friend," 'e sez, "You've did a Christian ack—
A noble deed that you'll be glad to tell
   An' boast uv to yer wife when you git back."
"Too true," I sez, reel chirpy, "She'll be proud,
    I'll blab it to the crowd—
        If I'm allowed."

"Good-bye! Good luck!" 'e sez. "I'll see to Rose,
   Make yer mind easy. Ierdine yer face.
Bless yeh! Good luck, young friend!" An' orf we goes—
   Me an' me conscience arguin' the case.
An', as we pick up speed an' race along,
    The rails make up a song:
        "Yer in all wrong!"

The Knight's Return

"Yer in all wrong! Yer in all wrong! Yeh blob!
   Why did yeh want to go an' 'unt fer Spike?
Yer in all wrong! Becoz yeh liked the job.
   That's wot. An' don't pretend yeh did n't like.
Yer in all wrong! Wot will yeh tell Doreen?
   Yeh'll 'ate to 'ave a scene.
            Don't yeh feel mean?"

Gawstruth I do! It ain't so much the fack
   That I 'ave soiled me soul be breakin' trust;
But 'ere's me lip swole up an' one eye black
   An' all me map in gen'ril bunged an' bust.
'Ow can a 'omin 'usband 'ave the neck
   To 'arf ixplain that wreck
            With self respeck?

An' then ther's Rose. Wot 'ave I got to say
   About that invite? 'Struth! Doreen an' Rose!
Arstin' strange dames (comparative) to stay
   Ain't done since knights 'ad buttons to their clo'es.
Wot's after, if I do pull orf the coop?
   I feel me spirits droop.
            I'm in the soup!

'Longside the line, a 'undred 'omes I see
   Uv 'appy 'usbands, peaceful with their wives.
They don't go out knight-erratin', like me,
   An' leadin' vi'lint, complicated lives.
They stops at 'ome, an' side-steps lash, to find
   Conjoojil pleasures kind,
            An' peace uv mind.

Rose of Spadgers

Two stations on, a w'iskered coot gits in
    I seem to sort uv rekernise, some'ow.
But all at once I place 'im, an' I grin.
    But 'e don't jerry; 'e's stone sober now.
It's 'im I scragged in Spadgers—number one—
    The late suspected gun.
              It's Danny Dunn.

"Sold that watch yet, ole cobber?" I remarks.
    'E grabs 'is bag, an' views me battered dile,
With sudden fears uv spielers an' their larks.
    But I ixplain, an' 'e digs up a smile.
"Ah, yes," 'e drawls. "We met two nights ago.
    But I was—well, you know—
              Well—jist so-so."

'E pipes me dile again, then stammers out,
    "I'm sorry, sonny. Stone the crows! It's sad
To see yer face so orful cut about.
    I never thort I walloped you so bad.
I'm sorry lad, that we should come to blows.
    Black eye? An' wot a nose!
              Oh, stone the crows!

I ease 'is guilty mind about me phiz,
    An' we're good cobbers in a 'arf a tick.
Then 'e wades in an' tells me 'oo 'e is.
    ('E ain't a bad old coot when 'e ain't shick)
"I ain't dead broke," 'e sez. "That night, yeh know,
    I was cleaned out uv dough,
              An'—well—so-so."

The Knight's Return

Lookin' fer land 'e is; an' 'as 'is eye
   Upon a little farm jist close to me.
If 'e decides to take it by-an'-by,
   "Why stone the crows! I'll look yous up," sez 'e.
"I need some friends: I ain't got wife nor chick;
   An' yous will like me quick—
        When I ain't shick."

I leave 'im tork. Me own affairs won't let
   Me pay much 'eed to all 'e 'as to say.
But, while 'e's spountin', sudden like I get
   A bright idear that brings one 'opeful ray.
One thing I 'eard pertickler while 'e spoke:
   'E is a single bloke.
        I lets that soak.

But later on I wished 'e'd sling 'is mag.
   The nearer 'ome I get the worse I feel;
The worse I feel, the more I chew the rag;
   The more I chew the rag, this crooked deal
I've served Doreen looks black an' blacker yet.
   I worry till I get.
        All one cold sweat.

I walk 'ome frum the station, thinkin' 'ard.
   Wot can I tell me wife? Gawstruth! I been
Eight long years wed, an' never 'ad to guard
   Me tongue before. Wot can I tell Doreen?
An' there she's waitin' 'arf ways down our hill....
   She takes one look.... "Why! Bill!"
        I stands stock still.

Rose of Spadgers

"Oh, yes, me face," I larfs. "O' course. Me face.
    I clean fergot. I—well—to tell the truth,
I—Don't look scared—I—Oh, it's no disgrace.
    That dentist. Yes, yes! Pullin' out me tooth.
Reel butcher. Nearly frachered both me jors.
    Yes, dear, lets go indoors."
              (Wow! 'Oly wars!)

"Poor Bill! Poor dear! 'E must 'ave been a brute."
    She kisses me fair on me busted lip;
An' all me fears is stilled be that serloot.
    Ar, wot a fool I was to 'ave the pip.
The game is mine before I 'ardly tried.
    Dead easy, 'ow I lied!
           I'm 'ome an' dried.

Yet. .... I dunno. Me triump' don't last long.
    'Twuz low down, some way, 'ow I took 'er in—
Like pinchin' frum a kid. I feel dead wrong.
    The parson calls it "conshusniss uv sin."
It might be; but it's got me worried now;
    An' conshuns is a cow,
           That I'll allow.

Take it frum me. To 'ave a lovin' wife
    Fussin' an' pettin' you, jist through a lie—
Like 'er this ev'nin'—crools all marrid life.
    If you can't look 'er fair bang in the eye
An' feel you've earned that trust frum first to last,
    You're 'eadin' downward fast ...
           But Rose—Oh, blast!

The Also-ran

I KNOW I'm dull, I know I got a brain
   That's only fit fer fertilizin' 'air.
I don't arst fer bokays: I ain't that vain;
   But fair is fair.
An' when yeh think yer somethin' uv a man,
It 'urts to find yourself a also-ran.

'Urts like one thing. To git sent to the pack
   When you 'ave 'ad idears you're ace 'an king
An' all the pitcher cards down to the Jack
   Is like to sting
Yer vanity. I thort I was some use,
An' now I'm valyid as a 'umble dooce.

Don't mind my sulks. I s'pose I 'as swelled 'ead;
   But gittin' snouted ain't wot I expeck.
Aw, they can 'ave it on their own! I'm full
   Up to the neck!
Never no more! I chuck good works right 'ere ...
But lets start frum the start an' git it clear.

I own I used me nut. Fer marriage brings
   Experience to stop yeh actin' rash.
I've missed the step before through rushin' things,
   An' come a crash.
I planned it out all careful frum the start;
Me taticks was a reel fine work uv art.

Rose of Spadgers

Me problem's this: The noos 'as to be broke
    Concernin' Rose. Doreen 'as to be told.
The 'ow an' when that bit of noos is spoke
    I've learnt uv old.
I'm shrood. I wait. I watch me chance to act.
The trick's to know the time an' place exact.

You blokes unmarrid ain't got no idear
    Uv 'ow successful 'usbands works their 'eads.
It's like a feller strugglin' to keep clear
    A thousand threads.
Once let 'em tangle, an' you take the blame.
You're up to putty; an' yeh've lost the game.

I picks a nice, calm, cozy, peaceful night.
    The supper things is washed; the kid's in bed
(I 'elped to wipe the plates) the fire burns bright;
    An' then I led
The tork around to tales uv Ginger Mick,
Cunnin' an' crafty like, an' not too quick.

"Funny," I sez, "that we should mention Mick.
    In town I met that girl—(Wot's 'er name? Rose)
By accident. Poor thing looks orful sick ...
    Well, I suppose
She 'as 'er worries. ... Lost 'er job, yeh know."
Doreen don't take much int'rest. She sez, "Oh?"

"Yes," I goes on; "a bit uv country air
    Is wot she needs. She's very sick——an' low.
She seemed——well——sort uv——'opeless with. ... despair."
    Doreen sez, "Oh?"
It's 'eavy goin'; but I sticks it, grim.
"Poor Mick!" I sez. "I often think uv 'im.

"Poor Mick!" I sez. (Well, any'ow, I mean
    Them words) "If you 'ad seen that girl, my dear,
You'd arst 'er up to stay." "Why," sez Doreen,
    "She's comin' 'ere
On Choosday next." (I jist choke back a shout)
"That's why I got the spare room tidied out."

"She's wot?" ... I can't say more. "Well," sez me wife,
    "Seein' you arst 'er, why all this su'prise?"
Seein' you 'ad a fight, an' risked yer life,
    An' got black eyes,
An' played the 'ero, as the parson says,
You ort to know. I've knowed," she sez, "fer days."

Snowy! To think that parson cove would go
    An' let me down to flounder in the mud,
An' scheme, an' lie, an' work the game reel low,
    To come a thud!
"Yeh mean to say," I arsts, mad as can be,
"Yeh've fixed all this without consultin' me?"

"Yeh mean to say I 'ave n't got the right
    To know wot's goin' on in my own 'ouse?
Yeh mean to say—" "There, Bill," she sez, "keep quite.
    Why should you rouse?
You tole me nothin'. Parson wrote to me;
An' we fixed things without yer 'elp," sez she.

Women! She sits an' tells me this dead cold!
    To think I've worked an' worried till I'm tired,
An' squeezed me brain a treat, jist to be told
    I ain't required!
"You was too modest, Bill, to let me 'ear
About that fight," she sez. "Now, were n't you, dear?"

Rose of Spadgers

Modest? Aw well, I s'pose I am—a bit.
    A feller can't go skitin' all 'is days.
But, spite uv 'er nice way uv takin' it,
    An' all 'er praise
An' that, I got to own I'm feelin' 'urt
Fet to git treated like a bit uv dirt.

Nex' mornin' I ain't feelin' none too good:
    That snub still 'urt. I potter round about;
Then go across to where 'e's choppin' wood
    To 'ave it out
With Wally Free about 'is thievin' cow.
But that pie-faced galoot *won't* 'ave a row.

I'll have the lor on 'im, I tells 'im straight.
    Me fence 'er out? 'E's got to fence 'er in!
The lor sez that. But all the lors I state
    Jist gits a grin.
That's all. 'E grins a sight too much, that bloke.
Clean through the piece, I seem to be the joke.

I know I'm dull. I know me brain's jist meant
    To nourish 'air-roots. But I 'ave me pride.
An' when I toils an' frets, an' then gits sent
    To stand aside,
I know me place: I don't need to be shown.
I'm done! An' they can 'ave it on their own.

A Woman's Way

WOMEN is strange. You take my tip; I'm wise.
    I know enough to know I'll never know
The 'uman female mind, or wot su'prise
    They 'as in store to bring yer boastin' low.
They keep yeh guessing wot they're up to nex',
An' then, odds on, it's wot yeh least expecks.

Take me. I know me wife can twist me round
    'Er little finger. I don't mind that none.
Wot worries me is that I've never found
    Which way I'm gittin' twisted, till its done.
Women is strange. An' yet, I've got to own
I'd make a orful 'ash uv it, alone.

There's this affair uv Rose. I tells yeh straight,
    Suspicious don't describe me state uv mind.
The calm way that Doreen 'as fixed the date
    An' all, looks like there's somethin' else be'ind.
Somethin'—not spite or meanness; don't think that.
Me wife purrs sometimes, but she ain't a cat.

But somethin'. I've got far too wise a nob
    To be took in by 'er airs uv repose.
I know I said I'd chuck the 'ole darn job
    An' leave 'er an' the parson deal with Rose.
But now me mind's uneasy, that's a fack.
I've got to manage things with speshul tack.

Rose of Spadgers

That's 'ow I feel—uneasy—when I drive
    Down to the train. I'm thinkin' as I goes,
There ain't two women, that I know, alive
    More dif'rint than them two—Doreen an' Rose.
'Ow they will mix together I dunno.
It all depends on 'ow I run the show.

Rose looks dead pale. She ain't got much to say
    ('Er few poor bits uv baggage make no load)
She smiles when we shake 'ands, an' sez Good day
    Shy like an' strange; an' as we take the road
Back to the farm, I see 'er look around
Big-eyed, like it's some queer new land she's found.

I springs a joke or two. I'm none too bright
    Meself; but it's a slap-up sort uv day.
Spring's workin' overtime: to left an' right
    Blackwood an' wattle trees is bloomin' gay,
Blotchin' the bonzer green with golden dust;
An' magpies in 'em singin' fit to bust.

I sneak a glance at Rose. I can't look long.
    'Er lips is trem'lin'; tears is in 'er eye.
Then, glad with life, a thrush beefs out a song
    'Longside the road as we go drivin' by.
"Oh, Gawd A'mighty! 'Ark!" I 'ear 'er say,
"An' Spadgers Lane not fifty mile away!"

Not fifty mile away: the frowsy Lane,
    Where only dirt an' dreariness 'as sway,
Where every second tale's a tale uv pain,
    An' devil's doin's blots the night an' day.
But 'ere is thrushes tootin' songs uv praise.
An' golden blossoms lightin' up our ways.

A Woman's Way

I speaks a piece to boost this bonzer spot;
    Tellin' 'er 'ow the neighbour'ood 'as grown,
An' 'ow Dave Brown, jist up the road, 'as got
    Ten ton uv spuds per acre, usin' bone.
She don't seem to be list'nin'. She jist stares,
Like someone dreamin' dreams, or thinkin' pray'rs.

Me yap's a dud. No matter 'ow I try,
    Me conversation ain't the dinkum brand.
I'm 'opin' that she don't bust out an' cry:
    It makes me nervis. But I understand.
Over an' over I can 'ear 'er say,
"An' Spadgers less than fifty mile away!"

We're 'ome at last. Doreen is at the gate.
    I hitch the reins, an' quite the eager pup;
Then 'elp Rose down, an' stand aside an' wait
    To see 'ow them two size each other up.
But quick—like that—two arms 'as greeted warm
The sobbin' girl.... Doreen's run true to form.

" 'Ome on the bit!" I thinks. But as I turn,
    'Ere's Wally Free 'as got to poke 'is dile
Above the fence, where 'e's been cuttin' fern.
    The missus spots 'im, an' I seen 'er smile.
An' then she calls to 'im: "Oh, Mister Free,
Come in," she sez, "an' 'ave a cup uv tea."

There's tack! A woman dunno wot it means.
    What does that blighter want with cups uv tea?
A privit, fambly meet—an' 'ere Doreen's
    Muckin' it all by draggin' in this Free.
She might 'ave knowed that Rose ain't feelin' prime,
An' don't want no strange comp'ny at the time.

Free an' 'is thievin' cow! But, all the same,
  'Is yap did seem to cheer Rose up a lot.
An' after, when 'e'd bunged 'is lanky frame
  Back to 'is job, Doreen sez, "Ain't you got
No work at all to do outside to-day?
Us two must 'ave a tork; so run away."

I went .... I went becoz, if I 'ad stayed,
  Me few remarks might 'ave been pretty 'ot.
Gawbli' me! 'Oo *is* 'ead uv this parade?
  Did I plan out the scheme, or did I not?
I've worked fer this, I've worried night an' day;
An' now it's fixed, I'm tole to "run away."

Women is strange. I s'pose I oughter be
  Contented; though I never un'erstands.
But when I score, it 'urts me dignerty
  To 'ave the credit grabbed out uv me 'ands.
I should n't look fer credit, p'raps; an' then,
Women is strange. But bli'me! So is men!

"Stone the Crows"

"WHY, stone the crows!" 'e sez. "I like 'er style,
　　But alwiz, some'ow, women 'ave appeared
Set fer to 'old me orf a 'arf a mile.
　　I dunno wot's agin me: p'raps me beard.
But, some'ow, when I speak 'em soft they run.
I ain't no ladies' man," sez Danny Dunn.

"I like 'er style," 'e sez. "Wot's 'er name? Rose.
　　The neatest filly that I ever see.
She'd run in double splendid. But I s'pose,
　　She'd never 'arness with the likes uv me.
Wot age you tell me? Risin' twenty-nine?
Well, stone the flamin' crows! She'd do me fine.

"I wonder can she milk? Don't look that kind.
　　But even if she don't I wouldn't care—
Not much. Stone all the crows! I'd 'arf a mind
　　To 'ave a shave an' 'ang me 'at up there.
But I ain't got the knack uv it, yeh know,
Or I'd been spliced this twenty year ago."

Ole Danny Dunn 'as been to pay 'is call
　　An' tell us 'e'll be settlin' down 'ere soon.
'E lobbed in on us sudden, ziff an' all,
　　An' ain't done nothin' all the afternoon
But lap up tea an' stare pop-eyed at Rose,
'E ain't said nothin' much but "Stone the crows!"

Rose of Spadgers

Now, as I sees 'im orf, down by the gate,
   'E's chirpin' love-songs like a nestin' thrush.
Rose 'as 'im by the w'iskers, sure as fate;
   Fer Spring 'as sent 'im soft all uv a rush.
'E's got the beans; an' so she's fixed fer life,
If Danny's game to arst 'er fer 'is wife.

An' so me scheme works out all on its own.
   I grabbed the notion that day in the train,
When Danny tole me that 'e lived alone.
   I reckoned, then, I'd 'ave to use me brain;
But 'ere 'e is, stonin' the crows a treat,
An' keen to sling 'is pile at Rose's feet.

I'll show 'em! Them 'oo thinks I got no brains
   Will crash when Rose is Mrs. Danny Dunn.
Doreen don't need to go to too much pains
   To show me that she thinks I've nex' to none,
When I take on a job I don't let go
Until I've fixed it, all sirgarneo.

"Listen," sez Danny. "Do yeh think a man
   'As any chance? I know I don't dress neat."
"Sling it!" I sez. "Don't be an also-ran.
   Go in bald-'eaded! Rush 'er orf 'er feet!
They don't know wot they want: women ain't got
No minds, till some strong man shows wot is wot.

"I'll 'elp," I tells 'im, "if you play the game.
   Don't give 'er time to think. Take 'er be storm.
Many's the lover's bowed 'is 'ead in shame
   Becoz 'e was afraid to woo too warm.
Be masterful! Show 'er 'oo's boss! 'Ave grit!
That's wot I done, an' come 'ome on the bit.

"Look at me now. I got a wife wot 'eeds
    My lightest wish. Uv course, I ain't unkind;
But I'm boss uv the show, becoz she needs
    A man to lean upon, an' guide 'er mind."
"By gum!" sez Danny; "but that must be fine.
That's 'ow I'd like to 'ave a wife uv mine."

I tells 'im there's a dance on Fridee night;
    'E must be there, tricked out in nobby clo'es
An' all spruced up. I'll see it fixed up right
    So 'e can make the goin' good with Rose.
"I don't dance much," 'e sez. "But p'raps me luck's
Changed round; an' stone the crows! I'll chance the ducks!"

So far, ribuck. I'm no back number yet;
    Although they treats me as brainless yob.
I may be slow to start; but, don't ferget,
    I still got some idears back uv me nob.
An' once I've got Rose wed an' fixed fer life
I might su'prise respeck out uv me wife.

I might, but—Listen. Can you tell me this:
    Why am I takin' all these speshul pains,
An' worried lest me plans will go amiss?
    Why am I so dead set to use me brains?
Dunno; no more than you; fer, spare me days!
A man's a puzzle to 'imself, some ways.

Listener's Luck

"MY sort," she sez, "don't meet no fairy prince." ...
    I can't 'elp 'earin' part uv wot was said
    While I am sortin' taters in the shed.
They've 'ad these secret confabs ever since
    Rose came. 'Er an' Doreen been 'eart to 'eart,
    'Oldin' pow-wows in which I got no part.

Not that I want to. This 'ere women's craze
    Fer torkin' over things is jist 'ot air;
    An' never reely gits 'im anywhere.
It don't concern me if they yap fer days.
    My bloomin' troubles! But, as I jist said,
    I can't 'elp 'earin' as they pass the shed.

"My sort," sez Rose, "don't meet no fairy prince."
    'Er voice seems sort uv lonely like an' sad.
    "Ah well," she sez, "there's jobs still to be 'ad
Down in the fact'ries. I ain't one to wince
    Frum all the knocks I've 'ad—an' will 'ave. Still,
    Sometimes I git fed-up against me will.

"Some women 'ave the luck," she sez; "like you.
    Their lives seem made fer love an' joy an' sport,
    But I'm jist one uv the unlucky sort.
I've give up dreamin' dreams: they don't come true.
    There ain't no love or joy or sport fer me.
    Life's made me 'ard; an' 'ard I got to be."

"Oh, rubbidge!" sez Doreen. "You've got the blues,
   We all 'ave bad luck some times, but it mends.
   An' you're still young, my dear; you 'ave your friends.
Why should you think that you must alwiz lose?
   The sun's still shinin'; birds still sing, an' court;
   An' men still marry." Rose sez, "Not my sort.

"Ah, wot's the use?" she sez. "You 'ave been good—
   Too good—an' it's ungrateful I should grieve;
   But when it comes the time that I must leave
All this an'—Oh, I should 'ave understood.
   I was a fool to come. I should 'ave known
   'Ow it would be. I should 'ave stayed alone."

An' then—Aw, well, I thort I knoo me wife,
   'Ow she can be so gentle an' so kind,
   An' all the tenderness that's in 'er mind;
As I've 'ad cause to know through marrid life.
   But never 'ave I 'eard 'er wisdom speak
   Sich words before. It left me wond'rin'—meek.

Yes, meek I felt—an' proud, all in the one:
   Proud fer to know 'ow fine my wife can be;
   Meek fer to think she cares fer sich as me.
" 'Ope lasts," I 'ear 'er say, "till life is done.
   An' life can bring us joy, I know it can.
   I know; fer I've been lucky in my man."

There's a wife fer yeh! Would n't any bloke
   Feel great to 'ear 'is wife say things like that?
   I know I've earned it; but it knocked me flat.
"Been lucky in 'er man." That's 'ow she spoke.
   "The dear ole simple block'ead," sez Doreen.
   " 'E's reel good 'earted, though 'e's orful green."

Rose of Spadgers

There's a wife for yeh! Green! Thick in the 'ead!
    To think she'd go an' tork be'ind me back,
    Gossip, an' paint me character that black!
I'm glad I can't 'ear more uv wot was said.
    They wander off, down by the creek somewhere.
    Green! Well, I said that women talk 'ot air.

I thinks uv Danny Dunn, an' wot I've planned.
    Doreen don't know wot I got up me sleeve;
    An' Rose don't know that she won't 'ave to leave,
Not once I come to light an' take a 'and.
    Block'ead won't be the name they'll call me then.
    Women can tork; but action needs us men.

Yet, I dunno. Some ways it ain't so fine.
    Spite uv 'is money, Danny ain't much catch.
    It seems a pity Rose can't make a match
That's reel romantic, like Doreen's an' mine;
    But then again, although 'e's old an' plain,
    Danny's a kinder fate than Spadgers Lane.

Bit later on I see Rose standin' by
    That bridge frum where Mick waves 'is last farewell
    When 'e went smilin' to the war, an' fell.
'Ow diff'rent if 'e 'ad n't come to die,"
    I thinks. Life's orful sad, some ways.
    Though it's 'ard to be sad on these Spring days.

Doreen 'as left, fer reasons uv 'er own;
    An' Rose is gazin' down into the stream,
    Lost, like it seems, in some un'appy dream.
She looks perthetic standin' there alone.
    Wis'ful she looks. But when I've turned away
    I git a shock to 'ear 'er larfin' gay.

It's that coot Wally Free; 'e's with 'er now.
    Funny 'ow 'is fool chatter makes 'er smile,
    An' shove 'er troubles under fer a while.
(Pity 'e don't pay more 'eed to 'is cow
    Instid uv loafin' there. 'E's got no sense.
    I'm sick uv tellin' 'im to mend that fence.)

'Er sort don't meet no fairy prince ... Ar, well.
    Fairy gawdfathers, p'raps, wot once was knights,
    Might take a turn at puttin' things to rights.
Green? Block'ead, am I? You can't alwiz tell.
    Wait till I wave me magic mit at Rose,
    An' turn 'er into "Mrs. Stone-the-crows."

The Dance

"Heirlums," 'e sez. "I've 'ad the trousiz pressed.
   Me father marrid in 'em, that 'e did.
See this 'ere fancy vest?
               See this 'ere lid?
Me gran'dad brought that frum 'is native land
In forty-two—an' then 'twas second-'and."

Clobber? Oh, 'elp! Pants uv wild shepherd's plaid,
   A coat that might 'ave knocked the cliners flat
When father was a lad,
              A tall, pot 'at
That caught the mange back in the diggin's days,
A fancy vest that called fer loud 'oorays.

But loud 'oorays don't 'arf ixpress my rage
   When Danny comes up'olstered fer the jig.
I've seen it on the stage,
             That comic rig;
But never at a country dance before
'Ave I seen sich crook duds as Danny wore.

"You want to crool my scheme," I sez, "with rags
   Like that? This ain't no fancy dress affair.
Wot sort uv tile an' bags
            Is them to wear?
But 'e don't tumble; 'e's as pleased as pie.
"By gum," 'e sez, "this ort to catch 'er eye."

The Dance

"You posin' fer a comic film, or wot?"
    I arsts 'im—"with noorotic togs like those!
Jazz clobber! Ain't you got
        No decent clo'es?"
But 'e's too tickled with 'imself to 'eed.
"This orter catch 'er eye," 'e sez, "this tweed."

It caught 'er eye, all right, an' many more.
    They starts to come before the daylight fades;
An', fer a hour before
        The crowd parades,
Ole Danny 'eld the centre uv the stage,
While I stood orf an' chewed me silent rage.

That's 'ow it alwiz is: I try to show
    'Ow I can use me bean in deep-laid lurks;
An' then some fool must go
        An' bust the works.
'Ere, I 'ave planned a coop in slap-up style,
An' Danny spikes me guns with gran'pa's tile.

Rose never seemed so free frum ugly dreams,
    Not since she came, as that night at the dance;
But my matchmakin' schemes
        Makes no advance;
Fer every time I gits a chance to score,
Doreen butts in, an' crools me pitch once more.

Reel thortless, women is. She ort to seen
    I 'ad intents—in spite uv Danny's clo'es—
An' that 'e was reel keen
        Concernin' Rose.
Not 'er. She larfs, an' chatters with the push,
As if rich 'usbands grew on every bush.

Once, f'rinstance, I gits busy when I seen
    Rose sittin' out; an' brings Dan on the run.
"Why, mercy!" sez Doreen.
         " 'Ere's Mister Dunn
Perlite enough to arst *me* fer a dance.
'E knows us marrid ones don't git much chance."

An' there she grabs 'im, fair out uv me 'ands!
    An' lets young Wally Free git off with Rose;
While like a fool I stands,
         Kickin' me toes
An' cursin' all the fool things women do.
I'd think 'twas done apurpis, less I knoo.

That's 'ow it was all night. I schemed a treat,
    Workin' shrood points, an' sweatin' blood, almost;
But every time I'm beat
         Right on the post.
All me matchmakin's bust—the task uv days—
Through Danny's duds an' my wife's tackless ways.

Nice chaperong she is! While Free an' Rose
    Dance 'arf the night Doreen jist sits an' beams.
When I seen that, up goes
         My 'opes an' schemes.
But all that Danny sez is, "Stone the crows!
Yeh'd think I'd took 'er eye, with them good clo'es."

When we git 'ome that night I shows me spleen
    By 'intin' Rose will be left on the shelf.
An' then I see Doreen
         Smile to 'erself.
"I would n't be su'prised," she sez, "to see
Rose marrid, some fine day, to Wally Free."

The Dance

To Wally Free! Yeh could 'ave knocked me flat
    With 'arf a brick. I seen it in a flash.
A grinnin' coot like that?
                Without no cash!
Besides, a man 'oo'd keep a thievin' cow
Like 'is, won't make no 'usband any'ow.

I'm sick uv everything. It ain't no joke.
    I've tried to do good works; an' now I've found
When you git 'elpin' folk
            They jist turn round
An' bite the 'and that feeds 'em, so to speak.
An' yet they sez the strong should 'elp the weak.

Wot rot!... I wisht I 'ad some reel ixcuse
    To push some face in, jist to ease me mind.
Spike Wegg, 'e 'ad 'is use—
            'Im an' 'is kind.
If I could give me ole left-'ook one swing,
I might feel kinder like to everything.

Spike Wegg

ME photer's in the papers! 'Oly wars!
A 'ero, I've been called in big, black type.
I 'ad idears the time was close on ripe
    Fer some applorse
To come my way, on top uv all me bumps.
Now it's come sudden, an' it's come in lumps.

I've given interviews, an' 'ad me dile
  Bang on the front page torkin' to a 'tec'.
  Limelight? I'm swimmin' in it to the neck!
    Me sunny smile
Beams on the crowd. Misun'erstandin's past;
An' I 'ave come into me own, at last.

But all the spot-light ain't alone fer me;
  'Arf, I am glad to say, is made to shine
  Upon that firm an' trusted friend uv mine,
    Ole Wally Free—
A man, I've alwiz said, 'oo'd make 'is mark....
But, case you 'ave n't 'eard the story, 'ark:

Spike Wegg—Yes, 'im. I thort, the same as you,
  That 'e was dished an' done fer in the Lane.
  I don't ixpeck to cross 'is tracks again;
    An' never knoo
That 'e 'ad swore to git me one uv those
Fine days, an' make 'is alley good with Rose.

Spike Wegg

Spike 'ad been aimin' 'igh in 'is profesh.
    Bank robberies, an' sich, was 'is noo lurk;
    An' one big job 'ad set the cops to work
        To plan a fresh
Campaign agin this crook. They want 'im more
Than ever they 'ave wanted 'im before.

They yearn fer 'im, reel passionit, they do.
    Press an' perlice both 'ankers fer 'im sore.
    "Where is Spike Wegg?" the daily 'eadlines roar.
        But no one knoo.
Or them that did 'ad fancies to be dumb.
The oysters uv the underworld was mum.

It was the big sensation uv the day.
    Near 'arf the Force was nosin' fer the bloke
    Wot done the deed; but Spike was well in smoke,
        An' like to stay.
Shots 'ad been fired; an' one poor coot was plugged.
An' now the crowd arsts, "Why ain't no one jugged?"

That's 'ow the land lies when, one day, I go
    Down to the orchid paddick, where I see
    A strange cove playin' spy be'ind a tree.
        I seem to know
The shape uv that there sneakin', slinkin' frame,
An' walk across to git on to 'is game.

Oh, yes; it's 'im; an' a reel vicious Spike.
    Venom is in the eye that looks in mine—
    A cold, 'ard, snaky eye. "Well, Bill, yeh swine.
        'Ow would yeh like
To make cold meat?" This is the pleasant way
'E greets me on a nice bright, warm, Spring day.

Rose of Spadgers

Though it is warm, I feel a sudden cold
    Creep up me spine. I 'speck to 'ear a gun
    Tork any minute; so I make a run
        To git a hold,
An' keep in close to use that upper-cut.
But Spike is fly this time, an' works 'is nut.

'E side-steps pretty. Then we git to grips.
    I plant a short-arm jolt; an', as I land,
    I see a flash uv somethin' in 'is 'and.
        Nex' thing, 'e rips
A knife beneath me guard an' gives a dig—
Sticks me fair in the bellers, like a pig.

It was red-'ot! I grunt, an' break away
    To 'old 'im orf. I'm battlin' fer me life—
    All-in, a cert; fer 'e's still got the knife.
        An', by the way
'E looks, I know it's either 'im or me
'As an appointment at the cemet'ry.

I've often wondered 'ow a feller feels
    When 'e is due to wave the world good-bye.
    They say 'is past life flicks before 'is eye
        Like movie reels.
My past life never troubled me a heap.
All that I want to do is go to sleep.

I'm gittin' weak; I'm coughin', chokey like;
    Me legs is wobbly, an' I'm orful ill.
    But I 'ave got some fight left in me still.
        I look at Spike;
An' there I see the dirty look wot shows
'E's got me where 'e wants me—an' 'e knows.

Spike Wegg

'E's smilin'. Not a pretty smile, I own.
    But, sudden, there's a fear springs in 'is eye;
    An', from be'ind me, some thing flashes by.
        I 'ear Spike groan;
I 'ear the squishy thud uv flesh on flesh;
An' gits idears there's somethin' doin' fresh.

I think that's where I fell. Nex' thing I see
    Is Spike Wegg down, an' fair on top uv 'im
    Some one that's breathin' 'ard an' fightin' grim.
        It's Wally Free!
It's good old Wally! 'E 'as got Spike pinned,
Both 'ands, an' kneelin' 'eavy on 'is wind.

So fur so good. But I ain't outed yet.
    On 'ands an' knees I crawls to reach 'em, slow.
    (Spike's got the knife, an' Wally dare n't let go)
        Then, as I get
Close up, I 'ear Rose screamin' then me wife.
I'm faint. I twist Spike's arm—an' grab the knife.

That's all. At least, as far as I'm concerned,
    I took no further interest in the show.
    The things wot 'appened subsekint I know
        Frum wot I learned
When I come-to, tucked in me little bed,
Me chest on fire, an' cold packs on me 'ead.

I 'ear they tied Spike up with 'arness straps
    An' bits uv 'ay-band, till the John 'Ops come;
    An' watched 'im workin' out a mental sum—
        Free an' some chaps—
Uv 'ow much time 'e'd git fer this last plot
An' other jobs. The answer was, a lot.

Rose of Spadgers

Then that nex' day! an' after, fer a week!
    Yeh'd think I owned the winner uv a Cup.
    Pressmen, perlice, the parson, all rush up;
        An' I've to speak
Me piece, to be took down in black an' white,
In case I chuck a seven overnight.

The papers done us proud. Near every day
    Some uv 'em printed photers uv me map
    (Looked at some ways, I ain't too crook a chap)
        But, anyway
I've 'ad enough. I wish they'd let me be.
I'm sick uv all this cheap publicity.

But I'm reel glad ole Wally's won a name.
    'E saved my life; I'm wise to that, all right.
    Besides, I alwiz said that 'e was white
        Since 'e first came
To live 'ere, but 'e never got 'is due.
Now 'im an' Rose—Ah, well; I fixed that too.

But sich is fame. Less than a month ago
    The whole thing started with a naggin' tooth.
    Now I am famis; an', to tell the truth—
        Well, I dunno—
I'd 'ardly like to bet yeh that I don't
Git arst to act in pitchers—but I won't.

Narcissus

A MAN'S a mug. I've worked the 'ole thing out
    To-day, down in the orchard where I sat
Runnin' the wheels red-'ot beneath me 'at,
An' wras'lin' fervud with a sudden doubt—
    A doubt wot's plugged me fair bang on the point
    An' jolted all me glad dreams out uv joint.

It's been a pearlin' day. The birds above
    Up in the trees sung fit to break their 'earts.
It seemed, some'ow, the 'ole world's makin' love,
    Ixceptin' me. An' then an' there I starts
To think things out an' git me bearin's straight,
Becoz—Well, I ain't been meself uv late.

I've flopped. It was the parson put me wise,
    Before 'e left. I 'ad been full uv skite.
    I was the 'ero uv the piece all right.
Me chest was out, me 'ead was twice the size
    It used to be. I felt I was king-pin.
    Did n't the papers 'ave me photer in?

I was that puffed with pride I never stopped
    To search me soul fer signs uv wear an' tear.
I loved meself so much I never dropped
    To any blot or blemish anywhere.
The Lord 'Igh Muck-a-muck, wot done the trick,
An' dug the Murray with 'is little pick.

Rose of Spadgers

When I think back on it I go all 'ot.
    I was that blind I never even seen,
    Nor looked to see no changes in Doreen.
I was content to 'ave 'er on the spot
    Dodgin' about the 'ouse in 'er calm way,
    To chirp, "Yes, Bill," to everything I say.

The parson punchered me. 'E's alwiz 'ad
    A trick uv callin' me by fancy names.
In town 'e christened me "Sir Gally'ad,"
    'Oo was, it seems, a knight wot rescued dames,
But never spoke out uv 'is turn to none,
Becoz 'is 'eart was pure. 'E took the bun.

But now "Narcissy" is the moniker
    'E wishes on me; an' I arst fer light.
    "Narcissy?" I remarks. "Don't sound perlite.
'Oo was this bird? There looks to be a slur
    Or somethin' sly about that cissy touch."
    "A bloke," 'e sez, " 'oo liked 'imself too much."

I looks quick fer that twinkle in 'is eye
    Wot tells me if 'e's kiddin' me or not.
But it ain't there. "Fair dinkum," I reply,
    "You don't mean—You ain't 'intin' that I've got—"
"I mean," 'e sez, "you should give thanks through life
That you 'ave been so lucky in your wife."

'E don't 'arp on the toon; but turns away.
    "Your daffydils," 'e sez, "makes quite a show."
    An' later, when it came 'is time to go,
'E shakes me 'and reel 'arty, twinklin' gay ....
    But, "lucky in me wife?" Where did I 'ear
    Somethin' like that before? It sounds dead queer.

Narcissus

I turns to 'er, after we've waved good-byes,
    To try an' figure wot the parson meant.
An' sudden, I see somethin' in 'er eyes
    I never noticed there before 'e went:
That troubled, mother look I've seen so plain
The times she's said, "Poor Bill! 'Ow is the pain?"

I seeks the orchard, with a sickly grin,
    To sort meself out straight an' git a grip.
    Them 'ints the parson drops give me the pip.
I don't quite see where daffydils comes in;
    But, "lucky in me wife!" Why, spare me days,
    Yeh'd think I beat 'er, by the things 'e says!

I tries to kid meself: to back me skite,
    An' 'old that wad uv self-content I 'ad.
It ain't no use. I know the parson's right:
    Clean through the piece I 'ave been actin' bad.
I've been so full uv Me, I've treated 'er
Like she was—well, a bit uv furnicher.

Yet, "furnicher" don't seem to put it good.
    Nothin' so wooden don't describe Doreen.
    All through the game, some'ow, she's alwiz been—
Well, somewhere 'andy, 'elpin' where she could,
    An' manidgin', an' ... Bli'me! Now I see!
    Wot she *did* manidge was the block'ead—me! ...

Well, I'm the goat. I s'pose I should 'ave seen
    I was n't 'ead an' tail uv all the show.
A bit uv putty in 'er 'ands I been!
    An' so bull-'eaded that I did n't know.
Only fer 'er things might 'ave—Spare me days!
I never will git used to women's ways.

Rose of Spadgers

Only fer 'er Rose might. . . . But wot's the use?
    Shakespeare 'as said it right: the world's a stage;
    An' all us 'uman ducks an' dames ingage
In actin' parts. Mostly the men cuts loose,
    An' fights, an' throws their weight about a lot.
    But, listen. It's the women weave the plot.

The women. . . . Well, it's been a bonnie day.
    Blue-bonnets, dodgin' in an' out the ferns,
Looks like blue chips uv sky come down to play.
    An' down the valley, where the creek track turns,
I see Rose, arm-in-arm with Wally Free.
The 'ole world's makin' love, ixceptin' me.

Huh! Women! . . . Yes; a man's a mug, all right. . . .
    I sees the sof' clouds sailin' in the sky,
    An' bits uv thistledown go driftin' by.
"Jist like men's lives," I think. An' then I sight,
    Fair in me cabbages, ole Wally's cow.
    That fence—But them plants ain't worth savin', now.

Women. . . . I wonder 'oo Narcissy was. . . .
    Green trees agin blue 'ills don't look 'arf bad . . .
I s'pose 'e got the cissy part becoz
    'Is ways was womanish. Well, serve 'im glad. . . .
That cow uv Wally's ort to milk a treat
With plenty good young cabbage plants to eat.

Women *is* often 'elpful—in a sense. . . .
    Lord, it's a lazy day! Before it fails,
    I better git a 'ammer an' some nails
An' dodge acrost an' mend that bit uv fence.
    It's up to me to try an' put things right,
    An'—well, I'll 'elp Doreen wash up tonight.

A Message
Armistice Day 1936

A Message

Armistice Day 1936

I got dreamin' that a message come in some mysterious way
From one ole pal of mine, gone West this many an' many a day,
   A bloke the name of Ginger Mick, a fightin' cove I knoo.
   (But 'e's Digger Corporal Mick Esquire, late A.I.F., to you)
'E got 'is on Gallipoli, an' sleeps there with the best,
Not leavin' very much be'ind, excep' one small request.
   "Look after things," was all 'e said, when 'e was mortal 'urt.
   Dead sure 'is mates—that's me an' you—would never do 'im
      dirt.

(Think of it in the Silence, with yer 'eads bowed low:
Do we keep the unspoke compact with the men we used to know?)

For I dreams it in the silence of a dark Remembrance Eve;
An' the message seems to tell me it is gettin' late to grieve.
   "But if you seem to miss us still, then get the sob-stuff o'er,
   An' think about the things wot we went an' fought a war.
Send up a pray'r an' drop a tear an' bend a reverent knee—
(Says Digger Corporal Ginger Mick, A.I.F., says 'e)
   But is them things we fought for still the things most dear to
      you:
   The honor an' the glory an' the mateship that we knew?"

(Think of it in the Silence, when the Last Post plays—
The splendid glimpse of Truth we 'ad, once, in the bitter days)

A Message

"Grief is a passin' compliment," the message seems to say;
But tears don't carry on the job for men that drift away.
    We 'ad small time or taste for such where guns was raisin'
        'ell,
    When we got busy plantin' blokes an' wishin' 'em farewell.
We blowed sad music over 'em—plain Digs, or Brass 'at Knuts—
But we played a quick-step comin' back, to show we 'ad the guts.
    Our speech was rough, our ways was tough—tough as our
        bloody game.
    Are the rough, tough, lads still honored, like when the Terror
        came?"

(Think of it in the Silence, when their spirits hover near:
The vision and the vows that held while still the land knew fear.)

'E's sleepin' on Gallipoli. At least, 'is bones is there:
Bones worth a ton of livin' flesh that won't play fair—
    Not till the terror comes again. "An' when it does," says 'e,
    If gods you've worshipped let you down, well, don't blame me."
'E's seen a lot, an' learned a lot most like, where 'e 'as gone;
An' 'eaven 'elp us when we meet if we ain't carried on.
    A vulgar person, Ginger Mick, a fightin' cove I knoo—
    (But Digger Corporal Ginger Mick, if you please, to you.)

(Think of it in the Silence; an', if you pray, pray deep
That all we 'ave an' all we are old loyalties shall keep.)

Glossary

A.I.F.—Australian Imperial Forces.
Alley, to toss in the—To give up the ghost.
Also ran, The—On the turf, horses that fail to secure a leading place; hence, obscure persons, nonentities.
'Ammer-lock (Hammer-lock)—A favourite and effective hold in wrestling.
Ar—An exclamation expressing joy, sorrow, surprise, etc., according to the manner of utterance.
'Ard Case (Hard Case)—A shrewd or humorous person.
Aussie—Australia; an Australian.
'Ayseed (Hayseed)—A rustic.
Back Chat—Impudent repartee.
Back and Fill—To vacillate; to shuffle.
Back the Barrer—To intervene without invitation.
Bag of Tricks—All one's belongings.
Barmy (Balmy)—Foolish; silly.
Barrack—To take sides.
Beak—A magistrate (possibly from Anglo-Saxon, Beag—a magistrate).
Beano—A feast.
Beans—Coins; money.
Beat—Puzzled; defeated.
Beat, off the—Out of the usual routine.
Beat the band—To amaze.
Beef (to beef it out)—To declaim vociferously.
Beller—The lungs.
Biff—To smite.
Bint—Girl.
Bird, to give the—To treat with derision.
Blighter—A worthless fellow.
Blighty—London.

Bli'me—An oath with the fangs drawn.

Blind—Deception, "bluff".

Blither—To talk at random, foolishly.

Blob—A shapeless mass.

Block—The head. To lose or do in the block—To become flustered; excited; angry; to lose confidence. To keep the block—To remain calm; dispassionate.

Block, the—A fashionable city walk.

Bloke—A male adult of the genus homo.

Blubber, blub—To weep.

Bluff—Cunning practice; make believe. v. To deceive; to mislead.

Bob—A shilling.

Bokays—Compliments, flattery.

Boko—The nose.

Bong-tong—Patrician (Fr. Bon ton).

Bonzer, boshter, bosker—Adjectives expressing the superlative of excellence.

Boodle—Money; wealth.

Book—In whist, six tricks.

Book—A bookie, q.v.

Booked—Engaged.

Bookie—A bookmaker (turf); one who makes a betting book on sporting events.

Boot, to put in the—To kick a prostrate foe.

Boss—Master; employer.

Break (to break away, to do a break)—To depart in haste.

Breast up to—To accost.

Brisket—The chest.

Brown—A copper coin.

Brums—Tawdry finery (from Brummagem—Birmingham).

Buckley's (Chance)—A forlorn hope.

Buck up—Cheer up.

Bump—To meet; to accost aggressively.

Bun, to take the—To take the prize (used ironically).

Bundle, to drop the—To surrender; to give up hope.

Bunk—To sleep in a "bunk" or rough bed. To do a bunk—To depart.

Bunnies, to hawk the—To peddle rabbits.

Bus, to miss the—To neglect opportunities.

Caboose—A small dwelling.

Carlton—A Melbourne football team.

Cat, to whip the—To cry over spilt milk; i.e., to whip the cat that has spilt the milk.

C.B.—Confined to barracks.

Cert—A certainty; a foregone conclusion.

Champeen—Champion.
Chap—A "bloke" or "cove".
Chase yourself—Depart; avaunt; "fade away". q.v.
Chat—To address tentatively; to "word", q.v.
Cheque, to pass in one's—To depart this life.
Chest, to get it off one's—To deliver a speech; express one's feelings.
Chew, to chew it over; to chew the rag—To sulk; to nurse a grievance.
Chiack—Vulgar banter; coarse invective.
Chin—To talk; to wag the chin.
Chip—To "chat", q.v. Chip in; To intervene.
Chiv—The face.
Chow—A native of far Cathay.
Chuck up—To relinquish. Chuck off—To chaff; to employ sarcasm.
Chump—A foolish fellow.
Chunk—A lump; a mass.
Clean—Completely; utterly.
Click—A clique; a "push".
Cliner—A young unmarried female.
Clobber—Raiment; vesture.
Cobber—A boon companion.
Collect—To receive one's deserts.
Colour-line—In pugilism, the line drawn by white boxers excluding coloured fighters—for divers reasons.
Conk—The nose.
Coot—A person of no account (used contemptuously).
Cop—To seize; to secure; also, s., an avocation, a "job".
Cop (or Copper)—A police constable.
Copper show—A copper mine.
Copper-top—Red head.
Count, to take the—In pugilism, to remain prostrate for ten counted seconds, and thus lose the fight.
Cove—A "chap" or "bloke". q.v. (Gipsy).
Cow—A thoroughly unworthy, not to say despicable person, place, thing, or circumstance. A fair cow—An utterly obnoxious and otherwise inexpressible person, place, thing or circumstance.
Crack—To smite. s. A blow.
Crack a boo—To divulge a secret; to betray emotion.
Crack hardy—To suppress emotion; to endure patiently; to keep a secret.
Cray—A crayfish.
Crib—A dwelling.
Croak—To die.

Glossary

Crook—Unwell; dishonest; spurious; fraudulent. Superlative, Dead Crook.

Crool (cruel) the pitch—To frustrate; to interfere with one's schemes or welfare.

Crust—Sustenance; a livelihood.

Cut it out—Omit; discontinue it.

Dago—A native of Southern Europe.

Dash, to do one's—To reach one's Waterloo.

Date—An appointment.

Dawg (dog)—A contemptible person; ostentation. To put on dawg—To behave in an arrogant manner.

Dead—In a superlative degree; very.

Deal—To deal it out; to administer punishment; abuse, &c.

Deal—A "hand" at cards.

Deener—A shilling (Fr. Denier. Denarius, a Roman silver coin).

Derry—An aversion; a feud; a dislike.

Dickin—A term signifying distrust or disbelief.

Digger—An infantryman; a comrade.

Dile (dial)—The face.

Dilly—Foolish; half-witted.

Ding Dong—Strenuous.

Dinkum—Honest; true. "The Dinkum Oil"—The truth.

Dipped—Mentally deficient.

Dirt—Opprobrium; a mean speech or action.

Dirty left—A formidable left fist.

Divvies—Dividends; profits.

Dizzy limit—The utmost; the superlative degree.

Do in—To defeat; to kill; to spend.

Done me luck—Lost my good fortune.

Dope—A drug; adulterated liquor. v. to administer drugs.

Dot in the eye—To strike in the eye.

Douse—To extinguish (Anglo-Saxon).

Drive a quill—To write with a pen; to work in an office.

Duck, to do a—(See "break").

Duds—Personal apparel (Scotch).

Dud—No good; ineffective; used up.

Dunno—Do not know.

Dutch—German; any native of Central Europe.

'Eads (Heads)—The authorities; inner council.

'Eadin'—"Heading browns"; tossing pennies.

Glossary

'Ead over turkey—Head over heels.
'Ead Serang—The chief; the leader.
'Eavyweight—A boxer of the heaviest class.
'Ell fer leather—In extreme haste.
End up, to get—To rise to one's feet.

Fade away, to—To retire; to withdraw.
Fag—A cigarette.
Fair—Extreme; positive.
Fair thing—A wise proceeding; an obvious duty.
Fake—A swindle; a hoax.
Final, to run one's—To die.
Final kick—Final leave.
Finger—An eccentric or amusing person.
Flam—Nonsense; make-believe.
Flash—Ostentatious; showy but counterfeit.
Float, to—To give up the ghost.
Fluff, a bit of—A young female person.
Fly—A turn; a try.
Foot (me foot)—A term expressing ridicule.
Footer—Football.
Frame—The body.
Frill—Affectation.

Funk, to—To fear; to lose courage.
Furphy—An idle rumour; a canard.

Galoot—A simpleton.
Game—Occupation; scheme; design.
Gawsave—The National Anthem.
Gazob—A fool; a blunderer.
Geewhiz—Exclamation expressing surprise.
Get, to do a—To retreat hastily.
Gilt—Money; wealth.
Give, to—In one sense, to care.
Gizzard—The heart.
Glarrsy—The glassy eye; a glance of cold disdain. The Glassey Alley—The favourite; the most admired.
Glim—A light.
Going (while the going is good)—While the path is clear.
Gone (fair gone)—Overcome, as with emotion.
Goo-goo eyes—Loving glances.
Gorspil-cove—A minister of the Gospel.
Graft—Work.
Grafter—One who toils hard or willingly.

305

Glossary

Grandstand play—Playing to the gallery.
Griffin, the straight—The truth; secret information.
Grip—Occupation; employment.
Groggy—Unsteady; dazed.
Grouch—To mope—to grumble.
Grub—Food.
Guff—Nonsense.
Guy—A foolish fellow.
Guy, to do a—To retire.
Guyver—Make-believe.

Handies—A fondling of hands between lovers.
Hang out—To reside; to last.
Hangover—The aftermath of the night before.
Hankies—Handkerchiefs.
High-falutin'—High sounding; boastful.
Hitch, to—To wed.
Hitched—Entangled in the bonds of holy matrimony.
Hit things up—To behave strenuously; riotously.
Hokey Fly, by the—A mild expletive, without any particular meaning.
Hot—excessive; extreme.
Hump, the—A fit of depression.
Hump, to—To carry as a swag or other burden.

Imshee—Begone; retreat; take yourself off.
Intro—Introduction; knock-down. q.v.
It (to be It)—To assume a position of supreme importance.

Jab—To strike smartly.
Jane—A woman.
Jiff—A very brief period.
Job, to—To smite.
Joes—Melancholy thoughts.
John—A policeman.
John 'Op (or Jonop)—Policeman.
Joint, to jump the—To assume command—to occupy the "joint", i.e., establishment, situation, place of business.
Jolt, to pass a—To deliver a short, sharp blow.
Jor—Jaw.
Jorb (job)—Avocation; employment.
Josser—A simple fellow.
Jug—A prison.

Keekin'—Peeping.
Keep one down—Take a drink.
Keeps, for—For ever, permanently.
Kersplosh—Splash.
Kick—Leave. Kick about—To loaf or hang about.
Kid—A child.

Kiddies—Children.
Kid, to—To deceive; to persuade by flattery.
Kid Stakes—Pretence.
King Pin—The leader; the person of chief importance.
Kip—A small chip used for tossing pennies in the occult game of two-up.
Kipsie—A house; the home.
Knob—The head; one in authority.
Knock-down—A ceremony insisted upon by ladies who decline to be "picked up"; a formal introduction.
Kock-out drops—Drugged or impure liquor.
Kock-out punch—A knock-down blow.
Knut—A fop; a well-dressed idler.

Lark—A practical joke; a sportive jest.
Lash—Violence.
Ledding—Leaden.
Leery—Vulgar; low.
Leeuwin—Cape Leeuwin on the South West coast of Australia.
Lid—The hat. To dip the lid—To raise the hat.
Limit—The end; the full length.
Line up—To approach; to accost.

Lingo—Language.
Lip—Impertinence. To give it lip—To talk vociferously.
Little Bourke—Little Bourke Street, Melbourne, Australia.
Little Lons—Little Lonsdale Street, Melbourne, Australia.
Lob, to—To arrive.
'Loo—Woolloomooloo, a part of Sydney.
Lumme—Love me.
Lurk—A plan of action; a regular occupation.

Mafeesh—Finish; I am finished.
Mag—To scold or talk noisily.
Mallee—A species of Eucalypt; the country where the Mallee grows.
Mash—To woo; to pay court. s. A lover.
Maul—To lay hands upon, either violently or with affection.
Meet, a—An assignation.
Mill—A bout of fisticuffs.
Mix—To mix it; to fight strenuously.
Mizzle—To disappear—to depart suddenly.
Mo.—Abbreviation of "moment".
Moll—A woman of loose character.

Glossary

Moniker—A name; a title; a signature.
Mooch—To saunter about aimlessly.
Moon—To loiter.
Mud, my name is—i.e., I am utterly discredited.
Mug—A fool; also the mouth.
Mug, to—To kiss.
Mug—A simpleton.
Mullock, to poke—To deride; to tease.
Mushy—Sentimental.

Nail—Catch.
Nark—s. A spoil-sport; a churlish fellow.
Narked—Angered; foiled.
Nark, to—To annoy; to foil.
Natchril—Natural.
Neck and neck—Side by side.
Neck, to get it in the—To receive severe punishment, i.e., "Where the chicken got the axe."
Nerve—Confidence; impudence.
Nick—Physical condition; good health.
Nipper—A small boy.
Nix—Nothing.
Nod, on the—Without payment.
Nose around, to—To seek out inquisitively.
Nothing (ironically)—Literally "something considerable".

Odds, above the—Beyond the average; outside the pale.
Oopizootics—An undiagnosed complaint.
Orfis (office)—A warning; a word of advice; a hint.
Oricle (oracle), to work the—To secure desired results.
Orl (orl in)—without limit or restriction.
'Ot Socks—Gaily coloured hose.
Out, to—To render unconscious with a blow.
Out, all—Quite exhausted; fully extended.

Pack, to send to the—To relegate to obscurity.
Pal—A friend; a mate (Gipsy).
Pard—A partner; a mate.
Part—Give; hand over.
Pass (pass 'im one)—To deliver a blow.
Pat, on one's—Alone; single-handed.
Peach—A desirable young woman; "fresh as a peach".
Peb (pebble)—A flash fellow; a "larrikin".
Phiz—The face.
Pick at—To chaff; to annoy.
Pick up, to—To dispense with the ceremoney of a "knock-down" or introduction.

Pilot cove—A clergyman.
Pile it on—To rant; to exaggerate.
Pinch—To steal; to place under arrest.
Pins—Legs.
Pip—A fit of depression.
Pitch a tale—To trump up an excuse; to weave a romance.
Plant—To bury.
Plug—To smite with the fist.
Plug along, to—To proceed doggedly.
Plunk—An exclamation expressing the impact of a blow.
Podgy—Fat; plump.
Point—The region of the jaw; much sought after by pugilists.
Point, to—To seize unfair advantage; to scheme.
Pole, up the—Distraught through anger, fear, &c.; also, disappeared, vanished.
Pot, a—A considerable amount; as a "pot of money".
Pot, the old—The male parent (from "Rhyming Slang", the "old pot and pan"—"old man").
Prad—A horse.
Pug—A pugilist.
Pull my (or your) leg—To deceive or get the best of.
Pull, off—Desist.
Pull, to take a—To desist; to discontinue.
Punch a cow—To conduct a team of oxen.
Punter—The natural prey of a "bookie". q.v.
Push—A company of rowdy fellows gathered together for ungentle purposes.
Push up the daisies, to—To be interred.

Queer the pitch—To frustrate; to fool.
Quid—A sovereign, or pound sterling.
Quod—Prison.

Rabbit, to run the—To convey liquor from a public-house.
Rag—Song in rag time.
Rag, to chew the—To grieve; to brood.
Rag, to sky the—To throw a towel into the air in token of surrender (pugilism).
Rain, to keep out the—To avoid danger; to act with caution.
Rat—A street urchin; a wharf loafer.
Rattled—Excited; confused.
Recomember—Remember.
Red 'ot—Extreme; out-and-out.

Glossary

Registry—The office of a Registrar.
Renege—To fail to follow suit (in playing cards); to quit.
Ribuck—Correct, genuine; an interjection signifying assent.
Rile—To annoy. Riled—Roused to anger.
Ring, the—The arena of a prize-fight.
Ring, the dead—A remarkable likeness.
Ringer—Expert.
Rise, a—An accession of fortune; an improvement.
Rocks—A locality in Sydney.
Rook, to—To "take down".
Rorty—Boisterous; rowdy.
Roust, or rouse—To upbraid with many words.
'Roy—Fitzroy, a suburb of Melbourne; its football team.
Ructions—Growling; argument.
Run against—To meet more or less unexpectedly.
Run 'is final—died.

Saints—A football team of St Kilda, Victoria.
Sandy blight—Ophthalmia.
Savvy—Commonsense; shrewdness.
Sawing wood—"Bluffing"; biding one's time.
School—A club; a clique of gamblers, or others.
Scoot—To hurry; to scuttle.
Scran—Food.
Scrap—Fight.
Set to—To attack; to regard with disfavour.
Set, to have—To have marked down for punishment or revenge.
Shicker—Intoxicating liquor.
Shick, shickered—Intoxicated.
Shinty—A game resembling hockey.
Shook—Stolen; disturbed.
Shook on—Infatuated.
Shyin', or Shine—Excellent; desirable.
Sight—To tolerate; to permit; also to see; observe.
Sir Garneo—In perfect order; satisfactory.
Skirt, or bit of skirt—A female.
Skite—To boast. Skiter—A boaster.
Sky the wipe—See "Rag".
Slab—A portion; a tall, awkward fellow.
Slam—Making all the tricks (in card-playing).
Slanter—Spurious; unfair.
Slap-up—Admirable; excellent.
Slats—The ribs.
Slaver—One engaged in the "white slave traffic".

Slick—Smart; deft; quick..
Sling—Discard; throw.
Slope, to—To elope; to leave in haste.
Sloppy—Lachrymose; maudlin.
Sluchy—A toiler in a scullery.
Smooge—To flatter or fawn; to bill and coo.
Smooger—A sycophant; a courtier.
Snag—A hindrance; formidable opponent.
Snake-'eaded—Annoyed, vindictive.
Snake juice—Strong drink.
Snare—To acquire; to seize; to win.
Snarkey—Angry.
Snide—Inferior; of no account.
Snob—A bootmaker.
Snout—To bear a grudge.
Snouted—Treated with disfavour.
Snuff, or snuff it—To expire.
Sock it into—To administer physical punishment.
Solid—Severe; severely.
So-long—A form of farewell.
Sool—To attack; to urge on.
Soot, leadin'—A chief attribute.
Sore, to get—To become aggrieved.
Sore-head—A curmudgeon.

S.O.S.—Signal of distress or warning, used in telegraphy.
Sour, to turn, or get—To become pessimistic or discontented.
Spank—To chastise maternal-wise.
Spar—A gentle bout of fisticuffs.
Spare me days—A pious ejaculation
Specs.—Spectacles.
Spell—Rest or change.
Splash—To expend.
Splice—To join in matrimony.
Spout—To preach or speak at length.
Sprag—To accost truculently.
Spruik—To deliver a speech, as a showman.
Spuds—Potatoes.
Square—Upright, honest.
Square an' all—Of a truth; verily.
Squeak—To give away a secret.
Squiz—A brief glance.
Stand-orf—Retiring; reticent.
Stajum—Stadium, where prize-fights are conducted.
Stiffened—Bought over.
Stiff-un—A corpse.
Stoke—To nourish; to eat.
Stop a pot—To quaff ale.
Stop one—To receive a blow.
Stoush—To punch with the fist. s. Violence.

Glossary

Straight, on the—In fair and honest fashion.
Strangle-hold—An ungentle embrace in wrestling.
Strength of it—The truth of it; the value of it.
Stretch, to do a—To serve a term of imprisonment.
Strike—The innocuous remnant of a hardy curse.
Strike—To discover, to meet.
Strong, going—Proceeding with vigour.
'Struth—An emaciated oath.
Stuff—money.
Stunt—A performance; a tale.
Swad, Swaddy—A private soldier.
Swank—Affectation; ostentation.
Swap—To exchange.
Swell—An exalted person.
Swig—A draught of water or other liquid.
Swiv'ly—Afraid, or unable, to look straight.

Tabbie—A female.
Take down—Deceive; get the best of.
Take 'em on—Engage them in battle.
Take it out—To undergo imprisonment in lieu of a fine.
Tart—A young woman (contraction of sweetheart).
Tater—Potato.
Tenner—A ten-pound note.
Throw in the alley—To surrender.
Time, to do—To serve a term in prison.
Time, to have no time for—To regard with impatient disfavour.
Tip—To forecast; to give; to warn.
Tipple—Strong drink; to indulge in strong drink.
Toff—An exalted person.
Togs—Clothes.
Togged—Garbed.
Tom—A girl.
Tony—Stylish.
Took—Arrested; apprehended.
Top, off one's—Out of one's mind.
Top off, to—To knock down; to assault.
Toss in the towel—See "rag".
Tossed out on my neck—Rejected.
Touch—Manner; mode; fashion.
Tough—unfortunate; hardy; also a "tug". q.v.
Tough luck—misfortune.
Track with—To woo; to "go walking with".
Treat, a—Excessively; abundantly.
Tucked away—Interred.
Tucker—Food.

Tug—An uncouth fellow; a hardy rogue.
Tumble to, or to take a tumble—To comprehend suddenly.
Turkey, head over—Heels over head.
Turn down—To reject; to dismiss.
Turn, out of one's—Impertinently; uninvited.
Twig—To observe; to espy.
Two-up School—A gambling den.

Umpty—An indefinite numeral.
Umptydoo—Far-fetched; "crook".
Upper-cut—In pugilism, an upward blow.
Uppish—Proud.
Up to us—Our turn; our duty.

Vag, on the—Under the provisions of the Vagrancy Act.

Wade in—Take your fill.
Wallop—To beat, chastise.
Waster—A reprobate; an utterly useless and unworthy person.
Waterworks, turn on the—To shed tears.
Welt—A blow.
Wet, to get—To become incensed; ill-tempered.
Whips—Abundance.
White (white man)—A true, sterling fellow.
White-headed boy—A favourite; a pet.
Willin'—Strenuous; hearty.
Win, a—Success.
Wise, to get—To comprehend; to unmask deceit.
Wise, to put—To explain; to instruct.
Wolf—To eat.
Word—To accost with fair speech.
Wot price—Behold; how now!
Wowser—A narrow-minded, intolerant person.

Yakker—Hard toil.
Yap—To talk volubly.
Yowling—Wailing; caterwauling.

A Note on the Text

C.J. Dennis was meticulous about the spelling and setting of his verse. To the frustration of his publishers, he insisted that variation simply reflected the Bloke's speech. "It would be inconsistent to be absolutely consistent," he wrote to George Robertson, "because the illiterate man is not consistent in his pronunciation of words—and there are no rules for bad grammar." Thus "with" would sometimes be spelt "wiv" and sometimes as "wif"; "sort of" would at times be "sorter" but also "sort o' "; "Saturday" could be both "Saturdee" and "Saturd'y". As the Bloke series progressed, however, Dennis and Fred Shenstone, his patient editor at Angus and Robertson, did standardise many words. *The Complete Sentimental Bloke* has adopted the latest known texts approved by Dennis. Every alteration has been checked against original manuscript material in the Mitchell Library, State Library of NSW (ML MSS 314). The variations mainly affect *The Sentimental Bloke* rather than the subsequent volumes.

A more significant change concerns the restoration of "The Battle of the Wazzir" sequence within *Ginger Mick*. As it retold an episode in Egypt where Australian troops did not behave themselves, the wartime censors insisted it be cut from the text in 1917. By 1919, Dennis had revised the proofs for future editions. It takes its rightful place for the first time with a complete text of *Ginger Mick*.

The three single poems interspersing the published books: "The Austra——laise", "Armistice" and "A Message" have been

A Note on the Text

selected for two reasons. First, they help to link the sequence as a single work. Secondly, they represent the raft of poems that Dennis wrote as the Bloke which were not published in book form. Most of these found their way into the Melbourne *Herald*, some in the last years of his life. The text for these was taken from *The C. J. Dennis Collection. From his "Forgotten Writings"* edited by Garrie Hutchinson (Lothian, 1987). Although the first version of "The Austra——laise" won a prize in a *Bulletin* competition for a national song in 1908, the text reproduced here is that of the leaflet issued to troops of the volunteer army in 1915.

For background material used in the Introduction, I would like to acknowledge primary sources held by the Mitchell Library, State Library of NSW (ML MSS 314), but also Alec H. Chisholm's *The Making of a Sentimental Bloke* (Georgian House, 1946) and *Selected Verse of C. J. Dennis* (Angus and Robertson, 1950); *C. J Dennis, The Sentimental Bloke* by Geoffrey Hutton (Premier's Department, Victoria, 1976); and *The World of the Sentimental Bloke* compiled by Barry Watts (Angus and Robertson, 1976). All other editions of the work of C.J. Dennis were published by Angus and Robertson.

Index of Poems

"A Gallant Gentleman" 136
Also-ran, The 269
Armistice 215
Australaise, The 65
"'Ave a 'Eart!" 253
Battle of the Wazzir, The 93
Beef Tea 47
Before the War 163
Call of Stoush, The 84
Crusaders, The 248
Dad 173
Dance, The 284
Digger Smith 177
Digger's Tale, A 188
Doreen 20
Duck an' Fowl 76
Dummy Bridge 168
Faltering Knight, The 226
Foreword 7
Game, The 132
Ginger's Cobber 102
Half A Man 200
Hitched 43
Holy War, A 237
In Spadger's Lane 111
Intro, The 13

Introduction (Moods of Ginger Mick, The) 73
Introduction (Rose of Spadgers) 221
Jim 206
Jim's Girl 192
Kid, The 56
Knight's Return, The 264
Letter to the Front, A 119
Listener's Luck 280
Logic and Spotted Dog 148
Mar 36
Mooch o' Life, The 61
Narcissus 293
Nocturne 242
Over the Fence 185
Pilot Cove 40
Play, The 23
Possum 154
Preface to the fifty-first thousand 5
Push, The 88
Rabbits 122
Rose 259
Sari Bair 98
Sawin' Wood 203

Singing Soldiers, The 107
Siren, The 32
Spike Wegg 288
Spring Song, A 9
Square Deal, A 210
Stoush o' Day, The 17
Straight Griffin, The 115
"Stone the Crows" 277
Stror 'at Coot, The 27
Termarter Sorce 231

The Boys Out There 196
To the Boys Who Took the Count 128
Uncle Jim 51
Vi'lits 151
War 80
Washing Day 145
West 181
Woman's Way, A 273

A&R CLASSICS

Have you read an Australian Classic lately?
HarperCollins invites you to take a fresh look with **A&R** Classics.

A&R Classics is proud to present a range of classic Australian writing that has captured the imaginations of generations of fans – books that are as fresh today as when they were first written.

Miles Franklin *My Brilliant Career* • ISBN: 0 207 19724 5
The classic story of love, ambition and rebellion.

Dymphna Cusack & Florence James *Come in Spinner* • ISBN: 0 207 19756 3
It's the 1940s and anything can be had – for a price. A vibrant portrait of three women and tough choices in wartime Sydney.

Henry Lawson *Selected Stories* • ISBN: 0 207 19708 3
A new selection of these timeless short stories, including favourites such as 'The Loaded Dog' and 'The Drover's Wife'.

Mudrooroo *Wild Cat Falling* • ISBN: 0 207 19736 2
As electrifying now as when it was first published, this searing and controversial novel shows what it is like to be black in Australia in the 1960s.

Eve Langley *The Pea-pickers* • ISBN: 0 207 19764 4
Steve and Blue are two young women who dress as men and pack apples and pick peas as they search for love and freedom.

Kylie Tennant *Ride on Stranger* • ISBN: 0 207 19740 7
The story of the wonderfully engaging Shannon Hicks, who takes on the world – and politics, business, religion and men – determined to find her own path.

George Johnston *Clean Straw for Nothing &*
A Cartload of Clay • ISBN: 0 207 19748 2
The Miles Franklin Award-winning sequel to *My Brother Jack*.
On a Greek island David Meredith faces the struggles with himself, and within his marriage.

Thomas Keneally *The Chant of Jimmie Blacksmith* • ISBN: 0 207 19716 4
From the author of *Schindler's List* comes this frank and moving account of tragedy on the Aboriginal and European frontier in the nineteenth century.

A.B. 'Banjo' Paterson *Collected Poems* • ISBN: 0207198675
From 'The Man From Snowy River' to 'Clancy of the Overflow', from 'The Geebung Polo Club' to 'Mulga Bill's Bicycle' – this volume brings together the complete poems of one of Australia's best-loved poets.

Barbara Baynton *Bush Studies* • ISBN: 0207196427
Written during the 1890s, Barbara Baynton's stories show women's experience of the bush, and she depicts the isolation, the heartache and the tragedies exacted by the land and the men within it.

C.J. Dennis *The Complete Sentimental Bloke* • ISBN: 0207197350
This is the 'definitive' *Sentimental Bloke* – for the first time published in one volume are the original *Songs of a Sentimental Bloke* and its sequels following the lives of Doreen, Ginger Mick, Digger Smith and Rose of Spadgers.

Ion L. Idriess *The Cattle King* • ISBN: 0207197822
For thousands of Australians Ion L. Idriess brought the outback to life. First published in 1936, *The Cattle King* is the rags-to-riches true story of cattle pioneer Sidney Kidman, who ran away from home at 13 with five shillings in his pocket.

Glenda Adams *Dancing on Coral* • ISBN: 0207197660
Published to rapturous reviews here and overseas, this story of the unforgettable young Lark's quest for adventure via a freighter voyage from Sydney to New York won the acclaimed Miles Franklin Award in 1987.

Peter Goldsworthy *Maestro* • ISBN: 0207197741
Since it was first published in 1989, *Maestro* has established itself as a modern classic. A young new arrival in Darwin meets the 'maestro', a Viennese refugee with a shadowed past. The occasion is a piano lesson, the first of many …

Drusilla Modjeska *Exiles at Home* • ISBN: 0207197431
This award-winning author's book is a landmark examination of the lives of Australian women writers in the period 1925–1945, including Miles Franklin, Katharine Susannah Prichard and Eleanor Dark among others. Immensely readable and full of fascinating insights into the creative process.

A&R Classics
An imprint of HarperCollins*Publishers*